CRIME IN CARTON HALL

A fiercely addictive mystery

CATHERINE MOLONEY

Detective Markham Mystery Book 16

JOFFE BOOKS

Joffe Books, London
www.joffebooks.com

First published in Great Britain in 2022

This paperback edition was first published
in Great Britain in 2022

Cover art by Dee Dee Book Covers

ISBN: 978-1-80405-336-2

PROLOGUE

When she set out for Old Carton on the morning of Sunday, 12 December, Annette Sullivan had no expectation that her weekend shift at the hall would yield anything other than the usual humdrum routine.

Situated on the outskirts of Bromgrove, Old Carton was a sleepy little hamlet of no great merit apart from the fact that it boasted Carton Hall, the ancestral home of the Twiss family, along with the up-and-coming Old Carton Artisan Centre which was tucked within the north-west boundary of the estate.

Annette never failed to experience a thrill at the sight of the medieval timber-framed manor house with its hotchpotch of Georgian and Victorian mock-Tudor embellishments, especially now when a December snowfall had transformed the chimneys and battlements into spun-sugar filigree confections worthy of a Disney production.

She always got excited at the approach of Christmas. Even now after the recent death of her dad, the familiar surge of festive anticipation would not be repressed, bubbling up inside her like an unstoppable outbreak of childlike optimism.

Dad had loved the parlours and 'withdrawing rooms' of Carton Hall, together with the strange little follies and mausoleum in the manor house grounds. And the ghost stories never failed to transfix him, especially the tale of the lady in black who allegedly glided about the place in the run-up to Christmas, eternally mourning her stillborn children and estrangement from her embittered husband who was forced to watch the estate pass to a second cousin. Ghost-hunters said the light changed in Lady Mary's boudoir when she was about to make a visitation. But no matter how tightly Annette screwed up her eyes in hopes of an extra-terrestrial happening, she had never yet beheld the unloved chatelaine.

Which wasn't to say that it might not happen. It was a question of being receptive to local vibes, so Annette hadn't entirely given up hope of a supernatural apparition.

She hardly ever came into contact with Sir Simon and Lady Twiss — remote god-like figures only glimpsed at a distance — but Christopher Hassett, the hall's assistant curator, was pleased by her enthusiasm and had promoted her to occasional tour guide when regular staff were absent. Catherine Metcalfe, the events manager, hadn't been keen, but Mr Hassett fought Annette's corner. 'She'll appeal to younger visitors,' he had insisted, and it was true. Somehow, she wasn't tongue-tied when it came to telling tourists about the history of the hall through the ages — as though the Twiss family had mysteriously ventriloquised her for their purposes. Talking about priest holes, hidey holes and secret closets, she found that her shyness vanished, as though she was the repository of an ancient legacy, fated to bequeath it to posterity.

Annette didn't have much to do with the Artisan Centre or the commercial side of the hall's operations, but there was always the possibility that one of the family might call in to the shop to review its stock. Mister Michael, the eldest son, was rarely seen, but Richard Twiss and his showbiz friends sometimes dropped by, creating a ripple of excitement among the staff that lasted for days, especially when the likes of Greg Wise and Anton Du Beke put in an appearance.

She loved seeing the shelves festooned with festive cards, decorations and gifts. Nothing gaudy, naturally. Miz Hoity

Toity Metcalfe was adamant about that. But the dainty Christmas tree ornaments, stationery and stocking-fillers (what her mother called 'geegaws') never failed to lift her spirits. And somehow, she felt her dad would approve. His favourite poem for the festive season had been John Betjeman's 'Christmas', with its reference to 'tissued fripperies' and 'sweet and silly Christmas things'. So it was as if the encroachment of baubles, bath salts and monogrammed novelties brought her closer to him. She certainly had every intention of using her staff discount card to splurge on treats for her little brothers and sisters so lately bereaved. And if Horseface Metcalfe had a problem with that, well for twopence she'd tell her where to stick it. If ever there was a time to spread some good cheer, Christmas was it. Mr Hassett said you couldn't put a price on that.

Not that she'd say no to a pay rise, of course. The Twisses paid just over the minimum wage to staff on the lowest rung. If she was being honest, she'd even be prepared to do it for less than that on account of working in such historic surroundings. Not many employees got to wander through stately picture galleries and boudoirs in their breaks. Annette could almost hear the rustle of petticoats and farthingales whenever she explored the cordoned off private quarters, mentally disappearing into a bygone world of shadowy plots and intrigue as she traversed dim shuttered passages and musty alcoves.

Plus, there was always the chance of bumping into someone glamorous. Someone like Charles Larrain who ran the aromatherapy concession in the Artisan Centre.

Hayley who worked alongside her in the shop scoffed at her crush on Mr Larrain.

'He's just a jumped-up ponce, luv,' she told Annette. 'A tuppenny toff. An' no more French than I am.'

But to Annette there was something wondrously alluring and exotic about the dark-eyed perfumier with his languorous drawl and come-to-bed expression. Something thrilling about the heavily accented tones which had enquired about the 'fresh little girl with the beautiful eyes'. Hayley insisted this was his standard routine, but Annette felt they had some-how made a *connection*. Nothing so crude as sex, but something indefinable and mysterious . . . something to do with the hall itself. As though echoes from the past reverberated down the centuries, reviving ancient gallantries from an armorial age.

'Too much Georgette Heyer,' was Hayley's sour verdict on such romantic flights of fancy, but Annette was neverthe-less loath to relinquish them.

Lost in thought, she crunched through deep snow to the basement tradesmen's door on the right-hand side of the building, beneath a pillared portico known as the Carriage Entrance, on account of its being reserved for quality folk who came in their grand equipages.

The staff locker room was a cramped untidy space, half storeroom half common room, with a service lift up to the shop on the ground floor. As she tugged off her duffel coat, beanie, Ugg boots and mittens, Annette speculated on the likelihood of her being able to take a peek at *The Power of Poison* exhibition in the Tapestry Room on the first floor. Curated by Margaret Twiss, who lectured part-time at Bromgrove University and took a kindly interest in Annette and her fellow workers, this had attracted considerable local interest. A two-page spread in the *Gazette* on the exhibition, alongside flattering pictures of the family and senior staff, displayed Catherine Metcalfe's 'pearly whites' to particular advantage.

Annette breathed a silent prayer of gratitude that La Metcalfe didn't come in on Sundays. Cosy Miss Evans, her immediate boss in the shop, and Mrs Irene Clark, Sir Simon's devoted PA, took a benign attitude to her fascina-tion with the hall's nooks and crannies. Even Carmel Scarron the sharp-tongued housekeeper turned a blind eye when she found the youngster 'stargazing' in front of the Twiss family portraits. Annette had the impression that the Twiss retainers took an indulgent view of her interest in those illustrious forebears, as though it demonstrated appropriate fealty to the dynasty.

She glanced at her wristwatch. A quarter to nine and no sign of anyone around.

There was no reason why she shouldn't take a quick look at the Tapestry Room.

She had heard Miss Evans speaking in awestruck tones about the engravings which depicted *ecartelage*, a fearsome medieval punishment that involved criminal poisoners being tied to four horses and then ripped apart as the horses galloped away in different directions. The drawings were really packing in the punters, according to her supervisor — only she had put it more genteelly — along with a new collection of astrologers' spell books and horoscopes on loan from the Reynolds Museum in Oxford. Mr Hassett had enthralled them with his description of a cabinet in the Tapestry Room, devoted to an Italian witch who sold potions to women who wanted rid of their husbands, finishing off some six hundred men with toxic brews disguised as holy water in glass flasks with the images of saints or hidden in makeup compacts.

And now she badly wanted to see these treasures for herself. Her old history teacher at Hope Academy had told them stories of Elizabeth I giving herself lead poisoning because of the gunk she slathered on her face, and she knew all about Rasputin and his cyanide-laced wine, but frankly that wasn't a patch on the black widows running amok in sixteenth-century Italy. Her little sisters would go mad for stories about wicked noblewomen bumping folk off, so fifteen minutes checking out Miss Margaret's latest finds would be time well spent.

Annette decided to go up by the service stairs at the far end of the basement — less chance of being spotted that way.

On the east-wing first-floor landing, she paused to contemplate the snow-clad lawns and shrubberies which stretched towards Old Carton Clough in the distance. The contrast of trees, hummocks and hedges showing black against the powdery mantle, gave her a curious pleasure, as though the vista formed part of some faery woodcut with the hall as its enchanted centrepiece.

Standing there, looking out at the winter landscape and the cold clear sky overhead, Annette suddenly became aware how still everything was. So still, it felt as if she was in the belly of some slumbering beast, breathing in time with its heartbeat . . .

She felt a sudden prickle of unease.

But everything was just the same as usual, right down to the familiar scents of beeswax polish and lavender, and the steady ticking of the mahogany longcase clock next to the State Anteroom, so-called because James I had apparently refreshed himself there on a royal progress to the North. The chamber housed the death masks of various Twiss magnates along with wooden and wax effigies used in funeral processions to the Pavilion, as the family mausoleum was known, and beyond this lay the Tapestry Room with its mementoes of brutal times past.

Then, from nowhere, Annette felt an overpowering repugnance which rooted her to the spot. As though some unseen presence eerily forbade her to proceed further.

She shook herself, baffled by the unexpected feeling of revulsion. True, the anteroom had always struck her as mildly disagreeable with its funerary models and dummies, so that she generally averted her eyes whenever she was obliged to cross it, but this morning was subtly different. The still close air of the ancient building momentarily clogged her throat with a sense of menace.

She shook her head again to clear it. At this rate she'd be caught lurking like some loony ghost-hunter instead of making the most of her opportunity! She forced herself forward, keeping warily close to the panelled wainscotting as though for protection then reeled backwards as soon as she entered the anteroom.

A crusted puddle of puke next to the periwigged figure of the seventh baronet whose haughty lips seemed almost to curl at the disgusting affront to family dignity.

Next to the congealed vomit a body stretched out, the congested complexion and foam-flecked features so distorted that it was some moments before Annette registered the identity of the man who lay before her, frozen in his death agony.

Charles Larrain. Rake, lothario and one-time epitome of glamour.

As long as she lived, she would never forget the sight.

His tall, elegant form was arched in a spasm so violent it made her think of pictures she had once seen at school of the contorted victims of Pompeii, arms and legs flexed in their ashy graves like demonic prize-fighters.

The Alley of Skeletons they called it.

And now Carton Hall had something to rival it.

The Anteroom of Death.

1. A TERRIBLE COLDNESS

It occurred to DI Gilbert 'Gil' Markham, sitting on his favourite bench in the terraced graveyard of St Chad's Parish Church on Monday morning, that he was on the same page as Annette Sullivan when it came to Christmas.

There had been some sad Christmases in his early life, but time was a great healer. Now when he thought of the past, he travelled back to the years before his family unit was irrevocably disrupted by the arrival of a stepfather and it was just him, his mother and brother draping their modest artificial tree with winking lights and squabbling amicably over where to place the garish felt Santas and furry reindeers. He smiled as he recalled the sinister Santa face which always went on top of the tree instead of the more traditional star or angel. Something about the floppy red hat, limp white beard and unnaturally radiant features had always unnerved him. But the peculiar little puppet had been passed down the generations, so his protests were to no avail.

His reminiscent smile faded as he recalled those other puppets at Carton Hall in the anteroom where Charles Larrain had been discovered the previous day . . .

'S'like Madame Tussauds,' DS George Noakes pronounced. 'Only creepier.'

The gloomy oak-panelled room held a range of effigies, some life-size but others just the head and torso, along with a collection of death masks in glass cases.

Noakes, predictably, didn't care for the Twiss squirearchy.

'The blokes are all pigeon-chested,' he declared. 'Prob'ly from the wigs an' all that furry clobber they dressed up in.'

'Not to mention the velvet and ermine,' Markham observed, noting the extravagant robes on the full-size mannequins.

'The women are a bit scary,' the DS continued, eyeing a haughty hook-nosed noblewoman clad in richly embroidered brocade. 'Mebbe that's why the fellas look like they've been squashed in the sack.' Since their investigation into an obesity clinic, Noakes's eyes had been opened to new aspects of gender warfare.

The pathologist Doug 'Dimples' Davidson, a bluff countryman and dead ringer for Tristan Farnon in the original *All Creatures Great and Small*, laughed at this.

'I'm not sure the Twisses would care for that interpretation, Sergeant,' he said. 'The effigies were actually meant to convey refinement and aristocratic breeding.'

'*Inbreeding* you mean,' the other grunted as he stooped to examine the effigy of a young child on its plinth. 'Most likely that's why this poor little bleeder never made it to his teens.'

Noakes squinted at the decorated oak tester on the wall above the child's head and then at the adjacent museum-style plaque.

'It's supposed to show a pair of monkeys,' he said rumpling his salt and pepper thatch so that it stood comically on end. 'King James kept 'em as pets an' gave one to little whatshisface when he came here on a visit cos the lad took a shine to it . . . called it Bombadil. *Hey*,' he brightened, 'ain't that the name of some bloke in *Lord of the Rings*?'

'Yes, but I don't think they were into Tolkien back then,' Dimples observed wryly. 'Anyway, it would seem the boy didn't live long enough to enjoy it.'

'Yeah, says here the chimp pined away an' died after the lad got smallpox an' snuffed it.' Noakes's shrewd piggy eyes had become suddenly compassionate as he contemplated the wistful wax figure in its full-length crimson robe with tiny lace jabot. 'Poor little bleeder,' he repeated before turning back to the pathologist. 'So, what did old Charles Aznavour die of then?' he demanded, his gaze roaming over the corpse bent in its fearful boomerang-like death throes.

'Charles *Larrain*,' Markham corrected him mildly. Noakes's chronic tendency to rechristen victims and suspects had on occasion got him into serious hot water, but the DI knew no one was more tenacious than his untidy, uncouth wingman when it came to tracking down a murderer.

'Well, the way that young lass talked about him, you'd have thought he were some frog pop star 'stead of jus' a shop-keeper,' the DS retorted.

It was certainly true that Annette Sullivan had spoken of the dead man with an ardour that suggested a teenaged crush, Markham mused. Noakes — father of perma-tanned Natalie, the apple of his eye — refrained from open raillery until she had been shepherded away for a cup of tea but then he had seen no reason to hold back. 'Sounded like the bloke thought he were God's gift,' he insisted.

'To answer your question, Sergeant,' Dimples inter-jected with heavy forbearance, 'I believe Mr Larrain was poisoned.'

'How?' The DS looked round the museum-like antecham-ber in bewilderment. 'I mean, how'd it get into his body?'

The pathologist held out a slim pouch in his gloved hand.

'I'd say someone tampered with his vape kit or whatever they call these e-cig contraptions these days.' He pursed his lips. 'Mercury vapour . . .'

'So he *inhaled* it then?' Markham asked, startled.

The medic smiled. 'It's not unheard of these days,' he told them. 'One of Vladimir Putin's critics made the mistake of calling him "the new Stalin". Next thing you know, he died of a heart attack — they think it was caused by someone spraying poison on the reading lamp next to his bed. The heat from the lamp vaporised the poison, see, and he was sitting right next to it. His bodyguards just stuck their heads in to say goodnight, so they got sick but survived.'

'Yeah, but that's the *Russkis*,' Noakes declared. As much as to say, *what else can you expect*? 'Stuff like that don' happen *here*.'

Dimples knew Noakes's xenophobia of old so didn't comment. 'It's more creative than other methods, I grant you,' he allowed patiently, 'but I'm pretty sure that's what you're looking at in this case.' He gestured at the body. 'Mr Larrain also had a hip flask in his pocket, so if the murderer contaminated that as well as the e-cig — with something like a pesticide, say — then we're talking a powerful double whammy.'

'But how the chuff could they count on Charlie boy wandering round the *château*?' The question was put with scornful emphasis on the last word just to show that the DS wasn't over-awed by his surroundings.

Dimples smothered a smile. 'I gather from Sir Simon's PA that Mr Larrain was in the habit of calling round at weekends.'

'But he's jus' someone from that poncey shopping centre — the artisan wotsit,' Noakes said crossly. 'What business did he have making free with the place an' strolling around without so much as a by your leave?'

The pathologist made a tutting sound. 'Now, now, that's not very democratic of you, Sergeant,' he said with a mischievous gleam in his eyes. 'The people at the hall think of themselves and the Artisan Centre as one big happy family.'

Noakes jerked a pudgy forefinger at the body. 'Not that happy by the looks of things,' he glowered.

Unabashed, Dimples continued smoothly, 'And in any event, Mr Larrain was a good friend of Richard Twiss. Took a keen interest in *The Power of Poison* exhibition too . . . Pretty much had carte blanche to go wherever he wanted.'

Noakes was not to be defeated. 'The security here's gotta be *pants*.'

'Fairly relaxed, yes,' the pathologist admitted. 'It appears the live-in staff set the alarms at the weekend, but family and friends have their own keys and know the codes.'

'So, basically, everyone an' their dog could've come traipsing through,' the DS concluded indignantly.

Dimples raised his hands apologetically. 'There hasn't been a burglary here in the last umpteen years, so the system had worked pretty well.'

Until now, said Noakes's expression.

'Time of death, Doug?' Markham cut in.

'Late Saturday night, around ten or eleven, but don't quote me on that.' The medic's face was sombre as he contemplated the body. 'The poor man died hard.' Unexpectedly he added, 'It's a coward's choice, poison.'

'They say it's a woman's weapon,' Noakes ruminated.

'Well, those Medici and Borgia dames were heavily into it,' Dimples agreed. 'But in our own times there's the likes of Crippen and Graham Young getting in on the act.'

'Oh yeah, Young was the bloke who knocked off his workmates.' Noakes never missed a true crime documentary on *CBS Reality*. 'Practised with weed killer when he were a kid an' then moved on to thallium . . . Always carried poisons on him cos it made him feel powerful, the sick git.'

'He was also a sexual sadist apparently,' Dimples added mischievously, aware that the DS had a surprisingly prudish streak.

Noakes shook his head. 'Dunno about that,' he replied. 'But he were screwy right from the off . . . his cousin said he sniffed her bottles of nail varnish to get high.'

'Well, there you have it, Sergeant,' said Dimples. '*Inhalation of toxic vapours.*'

The DS looked dubiously at the corpse. 'But I mean, tampering with an e-cig . . .'

'And most likely contaminating that hip flask,' Dimples pointed out. 'Perfectly doable if Larrain had put his jacket down somewhere.' A shadow crossed his face. 'I'd say the killer *enjoyed* doing this, really wanted to make him suffer. You're looking for a seriously troubled individual.'

The pathologist then gestured to two paramedics who had arrived with a gurney and were awaiting his signal to come forward.

'As if we needed telling,' Noakes burst out crossly after the sheeted stretcher had departed. He glanced round uneasily at the effigies and busts. 'An' if they've got a taste for this poisoning malarkey, they ain't going to stop at one victim, *no sirree*!'

Now as Markham sat contemplating the white-clad tombs and monuments, Noakes's prophecy came back to him.

They weren't going to stop at one.

He was struck with a terrible coldness that had nothing to do with the winter weather. A coldness that came from knowing there was a deranged enemy out there . . . the more deadly for being unafflicted by conscience or remorse.

There had been no question the previous day of their being granted an interview with Sir Simon and Lady Twiss, the family GP having attended so quickly that it was fair to assume they had him on speed-dial. In the meantime, Markham was prepared to wait until Dimples came back with the toxicology report.

The DI's thoughts turned to his team.

He had been startled during their last case when Noakes had bruited the possibility of quitting CID and setting up as a private investigator. There was no doubt that DCI Sidney — or 'Slimy Sid' as he was known to the rank and file — would sing a *Te Deum* at the prospect of his bête noire heading for pastures new. Noakes's chronic inability to follow the politically correct playbook (or 'woke bollocks' as he called it) and habit of saying just what he thought made him decidedly *persona non grata* with his superiors.

Personally, Markham relished his wingman's lack of any filter, valuing this quality as increasingly rare in an environment where people would do or say literally anything to climb the greasy pole. Noakes was an old-style copper with old-style values. 'Scrotes' and 'lowlifes' got zero sympathy, but there was a wellspring of tenderness for those who had no one to fight for them, coupled with a ferocious tenacity in bringing malefactors to justice that matched Markham's own. He also had a strain of poetic susceptibility in his makeup that was strongly at odds with his battered appearance and terrible dress sense, creating a mysterious psychic affinity with Markham whose troubled early life he had intuited without anything explicit ever passing between them on the subject. The DI had a feeling that the younger brother he had lost to drink and drugs would have liked Noakes.

Certainly, his partner Olivia Mullen found Noakes a 'kindred spirit', her roguish streak responding to the grizzled veteran's honesty and subversive resistance to the fashionable shibboleths espoused by DCI Sidney. She and Noakes shared a visceral dislike of Slimy Sid, whom she had rechristened Judas Iscariot on account of his jealousy of Markham and tendency to hog the glory at every opportunity. For his part, Noakes responded to the Pre-Raphaelite allure of Olivia's flaming red hair, willowy grace and musical contralto with a reverence to equal that of any medieval troubadour at the Courts of Love.

Noakes's formidable wife Muriel was markedly less enamoured of Olivia, sighing gustily to fellow members of the local WI that '*poor dear* Gilbert Markham was so easily *imposed upon*' — the implication being that her husband's boss, whose old-world courtesy and handsome mien were very much to her taste, had fallen victim to unspeakable sexual wiles.

Muriel and Noakes had met on the ballroom dance circuit, both being surprisingly proficient exponents of the art, with a chemistry which belied the prosaic reality of more than thirty years of marriage.

There had been a crisis during the notorious Bluebell investigation when Noakes discovered that he was not in fact Natalie's biological father and nearly chucked away his career as a result. To this day, Markham remained ignorant of what had transpired between the DS and his wife behind closed doors. But the couple had somehow weathered the storm, and Markham had noticed that Muriel had softened around the edges, though Olivia still mocked the older woman's social climbing and archly coquettish mannerisms.

For all Noakes's devotion to his bossy wife, she had failed in her endeavours to smarten him up — except for those occasions like church when he was 'on parade' — and his migraine-inducing wardrobe choices had passed into legend.

At least, Markham thought, he could count on DI Kate Burton to look the part.

Earnest and politically correct where Noakes was outspoken and tactless, she had experienced strong family opposition when it came to her choice of the police as a career. But she made a triumphant success of it, progressing through the ranks, a fast-track psychology graduate who was clearly 'going places'. The fact that she was now engaged to Professor Nathan Finlayson, a criminal profiler at Bromgrove University, failed to allay Olivia's jealous fear that Burton had never ceased to carry a torch for Markham. And it was undoubtedly true that their bond had only strengthened over the years, with the result that Burton's transfer to London had lasted a mere matter of months in the face of her professed desire to work with her former boss. Technically speaking, they were now the same rank, but she always deferred to him as her skipper. From time to time, he wondered if his selfish enjoyment of such flattering hero-worship had impeded Burton's professional development, but the pleasure of having such an intelligent and loyal subordinate made it easy to banish any lingering qualms.

Noakes and Burton had been initially highly suspicious of each other, since they were by temperament, upbringing and education as far apart as it was possible to be. But each had mellowed with the passage of time and shared the same dogged devotion to Markham, as well as an insatiable appetite for true crime documentaries. Noakes was always very sniffy about his colleague's academic leanings — there was no danger of him dipping into her beloved *Diagnostic and*

Statistical Manual of Mental Disorders — but he enjoyed chewing the cud with Burton and Nathan Finlayson, hoovering up all that the latter could relate about the psychopathic personality. For his part, Finlayson had grown fond of CID's resident curmudgeon, not even objecting when Noakes christened him 'Shippers' on account of his marked resemblance to the serial killer Harold Shipman.

Where Burton went, DS Doyle followed, the ginger-haired young detective having early hitched his star to hers. Armed with his newly minted criminal law degree, Doyle was undoubtedly another highflyer, but there was nothing obsequious or servile about him. He had remained devoted to his mentor Noakes, displaying a loyalty that showed he was his own man. Markham suspected he had never truly acclimatised to Southampton Row, secretly pining for Bromgrove, Noakes and the distinction of belonging to what station wits had designated Markham's 'Gang of Four'.

Well, the 'gang' was together again, and he had no doubt Sidney would agree to its deployment. Provided, of course, that he got results.

The cold clear day was bracing, and Markham was reluctant to exchange it for the fug of CID but he forced himself up from the bench, causing a squirrel to whisk out of sight behind a neighbouring tombstone.

Even though covered by snow, he knew the lines inscribed on it by heart:

> *Man is a single pilgrim, fighting unarmed amongst a thousand soldiers,*
> *Therefore enlist ye under the banner of thy God.*

A misappropriation of Victorian doggerel, according to Olivia, but somehow the words resonated with him, like an irresistible call to arms or a regimental quick march.

Dimples had said that poison was a coward's choice.

In that moment, he vowed he would force this hidden enemy to take the field.

* * *

CID was very quiet as Markham headed for his poky office with its unrivalled view of the station carpark.

Somebody — probably one of the civilian staff — had sorted a smattering of Christmas decorations, though he didn't give much for the chances of the little fibre optic tree, streamers and garlands making it unscathed through the festive period. The sprightlier members of the department would most likely use the tree for target practice, he thought with an amused shrug.

On the other hand, God help anyone who made off with those chocolate Santas he spied dangling from the lowest branches — Noakes regarded anything of the kind as his personal prerequisite.

The DS was notably keen on 'Crimbo', and his boss had literally seen the cogs turning in Noakes's brain as he calculated the domestic brownie points to be earned from a cull of 'posh smellies' at the Old Carton Artisan Centre. It was also useful to the investigation that daughter Natalie, in her capacity of upwardly mobile freelance beautician, would automatically have an entrée to the centre's various homeopathic and cosmetic outlets. Something of a man-eater in her salad days, Natalie was no longer the doyenne of Bromgrove's nightclubs, being respectably affianced to the son of a local entrepreneur who had briefly come under suspicion in a previous investigation.

However, like her mother, she was well disposed towards her father's handsome boss, which meant she would be highly amenable to the prospect of a role as unofficial intel-gatherer. The DI knew he would have to play his cards carefully, given Natalie's brush with danger during the Bluebell case and Noakes's protectiveness, but he suspected her nose for gossip was second to none.

Markham was amused to note that the door of Kate Burton's minuscule glassed-in domain — 'office' was stretching it for what was little more than a cubicle — featured a tasteful natural wreath (no tinsel, in keeping with her eco credentials) with a robin redbreast centrepiece. Was it his imagination, or was the bird cocking a wary eye at Noakes's frowsy desk nearby? If so, there was nothing to fear, the DS thoroughly approving of robins as being 'nice an' proper', reserving his wrath for politically correct 'winter festival BS where it could be *anyone*'s birthday' and where Christ was conspicuous by his absence. 'Like Hamlet without the prince,' Olivia chuckled at Noakes's perennial gripe, but Markham guessed his wingman — indelibly marked by a Methodist Sunday School upbringing — was genuinely outraged. 'Same with Easter,' the DS groused. 'That's why you've got kids who think it's all about some freaking bunny.'

Needless to say, Muriel Noakes's eminently tasteful Christmas card had already been delivered to CID by her proud spouse. Reflecting the good lady's recent flirtation with Catholicism, it depicted Our Lady, Undoer of Knots, with a sweet-faced Madonna whom Markham privately considered a vast improvement on some of the whey-faced precocious she-hypocrites and pasty infants of previous years. Perhaps Muriel's choice of painting could even be considered a favourable omen in light of the decidedly knotty conundrum posed by this latest murder.

As he settled in behind his desk, a minor commotion outside his door signalled the arrival of the threesome who he had no doubt were avid to get their teeth into the Carton murder.

Noakes certainly lived up, or down, to expectations in an eye-wateringly awful combo of a chunky crimson bobble jumper, decorated with what looked like capering penguins, bottle green cords and the ubiquitous George boots ('if it's good enough for the Paras, it's good enough for me'). Sidney would blow a gasket if he caught sight of this ensemble, Markham thought with an inward groan, though on the other hand Noakes might get away with it if they pretended he was involved in a local Save Arctic Wildlife campaign . . . On balance, it might just be safest to keep him well away from the higher-ups. If the worst came to the worst, Markham could always pacify Sidney by dangling the prospect of Noakes's imminent retirement (without mentioning his plans to branch out as a gumshoe . . .).

DI Kate Burton, nut-brown hair swinging in its trademark bob, looked immaculate in a sharply tailored navy trouser suit, black roll-neck jumper and suede ankle boots. Her slightly squashed, tip-tilted features were redeemed from absolute plainness by the intelligence of the brown eyes which were magnified to the size of enormous lollipops whenever she whipped on her high-prescription reading glasses.

DS Doyle, lanky but highly personable in his tweed jacket, slim-fit dark button-down and neat chinos, looked alert and eager. If he was a dog, Markham thought indulgently, he'd be wagging his tail.

Seeing Noakes rummage in the big paper bag with the McDonald's logo, Markham resigned himself to the fragrance of his wingman's usual grease-fest. And sure enough, out came the breakfast muffin, fries and coffee, causing Burton to wrinkle her nose fastidiously as her colleague proceeded to wolf down his supplies. Doyle merely grinned at this evidence of his mentor limbering up for the festive blowout.

'You gotta pace yourself, lad,' as the other invariably put it when it came to building stamina for the main event.

The DI knew better than to interrupt his wingman's fuelling up, but the latter made short work of the foodstuffs, enquiring with unmistakeable eagerness, 'Are we in on this one then, guv?'

'Yes, I've got the three of you for the Carton Hall murder, Noakes.' He frowned. 'And I have to say, it looks like it might be our most challenging yet.'

Seeing that Kate Burton had whisked a notebook and glasses out of her brown leather conference folder, Markham swiftly marshalled his thoughts.

'Right,' he said. 'The victim is Mr Charles Larrain, forty-five, perfumier from the Old Carton Artisan Centre and friend of Richard Twiss who's the second son of Sir Simon and Lady Edith.'

'As in "*friend*"?' Doyle asked, looking awkward as well he might with Noakes leering knowingly at the enquiry.

'We don't know if Mr Larrain and Richard Twiss were romantically involved,' the DI answered evenly. With a quelling glance at Noakes, he added, 'However if that should turn out to be the case, we will approach the issue with due restraint and discretion.' *As opposed to anyone trampling all over local sensibilities with their size twelves.*

Burton nodded approvingly.

'The Twisses have other children, isn't that right sir?' She still invariably addressed Markham as her superior and he had long since given up pointing out that they were now equals in rank. Deep down, he knew he liked her all the more for this continued mark of respect. 'That's cos you're her household god,' Olivia had commented waspishly, and he supposed there was truth in this but still refrained from correcting the misnomer, telling himself: *It is what it is.*

'That's correct, Kate. Michael Twiss, the eldest son, is in line to inherit. Then there's the youngest brother Philip Twiss who acts as the estate manager. And a sister, Margaret, who lectures part-time at the university.'

Burton busily scribbled away while the other two exchanged eloquent glances across her glossy head.

A university angle, Markham could almost hear them thinking. *God, she'll be in clover if there's a bunch of clever dicks involved.*

'Sir Simon's brother Gerald Twiss and his wife, Stella own Old Carton Farm,' Markham continued. 'Then there's Miss Isobel Farquhar, Lady Edith's sister, who lives in Old Carton Dower Cottage with her unmarried daughter Frances.'

'Worse than *Downton Abbey*,' Noakes grumbled, poking around in his McDonalds bag in the forlorn hope of finding stray fries to gobble.

'What about staff at the hall, sir?' Doyle asked.

'I'm not totally clear about the set-up yet . . . I gather there's a Christopher Hassett who's the assistant curator. He helps arrange exhibitions like this latest offering: "The Power of Poison".'

Burton looked even more enthralled on hearing this.

Noakes scowled. *That's all we need. Her going all misty-eyed over a load of medieval twaddle the la-di-da lot have cooked up to get the punters in.*

Perfectly aware of his wingman's malevolent inner monologue, Markham suppressed a smile.

'I believe there's also an events manager who divides her time between the hall and the Artisan Centre,' he continued. 'Name of Catherine Metcalfe. In terms of household staff, Sir Simon has a PA, Mrs Irene Clark. There's also a housekeeper, Carmel Scarron, whose son Patrick acts as a sort of groundsman.'

Burton was clearly disappointed. 'It doesn't sound all that lavish.'

'That's the way with so many so-called stately homes these days, Kate. Pretty much run on a shoestring,' Markham told her. 'The family's well embedded locally, so I imagine they get extra help from the village when they need it. They're pretty thick with a clutch of local worthies — the vicar and his wife, churchwardens and so forth.' He grinned, his austere features softening in a rare, charming smile. 'I believe Mrs Sidney serves on Bromgrove's Heritage Committee with Lady Twiss.'

'Oh *well*,' Noakes said with heavy sarcasm. 'You can say bye-bye to fingering any of the poshos, guv.' The DS stuck out his pinkie in a parody of teatime gentility. 'Can't be having any of the *Downton Abbey* brigade in the frame, dontcha know.'

'Get that chip off your shoulder, Noakesy,' Markham told him sternly. 'We're going in with no preconceptions, and I think the DCI appreciates that.'

Noakes looked thunderous. *Yeah, like chuff he does.*

But actually, Markham had seen another side to the DCI in recent investigations. A willingness to park his undoubted predilection for social standing and celebrity — the product of a difficult start in life — in favour of giving Markham a decent run. He couldn't flatter himself that Sidney had suddenly conceived some sort of personal regard for him, resentment of his Oxbridge credentials and meteoric rise in CID were too deeply ingrained for any such volte-face, but *something* had brought about a transformation. Markham was simply grateful for the positive consequences. Maybe it was just that the instincts of a decent copper were not entirely crusted over with the corrosive effects of high office. Olivia scoffed at the notion of Markham's boss having had any such Damascene conversion, but he felt nonetheless that it was so.

'So, what's next, sir?' Burton asked simply, bringing him back to the present.

'A recce of the hall this afternoon,' the DI replied. 'I want to get a feel for the family and staff while we're waiting for Dimples to report back about the toxicology.'

Seeing that Burton was regarding him expectantly, Markham explained the pathologist's theories.

His fellow DI thought hard. 'He really thinks it's cyanide and—'

'Rat killer,' Noakes interjected peremptorily.

'Or possibly hydrobromide of hyoscine,' Markham amended. 'Either way, fatal poisons administered by means of Mr Larrain's e-cigarette and hip flask.'

'*Sneaky*,' Noakes declared.

'Indeed,' Markham agreed. Repressing a shiver, he added, 'There's something devious and deliberate about the way in which Mr Larrain was dispatched.'

'A highly intelligent coward,' Burton said solemnly, unconsciously echoing the pathologist.

'An' a freaking sadist.' Noakes wanted no one to be in any doubt about that.

'Which is why we need to move *fast*,' the DI told them.

There was no need to add: *Otherwise, we've got a serial killer on our hands.*

2. THE ITALIAN SOLUTION

Monday afternoon found the team back at Carton Hall. Family and staff, however, were nowhere to be seen, except for Christopher Hassett the assistant curator of 'The Power of Poison' exhibition.

A tall, slightly stooped man who looked to be in his early fifties, Hassett was nonetheless attractive in a donnish sort of way, horn-rimmed spectacles and dark hair streaked with silver lending him a certain distinction. His cultured voice added to the impression of refinement, and he had the air of one comfortable in his own skin. With fine instincts, after the introductions had been performed, he said nothing about the previous day's discovery other than to express his shock on hearing of the murder.

'I've arranged with family and staff to make themselves available for interviews tomorrow morning, Inspector,' he said. 'I hope that's agreeable to you.' When Markham confirmed that it was, he continued: 'Perhaps in the meantime you'd like to explore the hall?'

'"The Power of Poison" exhibition appears to have attracted favourable publicity,' the DI said courteously. 'If it's not too much trouble, perhaps you wouldn't object to us taking a look.'

The curator was clearly pleased by the request and escorted them through the State Anteroom, where a swarm of SOCOs were still at work, to the Tapestry Room.

'*Hey*, that's the same thingummyjig picture we saw in Sherwin College,' Noakes declared on spying a tapestry at the far end of the room. 'The Field of Wotsit where Henry VIII an' the Frenchies had this big picnic.'

'Well spotted, Sergeant.' Hassett smiled approvingly, impressively understanding Noakes's botched description. 'Yes, it's a Flemish depiction of *The Field of the Cloth of Gold* where Henry and King Francis tried to outdo each other.' He chuckled. 'Henry even brought along a pair of monkeys covered in gold leaf, and Francis took such a shine to them that he wanted them in attendance at every banquet.'

'King James liked 'em as well,' Noakes threw a triumphant look towards Kate Burton as though to say, *I can do the boffin stuff too*. 'An' he gave one to that little beggar next door . . . the lad who died young.'

'Right again, Sergeant.' The curator was pleasantly surprised by the response of the big detective who stood rumpling his bushy hair so that it sprouted rampantly erect in little prongs as though to reflect unbridled enthusiasm. Markham couldn't help but smile.

Hassett proved to be an agreeable guide, with a gift for imparting quirky nuggets of historical lore.

'It says here that Henry VIII's people had to kiss all his bedsheets an' pillows to prove they hadn't smeared 'em with poison,' Noakes exclaimed delightedly, peering at a wall display.

'Oh, that's nothing, Sergeant,' Hassett laughed. 'Edward VI's courtiers were even more paranoid, so they used to dress a boy of the same size in his clothes and wait to see if he cried out in pain. There were conspiracies everywhere . . . You couldn't even be sure of the doctors. There was a famous case where a gentleman at King James's court died in agony after his enemies bribed a doctor to give him a sulphuric enema.'

'I remember that!' Kate Burton exclaimed. 'James had all these male favourites. One of them called Robert Carr had affairs with men and women . . . When Carr eventually decided to settle down, some ex-boyfriend kicked up a fuss and began badmouthing the woman he wanted to marry. James imprisoned this awkward character in the Tower of London on some pretext or other, and that's when Carr and his lady friend saw their chance and got the dodgy doctor to finish him off.'

The curator was openly admiring. 'Well remembered. Yes, Sir Thomas Overbury died an excruciating death.'

'I bet the doc copped it while Lord an' Lady Muck got off scot-free,' Noakes put in with lugubrious satisfaction.

Hassett gave a wry smile. 'Well, King James conducted some sort of show trial but essentially yes, they tap danced away from it while the doctor and the other conspirators ended up being executed.'

Noakes shook his head sorrowfully, though Markham reckoned he was secretly gratified to have his prejudices confirmed.

But Hassett wasn't averse to a little moralising. 'What goes around comes around, Sergeant,' he said. 'The guilty couple had no joy of their marriage, and the wife died in unbearable pain at forty-two, riddled with cancer.'

Doyle cut in, obviously having no intention of allowing his colleagues to make off with the intellectual laurels. 'Weren't the Italians supposed to be experts at bumping people off with poison?' he asked.

'After the Overbury case, it was the English who carried that stigma for a time,' Hassett replied. 'But it's true that skill with poisons was considered practically an Italian birthright.'

'Presumably that's why Catherine de Medici looms so large in the exhibition,' Markham observed, admiring a life size mannequin dressed in mourning with a black head dress and flowing gauze veil, the sombre effect relieved only by a huge white cartwheel ruff.

'Ah yes, the original Black Widow . . . Wore perpetual mourning as a sign of devotion to King Henri who died after a joust went wrong.'

'But didn't he have affairs with other women?' Burton asked the curator.

'Correct, but she was still crazy about him,' Hassett replied. 'Even went so far as to drill holes in the floor of her apartment so she could watch him being pleasured by his mistress in the room below and pick up some lovemaking tips.'

Markham could tell that the curator rather enjoyed the effect of this revelation on Noakes, who now regarded the mannequin with a distinctly disapproving expression.

'Wasn't she the one behind a big massacre in Paris?' Burton enquired hastily before Noakes could voice his displeasure.

'Yes, the St Bartholomew's Day Massacre when the Catholics set about killing as many Huguenots — Protestants — as they could lay their hands on. Some playwright said that because of it her memory would be wrapped in bloody crepe till the end of time.'

Burton was on a roll now. 'There were rumours about her committing incest with her sons too, weren't there?'

Noakes looked more po-faced than ever, eliciting a chuckle from the curator.

'Oh, Catherine was up to all sorts . . . black magic, astrology, voodoo . . . You name it, she'd had a go. When she was trying to get pregnant, she drank urine from pregnant livestock and wore a locket stuffed with a cremated frog.'

'*Eeeeugh!*' burst from Doyle.

Hassett grew expansive. 'The sons were tubercular and downright weird . . . the youngest was a pockmarked hunchback,' he continued, 'while the middle one turned out to be a religious maniac when he wasn't having affairs with the best-looking male courtiers . . . And you might be right about the incest, given that she told the middle son if she were to lose him, she would have herself buried alive in his grave.'

Observing Noakes's look of extreme distaste, the curator added, 'They were brutal times, Sergeant, and Catherine resorted to any number of tactics to wield power. Poison was one method. Sex was another.'

'How come, seeing as she were so bad at it?' Noakes asked, intrigued despite himself.

'She had what was called her "flying squadron" of beautiful ladies-in-waiting and used them to seduce noblemen for political ends.'

'Wasn't there a daughter?' Burton interposed swiftly, again cutting off any of Noakes's remarks.

'Yes, Marguerite. But Catherine never had much time for her, just the sons.' Hassett gave a thin smile. 'In the end none of them lasted long on the throne and the crown passed to Marguerite's husband whom Catherine hated on account of him being a Protestant.'

'Sounds a wrong 'un,' was Noakes's trenchant verdict on 'The Italian Woman'.

'She was very superstitious . . . Always consulting soothsayers and the like. One of them told her to beware of Saint-Germain if she wished to live for a long time. So she avoided the chateau of Saint-Germain like the plague. But the prophecy caught up with her, because the priest who gave her the last rites was called Julien de Saint-Germain.'

'Got her just desserts then,' Noakes grunted.

'Well, she lived to be seventy-one . . . The autopsy showed she had rotten lungs, a blood-soaked brain and an abscess in her left side. Something went wrong with the embalming process, and she began to smell so bad that they decided to bury her at night in an unmarked grave . . . Later on, she was moved to the traditional mausoleum, but during the French Revolution a mob dug her up and chucked her bones into a mass grave along with all the other royals.'

'Serves her right for being a witch,' asserted Noakes in the tones of a modern-day Torquemada.

'As I say, she was a product of her times, Sergeant. Palaces back then literally *heaved* with poisons of all kinds. And medicine was a case of kill more than cure. Whenever one of the Spanish royals fell ill, the doctors would dig up saintly body parts and entire corpses from churches and monasteries and put them in bed with the invalid . . . That's when they weren't using unicorn horn or rooster dung as prophylactics.'

Noakes was obviously beginning to feel that maybe his breakfast muffin hadn't been such a bright idea. 'She looks like a toad with them bulging eyes,' he muttered with a last baleful glance at Catherine de Medici.

'Not a looker, certainly,' their guide informed them. Then with a wry smile: 'One wit said that she was a beautiful woman when her face was veiled.'

Noakes guffawed appreciatively before moving along to the cabinet containing engravings of the punishments for poisoners, including the fearsome *ecartelage*. Meanwhile, as Burton and Doyle examined a display about Nostradamus, Markham wandered over to another mannequin whose label proclaimed her to be Henrietta Stuart, daughter of Charles I who became the exiled Duchess of Orleans after her father's execution.

'Now *her* husband really *was* a toad,' Hassett said coming up alongside him. 'Bisexual and all-round bastard who made her life a misery. He was jealous of her popularity too and thrilled when one of his tame astrologers predicted that he would have more than one wife. By the end, he was pretty much exclusively homosexual . . . widely suspected of having poisoned Henrietta, but nowadays they think she had a perforated ulcer.'

'And *did* he end up marrying again?' Markham asked curiously.

'Yes, that prophecy did turn out to be true.'

'I don't see any modern poisoners in here,' the DI observed looking around him. 'No Dr Crippen or William Palmer . . . The focus seems to be predominantly Renaissance?'

'Ah, that's down to Margaret Twiss.' Markham was interested to note a slight tinge of colour in the man's sallow cheeks as he said her name. 'She's a Renaissance specialist, very highly regarded in her field.'

'And what about you, sir? What do you specialise in?' The DI was interested to know more of Hassett's background.

'I was a lecturer in art history at Goldsmiths College, followed by a stint at Sotheby's. I'm a native of these parts, so when I tired of the London jungle and heard about a position at Carton, I jumped at it.' A self-deprecating shrug. 'I inherited my parents' house in the village when they died, so it looks like I'm here for the long haul.' There was a faint undertone of dissatisfaction as he said this, which made Markham wonder if the position at the hall had somehow failed to deliver, but perhaps that was only a fleeting impression.

An agreeable interlude followed, with his colleagues proving insatiable for stories of horoscopes, spells and Black Masses. And for all his disapproval of the juicier anecdotes, Noakes was visibly hooked on details of powders and potions.

Absorbing the splendours of the exhibition, Markham wondered if *this* was where their killer had conceived the plan to murder Charles Larrain. Was there something in the very air of Carton Hall conducive to plotting death by poison?

As though aware of what the DI was thinking, Christopher Hassett wound up the tour with an allusion to the ghost of Lady Mary and the story that she had been poisoned by her husband.

'Do *you* believe it, Mr Hassett?' Markham asked.

'I'm not sure that I do,' the other replied after a thoughtful pause. 'He was a well-known lothario with many enemies, so fomenting rumours was one way to make trouble. And nothing was ever proved against him.' A sudden puckish grin. 'But it's great box office, so we're happy to talk up the legend.'

At that point, Hassett tactfully melted away so that the detectives could explore the premises at their leisure. 'There's refreshments for you in the housekeeper's room when you're ready,' he told them. 'You can't miss it — off the corridor behind the Great Hall.'

The two-storeyed manor exhibited a fascinating mixture of historical styles, from Tudor carved oak furniture and intricate Jacobean ceilings through to the Victorian Gothic of the library and main parlour. Noakes was delighted to detect the motif of monkeys repeated throughout the various rooms and even in the stained glass of the tiny chapel, though Markham disliked their simian capering, especially those images which showed the creatures with mouths stretched wide and teeth bared. They made Burton uncomfortable too. 'Like wicked little gargoyles,' she said uneasily.

While charmed by the monkeys, Noakes was warier of the astrological and magical items which turned up in just about every room, together with death masks, witch bottles and cunning little memento mori such as coffin-shaped snuff boxes. The many allegorical paintings which featured gurning skeletons cavorting with assorted nobility also 'creeped him out'. However, he was quite taken with a series of Pre-Raphaelite illustrations of the tomb scene from *Romeo and Juliet*, somewhat to the surprise of his colleagues who recalled his scathing denunciation of Pre-Raphaelite paintings in a previous investigation as 'S&M for Victorians'. However, the DS stuck to his guns.

'Them lasses we saw last time looked like they'd had too many pies,' he declared, mastiff's head on one side like a connoisseur. 'But *she's* okay.' He pointed to a Frederic Leighton reproduction. 'Ackshually, she reminds me of your Olivia,' he told Markham, ears turning slightly pink as he offered this insight.

Doyle smothered a grin. *God, what was it with Noakesy's crush on Olivia Mullen . . . ? It had to be the worst kept secret in CID. Anyone'd think she'd cast a spell on him or something.*

Impenetrably grave, Markham acknowledged the compliment with his usual cast-iron courtesy. 'A flattering comparison, Sergeant.'

Burton shifted impatiently. 'Maybe all this points to the killer being someone who works here, or a regular visitor . . . someone who developed a fixation with poison,' she said. 'After all, that's how Romeo and Juliet die, right?'

'What was it they took?' Noakes asked, temporarily diverted from his perusal of willowy nineteenth-century heroines. 'I mean, Shakespeare never said, did he?' He scratched his bristly chin. 'Had a bit of a thing about poison, though, old Willy Shakes. I remember from O level . . . someone pouring stuff into his brother's ear . . .'

'That's *Hamlet*,' Doyle piped up. 'It was most likely hemlock or deadly nightshade.'

'Deadly nightshade's the same as belladonna,' Burton informed them. 'I read somewhere that Elizabethan ladies used drops of it to make their eyes sparkle.'

'Let's find the housekeeper's room,' Markham said firmly. 'Then we can thrash this out in comfort.' He also wanted to take the conversation somewhere more private, since he could not rid himself of an impression that the wainscoted walls had ears.

Or maybe it was something about those omnipresent primates which reminded him of the flying monkeys from *The Wizard of Oz* . . .

Nothing loath, the team made their way down to the corridor behind the Great Hall, easily locating the housekeeper's room next to the kitchen where they found tea and coffee urns along with a freshly baked Victoria sponge.

'Mrs Mop knows how to make folk feel welcome,' Noakes said appreciatively, losing no time in tucking in. 'So, what do we reckon the killer used on poor Charlie boy then?' he asked through a mouthful of cake.

'Dimples should have the toxicology results back by tomorrow morning,' Markham said. 'Unofficially, his money's on mercury for the e-cig and insect powder in the hip flask.'

'How did the killer get hold of the mercury?' Doyle mused. 'I mean, it's not like you can just pop along and ask the chemist . . . Isn't there a Poisons Book and all that palaver?'

Burton frowned. 'There's mercury in all kinds of products . . . ointments, disinfectants, fungicides, stuff like that.'

'In thermometers too,' Noakes chipped in.

She nodded slowly. 'You'd be able to pick up liquid mercury from a chemical supply store. They have it in all kinds of places . . . school chemistry labs and industrial sites. I think you can even get it off Amazon.'

'Mercury poisoning . . . that's what the Mad Hatter had in *Alice in Wonderland*,' Noakes told them solemnly. 'Cos hatmakers used mercury on the felt an' then breathed it in.'

Markham joined the debate. 'Apparently liquid mercury's most dangerous when it vaporises,' he said. 'The fumes are odourless and can be very quickly absorbed.'

'So Mr Larrain could've been puffing away without realising the risks?' Doyle asked.

'Precisely.' Markham's face was grave as he added, 'It's a neurotoxin that can trigger psychosis and pulmonary failure.'

Doyle thought for a moment. 'Okay, so he'd be at risk of hallucinations and his lungs packing up, but the killer couldn't count on the mercury being fatal.'

'They could if they made sure to supplement it with something else,' Burton observed. 'Larrain knocked back paraquat or something toxic from the hip flask,' she pointed out. 'Even a tiny sip of weedkiller can be fatal.'

'An' if they had a thing for poisons, mercury might've been special to them for some reason,' Noakes conjectured. 'An' they wanted him to really suffer.'

'They still couldn't be sure someone mightn't come across Larrain in time to get medical help,' Doyle persisted.

'I'd say the risk of outside intervention was minimal, Sergeant,' Markham countered. 'The killer knew the hall was pretty much deserted on Saturday night and had either lured Mr Larrain there or was aware he had plans to visit his favourite rooms, given that he pretty much had the run of the place as Richard Twiss's close friend.'

'At some point beforehand, they must've tampered with the vape kit and hip flask,' Burton speculated. 'Most likely when he was at the Artisan Centre . . . perhaps at work with his jacket hanging up, so the killer had time to doctor his gear—'

'Or substitute identikits,' Doyle ventured.

'*Nah*, flash gits like him would have everything custom made an' monogrammed,' Noakes objected. 'The killer would've had to sneak off with his jacket an' get it back without anyone seeing.'

'We'll need to plot Mr Larrain's movements on Saturday and establish precisely who had access to him,' Markham said. 'If we're finished,' with a meaningful glance at Noakes who had just sneaked a second slice of cake, 'I want to get an incident room set up.'

'*Here*, boss?' Burton asked eagerly, visibly delighted at the prospect of working in such historic surroundings.

'Well, if Mr Hassett can find us a suitable corner, I think that might be best. The hall will be closed to the public this week while the SOCOs finish up, so at least we won't have to worry about tourists and rubberneckers.'

Like Burton, Markham relished the idea of basing his team at the hall. There was something theatrical and magical about the place, from the old-fashioned handsome furniture and faded Persian carpets to the high windows which presented such an agreeable contrast to the cramped claustrophobia of their shabby quarters in CID. And whereas there was little opportunity to appreciate the snowscape from Bromgrove police station with its slush-covered pavements, here every view offered an aesthetically pleasing prospect of unsullied white brilliance thrown into sharp relief by the black-branched trees of neighbouring copses.

* * *

Later that evening, over a Chinese takeaway with Olivia, Markham tried to sum up Carton's appeal.

'Architecturally, it's rather bizarre,' he said. 'The Tudor part has lots of geometrical timber patterning — very romantic and picturesque — and then there're these extensions dating to the eighteenth and nineteenth centuries tacked on.'

'We used to do school trips there every year,' Olivia said. 'That was before Call-Me-Tony and Old Mother Lipscombe started pushing their woke agenda and banned any visits to places that were "culturally suspect".'

An English teacher at Hope Academy (popularly known as 'Hopeless'), Olivia regularly found herself at odds with the insufferably right-on Headteacher and Assistant Head whose antipathy for imperialist antecedents hobbled her ambition to expand the school curriculum.

Markham chuckled. '*Ah*, I take it the hall has a connection with colonialism.'

'Pretty tenuous, if you ask me . . . Some distant cousin owned slaves.' She speared a pork ball as intently as though it was a tender part of Anthony Brighouse's anatomy. 'It made no odds to the gruesome twosome that the Twisses who owned Carton Hall actually supported the *abolition* of slavery. Once they got a whiff of the plantation in Jamaica, it was goodbye to any more extra-curricular outings that might,' she air-quoted savagely, '"cause offence".'

'In fairness to them, I suppose they're trying to be inclusive and redress the balance, so that youngsters have some idea of the bigger picture.'

She punched his arm mock-indignantly. '*Whose side are you on*?' And with a distinctly acid undertone, 'Sounds to me like you've got a bad case of Kate Burton.'

He chose to ignore that.

'Cheer up, Liv. One day they'll get promoted out of Hope and you'll be free of Cancel Culture.'

'The local authority will probably foist another pair of zealots on us,' she said gloomily. Then more brightly, she continued, 'I like the sound of "The Power of Poison" exhibition, Gil . . . There's something fascinating about the Renaissance and all those courtiers at each other's throats.' She giggled. 'A bit like CID.'

'Maybe that's why the team went a bundle on it,' he replied drily. 'You should have seen Noakesy . . . he really had a ball.' With a reminiscent smile, he added, 'He couldn't get enough of Catherine de Medici . . . Loved the story of the poisoned gloves.'

Olivia's eyebrows shot up. '*Oh*?'

'Catherine whisked this visiting Protestant royal off for a shopping expedition. The lady in question loved perfumed gloves—'

'That figures, with everyone in those days stinking to high heaven, and folk needing to cover it up,' Olivia laughed. 'I remember reading that Elizabeth I took a bath once a month *whether she needed it or not!*'

'Precisely,' Markham chuckled. 'Well, Catherine took her guest to buy gloves from this perfumier who secretly doubled as her poisoner. Like everyone else in those days, the poor woman wanted her gloves strongly scented to obliterate body odour and disguise the reek of the dog dirt tanners used to make gloves supple. She knew the perfumier Master Bianco had a bad reputation, but she shrugged off the rumours.'

'*Uh-oh*, somehow I think you're going to tell me it ended badly.'

'Yep . . . She died shortly afterwards. The post-mortem showed the rupture of an abscess on her lungs, but most people believed Catherine had arranged for the gloves to be poisoned.'

Olivia rolled her eyes. 'Isn't there a saying, "One must suffer to be beautiful" . . . Sounds like that poor doomed princess or whoever she was took it to extremes!'

'She was a queen apparently. The queen of Navarre.'

'Where's that?'

'Oh, it doesn't exist now. In those days, it was some tiny state sandwiched between France and Spain.'

Markham helped Olivia to more chow mein and poured himself another generous glass of his favourite Châteauneuf-du-Pape.

'Poison was an occupational hazard for all kinds of folk,' he observed, 'not just the nobility. Kate told me painters used a white paint made of lead mixed up with arsenic. So when they sucked on their brushes to create a more pointed tip, they were actually poisoning themselves . . . She said that's most probably what happened with Caravaggio, and it didn't help that he smudged painted canvases with his fingers or rags without washing his hands afterwards.'

As he dished up some more sweet and sour pork, Markham missed the slight narrowing of Olivia's eyes at the mention of Kate Burton but her voice was level when she said lightly, 'Musicians too.'

'How so?'

'Well, you know everyone thinks Mozart was poisoned by his jealous rival Salieri, like in the film *Amadeus*? There's a new idea doing the rounds that says he might have caught a streptococcal infection from horses because he was always dashing around in carriages.'

'Intriguing.' Markham smiled with a tenderness that would have astonished the detractors who called him 'Lord Snooty' because of his aristocratic aloofness. The hawklike features softened still further as he went on to give Olivia an account of his day.

'So we're going to base ourselves at the hall for now,' he concluded.

'I suppose it has the advantage of keeping George well away from Judas Iscariot,' she observed. 'By the by, what news of his plans to retire?'

'I think there may be some resistance from Muriel to the idea of him setting up as a private investigator.'

Olivia flashed him a grin of complicity. '*I'll bet.*'

'But I reckon it's definitely on the cards . . . I even have a feeling he hopes to persuade Doyle to come in with him.'

'Any chance of that happening?'

Markham shook his head. 'I doubt it. Doyle's very thick with Noakesy, but it's too much of a gamble.' He sighed. 'I suspect this may be our last outing together in CID.'

She reached for his hand. 'Better make sure George's career ends on a high. "*Fab Four Solve Poison Riddle*".'

He returned the pressure, but his face was shadowed.

'It's the most baffling case I've ever encountered, Liv.'

Later that night in bed, with Olivia curled up next to him, Markham found himself restless. In his nostrils was the scent of Carton Hall with its patina of centuries of beeswax overlaid with a faint overlay of must and damp. A sweet and sour fragrance all of its own.

There had been a surreal quality to the events of the day, as though he and the team were themselves effigies being manipulated into position by an invisible hand. His last conscious thought was the memory of Catherine de Medici's black mourning veil and the waxen countenance of the Poisoner-Queen.

Wrapped in bloody crepe till the end of time.

3. BORROWED LIKENESS

Markham rose very early on Tuesday 14 December, taking strong black coffee into his study so as not to disturb Olivia.

Their apartment at the upmarket complex known as the Sweepstakes overlooked Bromgrove North Municipal Cemetery, a vista he never tired of contemplating.

Now as he regarded the snowy counterpane that coated the graves and monuments under a pewter sky faintly streaked with red, he thought how strange it was that the dead should lie so perfectly still while the planet spun on its axis like a plaything of God.

Yet, however strong his awareness of human insignificance in the cosmic scheme, Markham never forgot the individuality of murder victims, the proximity to graves and monuments helping him to keep their memory close. At this time of the morning, with the landscape outside the bay window so blindingly white, he could almost imagine the walls of the flat falling away and the ceiling opening to give him a glimpse of that other world with its special kind of life that did not exist on earth at all . . .

There was something about it in the Bible — words that he had heard recited at innumerable funerals and memorial services down the years . . . Something about souls who wore glistening white robes and carried palm branches, who walked, mingled, and sang a special heavenly language, totally at peace, all striving gone.

Noakes, curiously, never scoffed when Markham dropped hints of this obscure yearning after a better existence for his murdered dead. His own unshakeable religious faith — that sturdy Methodism — was part of his DNA, and he experienced no such supernatural apprehension. But he showed great respect for the guvnor's 'otherworldly side' and was manifestly proud of having a boss so far removed from the common run of CID supremos. Perhaps too he remembered the boss's younger brother, long since lost to drink and drugs — the sibling Markham had been unable to protect from their abusive stepfather — and understood the DI's preoccupation with another world free of clouds and bewilderment.

Markham knew that Slimy Sid took a dim view of feyness — what he was pleased to term 'Markham's Oxbridge airs and graces' — and was therefore careful to curb any imaginative impulses when briefing the DCI. But it was difficult to remain unaffected by the strange ambience of Carton Hall which he suspected somehow played a part in the psychological makeup of their poisoner.

At least there were no next-of-kin to be contacted, Charles Larrain being an only child whose parents had died in Canada many years previously. Markham never shirked the condolence visits — never shunted them on to his subordinates — but on this occasion could not help feeling a guilty relief at being spared that task.

His mind turned to the team's tasks for the day.

He and Noakes would interview family and staff while Kate and Doyle took Old Carton Farm and the Dower Cottage. He could only hope that his wingman's notorious dislike of forelock-tugging wouldn't tip over into outright truculence, but he sensed that Noakes too had succumbed to the eerie, almost unearthly, allure of the hall and was on that account less likely to antagonise the Hunting-Shooting-Fishing Brigade.

God only knew what kind of attire his wingman would fix on for interviewing the Twisses. Something tweedy and porridge-coloured no doubt, as being most suitable for a rural interlude. Not forgetting the trusty regimental tie, to underline his patriotic credentials and general reliability.

The DS was bound to ruin the overall effect with an appalling deerstalker or some other dubious accessory. With any luck, he could be passed off as endearingly eccentric rather than downright offensive. At least the Twisses were unlikely to spout any of the 'woke twaddle' guaranteed to bring out his combative streak. And Noakes's genuine interest in the hall — from coalholes to trapdoors and closets — was surely a passport to acceptance. To say nothing of his fascination with 'The Power of Poison' exhibition.

Markham shifted uneasily at the memory of the dream he had last night. He could still feel the heavy folds of that Italian woman's mourning weeds dragging him down. Could almost smell their choking mustiness . . .

He gulped down his rapidly cooling coffee and took one last look out of the window.

Snow-laden trees in the cemetery, white and stark, reared up against the leaden sky. There was something almost supplicatory about their heavy-laden boughs, as though, like him, they sought to reach up to heaven and penetrate its secrets.

Perhaps it was a trick of the light, but he fancied he saw a pale smudge against the thicket of black-branched birches on the graveyard's far periphery. Then it moved and was gone. It gave him a disagreeable sensation. *The watcher watched.* In that instant, he recalled the team's last investigation at an Oxford museum exhibition devoted to polar exploration, when they had learned that travellers at the South Pole were often haunted by the feeling there was an extra person walking beside them . . .

He shook his head, as if to banish his increasingly dark thoughts. The daylight was getting stronger. Time for another coffee before he drove to Noakes's to give him a lift to Carton Hall.

Padding out to the galley kitchen, he wondered how the dynamics of the team would shift once Noakes finally cashed in his chips. Sidney would most likely see if as an ideal opportunity to foist some dynamic whiz-kid, fluent in politically correct psychobabble, on him. Said wunderkind would also no doubt be recruited to spy on Markham's unit and report back to 'the gold-braid mob'. Not at all an inviting prospect, though at least he knew he could count on loyalty from Kate and Doyle . . .

He shrugged off such depressing thoughts as an unnecessary distraction given that they had a deranged poisoner on the loose. A late-night call from Dimples had confirmed the cause of death as myocardial infarction following mercury inhalation combined with ingestion of strychnine.

'Now here's the thing,' the pathologist had concluded. 'According to his medical records, Larrain had significantly decreased resistance to toxic agents compared with most people. A double hit of that kind was always going to be catastrophic.'

'Assuming he was disorientated from the effects of the mercury, couldn't he still have spat out the weedkiller or pesticide or whatever it was?'

'His gag reflex didn't kick in,' was the blunt response. 'Even if someone had been on hand to induce vomiting, it would most likely have been too late with him going into shock like that . . . His whole system shut down almost immediately, so if the heart attack hadn't killed him, organ failure would have done.'

Neither man had commented on the appalling image of Larrain spasming uncontrollably and writhing in agony while his killer stood feet away watching and waiting.

Now as he showered and dressed, Markham wondered anew about 'The Power of Poison' exhibition.

Had it acted as *inspiration* for the murderer? Were they looking for someone who had a deep-seated affinity with the poisoner's art, or had the exhibition merely afforded a convenient opportunity to dispatch Larrain in circumstances that satisfied some sick quirk of personality?

Either way, it added up to a killer quite unlike any they had hunted before . . .

Noakes's bucolic wardrobe was indeed of the porridgy variety, Markham reflected a short time later as the DS crunched his way over to the car. But he supposed it could have been infinitely worse and was grateful that the oilskin fishing hat didn't strike too discordant a note when taken with the overall 'winter grunge' look.

Driving carefully along ruts and ridges that sparkled dangerously in the weak early-morning sun, the DI brought his subordinate up to speed on the post-mortem findings.

'So poor old Aznavour weren't the strongest to start with,' Noakes commented. 'Most likely the killer knew he'd go into anaphylactic wotsit an' peg out soon as the poisons got into his bloodstream . . . thrashing about like he had rabies or summat.'

As ever, Noakes had the gift of painting a picture with a few well-chosen words, the canine comparison reminding Markham of Larrain's froth-flecked features and the corpse arched in its death throes. All under the implacable gaze of a torturer who watched from among those strange effigies of the State Anteroom which looked fiercely nowhere and stared with extraordinary intensity at nothing.

'There's a cold-blooded deliberation about it all,' he agreed.

'What tack are we going to take with the twisted Twisses?' his wingman enquired jocularly.

'Well, for starters we need to ensure they don't get straight on to the blower and complain to the DCI about any want of courtesy on our part,' Markham said with a dead-eyed sidelong glance at his colleague. 'Remember, Mrs Sidney and Lady Twiss both serve on that Heritage Committee.'

'The missus'd be good at that,' Noakes ruminated evasively. 'National Trust an' flower arranging an' all that jazz.'

It seemed as though Muriel Noakes's social aspirations were the surest guarantee of a housetrained DS, Markham thought suppressing a chuckle. By the sound of it, there would be no sideshow of the Revolting Peasants variety. A part of him realised that he was almost disappointed at the prospect of Noakes reining himself in, but the sensitivities of the local community required careful handling.

However, the DS wasn't totally squelched, defiantly whistling 'All Things Bright and Beautiful' as they juddered along to Carton Hall.

Markham's lips quirked at the well-remembered lyrics:

The rich man in his castle. The poor man at his gate. God made them, high or lowly. And ordered their estate.

One way or another, George Noakes always had to have the last word.

After this, they travelled for a time in companionable silence.

Eventually Noakes broke the tranquillity.

'I've jus' seen a robin redbreast,' he said. 'Thass meant to be lucky, right?'

'I believe so . . . Or it can symbolise a visit by the dead.'

'There's a story about it being red cos of getting its chest burned when it was fanning the fire to keep Baby Jesus warm.' It was very apparent that Noakes preferred this legend to any notion of ghostly revenants.

'I like robins on Christmas cards,' he continued inconsequentially. 'The missus likes 'em too . . . it's tradition, see.' Then unexpectedly he added, 'The Twiss Family Robinson had a decent crib in that big fireplace downstairs.'

'I hadn't spotted that, Noakes.'

'Oh aye, it were there alright, a miniature cave with the ox an' ass an' everything . . . better than a stable in my book.'

'How so?'

'Well, they used caves for the animals back then. Plus, it shows Jesus were *badly off* . . . Didn't even get to be born in the city, an outsider from day one. Stands to reason he were always dead keen on poor folk.'

Markham found himself oddly touched by this observation, shedding as it did new light on his sergeant's inveterate compassion for the underdog.

'Our Nat played Mary when they did it at primary school,' the DS reminisced happily. 'They had live animals an' everything.'

The DI had a sudden disconcerting image of Natalie Noakes wearing a long blue veil, with her eyes cast down and her hands plastered together, finger to finger . . . Joseph and the Shepherds would have been cast quite in the shade.

Noakes continued his whistling. At least these pious recollections served to put him in good humour.

Now they had passed through the lodge and approached the long winding path to Carton Hall.

As they got out of the car, it seemed to Markham that the silence of the snow-covered countryside fell more heavily on his ears than the town's noisiest traffic hum. Inhaling the bitingly cold air which set his lungs on fire, he felt suddenly light-headed, almost drunk, as though he stood outside himself.

But the sensation passed. Noakes trudged ahead of him to the entrance, depressing the great brass doorbell with his customary impatience.

* * *

Markham wasn't sure exactly what he had been expecting with the Twisses. Something *Downton Abbey*-ish and fruitily squirearchical if he was honest.

In the event, Sir Simon and Lady Edith were almost nondescript. The former, in well-worn tweeds, had a surprisingly youthful pink scrubbed face ('like Pigling Bland, or a peeled prawn', as Noakes put it to Doyle afterwards), and sensual, good-natured features that were somewhat at odds with the swept-back thinning white hair. He projected a slightly helpless, absent-minded air, as of the world being too much for him, but Markham suspected this was an affectation. His wife, whippet-thin with sharp angular features and hooded eyes, gave nothing away, merely echoing her husband's conventional expressions of surprise and shock.

Richard Twiss was swarthily handsome with a well-tended black moustache and long dark hair, artfully dishevelled, that gave him the appearance of a rock star. Markham noticed that he had long, elegant hands with tapering fingers, like those of a musician. His striking appearance was marred only by a large mole between his right eye and nose. Chain-smoking and tense, he gave the appearance of one whose emotions were very close to the surface. His eyes kept swivelling to his mother, and Markham wondered if covert messages were passing between them somehow. Certainly, the youngest son Philip — also handsome with curly dark hair, tanned skin somewhat pitted by acne and lustrous black eyes, though undersized by the side of Richard — likewise kept a wary eye on his mother, as though waiting for her to feed him his lines.

Margaret Twiss, on the other hand, seemed to be outside the charmed circle of mother and sons. Also very striking with long black hair, dead-white complexion, a generous mouth and doe eyes, she said little and stood somewhat apart from the rest of the family wearing an expression of ironical forbearance. The eldest son Michael, who arrived after the others, did not share the good looks of his siblings. Tall and sallow-cheeked, with lustreless brown hair and a reedy voice, he had a listless hypochondriacal air which was in marked contrast to the vitality of his brothers and sister.

Unsurprisingly, when it came to alibis, all of the family claimed to have been virtuously abed, though there was a tell-tale slither of Richard Twiss's eyes towards his mother that did not go unnoticed by Markham and Noakes.

Afterwards, installed in a bow-windowed room on the first floor at the front of the house, with lots of furniture of a faded blue, a profusion of sporting prints and any number of thin-legged chairs and tables, the DS lost no time in fingering his prime suspect.

'Ricardo weren't telling the truth about Saturday night,' he grunted. 'An' you could see his old mum knew it . . . God, she's a real hatchet-face. Amazing how she an' Baron

Hard-up managed to produce a looker like the daughter. Did you see the *state* of his lordship's jacket!' Noakes contemplated his own donkey-jacket with some complacency. 'All frayed an' falling apart at the seams.'

Markham refrained from pointing out that the well-worn look of 'shabby gentility' was invariably favoured by families like the Twisses in a species of inverted snobbery that deplored any appearance of trying too hard or putting forth one's best. Better to encourage his wingman's belief that he had put one over on the aristos from the outset.

'Yes, judging by his demeanour, I'd agree that Richard Twiss most probably wasn't tucked up in bed. Though we've got nothing to break that alibi as things stand.'

'The bloke's a ponce, guv. He had an earring an' all.'

Markham supposed it might be considered progress that Noakes hadn't immediately unleashed his usual dithyrambs about homosexuals.

'The fact that the man has an unconventional appearance is neither here nor there, sergeant,' he said repressively.

But Noakes had the resilience of India rubber. 'If him an' Aznavour were *at it*, then we could be looking at a lovers' quarrel.' The DS's lower lip shot out, giving him the look of a mutinous child. '*Crime passionnel*,' he added in an execrable *allez-oops* accent. 'Plus, Lady Hatchet-Face said,' this in a niminy-piminy voice, '"Mr Larrain had a colourful private life". *Colourful* as in he weren't choosy about who he shagged.'

'Spare me the scatological language, Noakes. The fact that Mr Larrain may have been bisexual does not incriminate Richard Twiss, and certainly not based on his looks.'

The DS changed tack. 'You could tell the rest of 'em didn't like Aznavour. An' another thing.' Markham braced himself, but the other merely pointed out, 'They weren't surprised someone murdered him.'

Markham nodded, relieved. 'Which suggests that the man had his fair share of enemies.'

There was a diffident tap at the door and Christopher Hassett appeared.

'Good morning, gentlemen. I hope the room suits.' He must have detected something in Noakes's expression because he added apologetically. 'It's a bit over-feminine and cluttered, I know.'

'Think nothing of it, sir,' Markham reassured him courteously. 'Inspector Burton will be arranging the computers and phones, so it's just a case of keeping my team fed and watered.'

Hassett's expression cleared. 'Oh, Mrs Scarron will see to all of that, never fear.' He smiled shyly. 'When it comes to hospitality, she always takes the view that the honour of the house is at stake.'

Noakes looked as if he thoroughly approved such laudable sentiments.

'She'll be along shortly,' Hassett concluded, 'and I'll send Sir Simon's PA down once she's sorted the morning mail.'

'Excellent, thank you Mr Hassett.'

As the curator seemed disposed to linger, Markham brought up the woman who had haunted his dreams the previous night.

'I found it difficult to get those poisoning royals you showed us out of my head,' he said waving the other to a chair.

Hassett grinned, suddenly looking much younger. 'Catherine de Medici tends to have that effect on visitors,' he said. 'Of course, she lived in an age of eclipses, comets and other unusual sights, so it's not surprising she had such a fascination with the black arts.'

'The voodoo woman, right?' Noakes said, piggy eyes alert with interest.

'The very same. She was rumoured to have second sight . . . regularly woke screaming in the night and prophesying the death of a loved one. She foresaw her husband's death . . . begged him not to take part in the fatal joust . . . dreamed that he lay wounded, bleeding in the face. And then *hey presto*, his opponent's lance shattered, and splinters went into his eye. Once the infection took hold, the king was doomed.'

'Did they cut off the other bloke's head?' Noakes asked eagerly.

Hassett chuckled.

'The gallant knight begged the king to cut off his head and hands, but Henri said he hadn't committed any offence. Mind you, the court doctors went and got hold of the decapitated heads of criminals who had been executed the day before to see if they could reproduce the king's wounds on the skulls and work out a way to cure him.'

'*Chuffing Nora.*' Noakes was visibly enthralled. 'Mebbe the king dying like that was a punishment cos of his missus getting up to witchcraft.'

'She was a sinister woman and no mistake.'

'No oil painting neither.'

'True, Sergeant. When it was late and getting dark on the day, she made her entry into Lyon to be crowned, unkind people said the king wanted the coronation to take place under cover of night so that no one would notice her ugliness.' Hassett paused, eyeing Noakes's portly frame. 'She was a chronic overeater and got very stout . . . one reason why she developed gout.'

'Yeah, well it were prob'ly wall to wall banquets in them days,' the DS said a trifle self-consciously.

'But it didn't stop her hunting and hawking . . . all the usual royal pursuits.'

'An' perving,' Noakes interjected beadily.

Hassett looked startled.

'I believe my sergeant is referring to the rumours of incest,' Markham clarified hastily.

'*Ah*, I'm with you now. Yes, that's right, those stories dogged her all her life. She was obsessively protective of her children — always consulting astrologers who performed tricks with pentacles and crystal balls. One of them summoned the spirits of the sons and told her that the number of times their faces circled a mirror corresponded to the number of years they would reign.' A harsh bark of laughter. 'Actually, they were spot on in predicting that her line would die out . . . That's why she was so ruthless when it came to punishing traitors — having them sewn into sacks and dumped in the river Loire to drown or turning beheadings into a spectator sport. Her sons were cruel as well, and all of them were disfigured in some way; the eldest was so bad, he was said to be leprous while the middle one had a suppurating fistula on his face and the youngest was practically a dwarf.'

'What about the daughter?' Noakes enquired.

'Oh, she was beautiful, but being a girl meant she didn't really count . . . ended up becoming something of a nymphomaniac.'

'S'like the Kardashians or summat,' Noakes observed with relish.

Again, there came that charming grin which took years off the man. 'A very apt comparison, Sergeant. I imagine that's why our visitors can't get enough of these medieval misfits.'

A soft knock at the door announced the housekeeper's arrival.

She smiled indulgently at the curator. 'Giving them the talk are you, Mr Hassett?'

'You know me, Carmel . . . The merest whiff of an audience and I get carried away.' He gestured expansively at Markham and Noakes before adding, 'I'll leave you in Mrs Scarron's capable hands, gents.' And with that, he was gone.

Carmel Scarron was a wiry no-nonsense little woman who put Markham in mind of a 1920s housekeeper. Janet MacPherson from *Dr Finlay*, or something of the sort. He suspected she played up to the stereotype of the faithful retainer — indeed, had absorbed it so faithfully into her DNA that her own personality had become subsumed in the role. Despite the grey old-lady pin curls, her energetic manner suggested that she was younger than she looked. But something about her made Markham uneasy. And curious.

'No chance of getting her to dish the dirt,' Noakes lamented after she had departed to arrange some refreshments.

'It was more than that,' Markham said slowly. 'I had the impression she was holding something back . . .'

'What, you mean you thought her alibi were dodgy, guv?' Noakes enquired doubtfully. 'Seemed kosher to me . .

. I can see her getting stuck into the Horlicks an' *News at Ten* like she said.'

'No, not that . . . It was just a flicker, something behind her eyes when I mentioned the poison exhibition.' Gone so quickly, that Markham couldn't be sure he hadn't imagined that look of furtive apprehension, as though a lightbulb had gone on.

'Well, they all know from the lass who found the body that Aznavour puked his guts out right next door to the exhibition . . . So most likely they're freaked about some screwball running around putting cyanide in their drinks.'

'Hmm.' The DI still felt that niggle of unease. 'No doubt that's it.'

Another rap at the door interrupted these speculations.

This time it was Catherine Metcalfe, the events manager from the Artisan Centre. Attractive and well-groomed, with aquiline features framed by a frosted blonde bob and startlingly blue eyes, she gave the impression of being pure state-of-the-art Sloane right down to the clipped vowels and strangulated accent. But something about her didn't ring entirely true to Markham . . . as though she was trying too hard.

To the detectives' surprise, it transpired that she was Michael Twiss's girlfriend. 'Punching above his weight,' as Noakes put it after the interview. She had apparently spent the night at her own flat in Bromgrove town centre, which in terms of an alibi was as unsatisfactory as the rest.

Unlike the rest, though, she was frank about not liking Charles Larrain, though it appeared this stemmed primarily from his interference with her remit, specifically his attempts to 'sissify' the Artisan Centre with 'new age tat'. The DS threw Markham a glance of triumphant vindication on hearing this.

'Wonder how Burton an' Doyle are getting on at the Farm and Dower wotsit,' Noakes mused as the door closed behind the events manager. Scratching his paunch lazily in a fashion that was singularly ill-suited to the elegant surroundings, he added, 'At least Mister Curator were worth listening to but as for the rest of 'em . . .' An eloquent shrug said it all.

The DI sighed. 'We need to speak to Sir Simon's PA,' he said. 'And then, once we've heard from Kate and Doyle, I want to check out that Artisan Centre.'

'Not before we've had our elevenses,' Noakes cut in anxiously.

'Oh, I've no doubt you'll do full justice to Mrs Scarron's hospitality.'

Sarcasm was wasted on the DS.

'Thass alright then,' he said jovially. Wandering to the bay window, he declared, 'It's snowing again, guv.'

The two men stood side by side watching fat flakes falling from sullen skies that seemed to press up against Carton Hall.

The winter landscape had an air of brooding anticipation that unsettled Markham.

Stiff and stark and cold . . . in the borrowed likeness of shrunk death.

4. PITIFUL DAY

In the event, Mrs Scarron's elevenses proved eminently satis-factory, with home-made shortbread and two types of cake. Markham normally ate sparingly on such occasions, but for once found himself both hungry and thirsty, doing full jus-tice to the excellent coffee and decadent chocolate fudge cake.

'Them Twisses should be right lard buckets with grub like this,' Noakes observed ruefully. He sounded as though there was no justice in the world. 'But there's not a pick on any of 'em.'

Markham grinned. 'Must be the aristocratic metabo-lism, Sergeant.'

'Well, Mrs Thing's wasted on 'em,' the DS grunted. Replete (for the time being), he betook himself once more to the window.

Despite the housekeeper having lit a wood fire in the ele-gant stone fireplace, it didn't entirely keep out a keen draught that nipped round their ankles.

''S no wonder they all wear them quilted jackets,' Noakes muttered. 'Must be brass monkeys in a place like this.'

'I imagine there's central heating in the private quarters,' Markham pointed out, 'but we're in the historic part of the building.'

'Oh aye,' the other grouched, looking as though he could have dispensed with medieval authenticity.

At that moment, the door opened to disclose Burton and Doyle, their faces pinched with cold. They brightened visibly at the sight of the refreshments, thawing out over hot drinks and cake.

Kate Burton, predictably, wasted little time in bringing them up to speed on the other branches of the family.

'Gerard Twiss is in his early seventies, but very spry and dapper,' she said. 'The wife, Stella, is a good bit younger — pretty in a faded sort of way. Comfortably off by the look of things . . . typical farming couple really. They're each other's alibi for Saturday night.'

Noakes groaned theatrically. 'Wouldn't you jus' sodding know it . . . It's the same here,' he groused. 'Like some toff version of *The Waltons* . . . Nobody out on the razz 'cept mebbe Rikki-Tikki-Tavi.'

Accustomed to Noakesian invective, Kate turned expectantly to Markham for a translation.

'Mr Richard Twiss didn't appear entirely comfortable when the subject of alibis was under discussion,' the DI explained.

'Too right,' the DS snorted. 'Kept looking at Mommie Dearest . . . dead shifty.'

Burton didn't appear to think this was much to go on.

'Did Gerard and Stella open up about the family dynamics?' Markham asked.

'They were pretty cagey,' Doyle replied, long legs tucked somewhat awkwardly under his spindle-legged Hepplewhite chair. 'Sounded quite fond of the younger ones, Philip and Margaret. Reading between the lines, Lady T spoils the boys and doesn't have time for her daughter . . . They didn't say much about Michael and Richard.'

'Anything about Mr Larrain?' Markham pressed.

Doyle pulled a face. 'You could tell they weren't keen . . . Said the polite stuff about terrible tragedy blah blah, but it was just the way they carefully didn't look at each other.'

'Stella's an antiquarian,' Burton said.

Noakes looked underwhelmed. 'What's one of them when it's at home?'

'Into history and all that.'

The DS cast a meaningful look towards Doyle. *Wouldn't you know she'd sniff out the local egghead.*

'She did an MA in Renaissance Studies at the university. It's one of the reasons she's close to Margaret,' the DI continued.

'Mebbe it's more than that,' Noakes said consideringly. 'When you think about how Aznavour were killed, the poisoning, them effigy thingies an' that creepy exhibition . . .' In his experience, "intellectual types" were capable of anything.

Burton blinked at 'Aznavour' but carried on gamely. 'Well, Stella and Margaret are certainly into Catherine de Medici and Co,' she agreed. 'Stella was a fount of information. Apparently, Catherine was known as Madame La Serpente or the Black Queen . . . but,' she eyed her colleague warily, 'there was a fair amount of racism in the mix on account of her being an Italian.'

'Oh yeah,' Doyle was interested. 'The curator guy said the Italians had a bit of a reputation.'

'That's right . . . for hiring assassins and poisoning their enemies,' Burton said. 'Actually, Stella might've kept shtum about her in-laws, but when you were out in the yard with Gerard,' she nodded at Doyle, 'she opened up about the hall and its treasures.'

Noakes grimaced. 'You mean all the black magic oojah?'

'Stella said the Black Queen had this sorcerer who made life size bronze effigies of people she wanted to kill.'

The DI could tell Noakes was hooked.

'It was all very realistic,' she went on. 'Right down to the long hair . . . Anyway, there were these screws that allowed their limbs to move and their chests and heads to be opened up . . . The sorcerer locked himself away to cast their horoscopes and did stuff with the screws based on what he found . . . Apparently when various folk turned up dead, there were these strange marks on their bodies that nobody understood.'

Noakes stared at her. 'So, the queen were calling up supernatural powers or summat?'

Burton nodded solemnly. 'Yes, something like that . . . It's one reason Margaret got so interested in those wax effigies people had at funerals.'

The DS shuddered. '*Jesus.*' Then, knowing Markham was notoriously touchy about blasphemy, he hastily amended, '*Chuffing Nora* . . . Talk about a freaky family.' He rumpled the salt and pepper hair so fiercely that the thatch stood bolt upright, giving it the appearance of a bizarre crest. 'What did Auntie Stella reckon to Ricardo an' Aznavour then? Were they,' he groped for an acceptable form of words, 'an *item*?'

'She wouldn't be drawn on Larrain,' Burton sighed. 'Fobbed me off with some historical rigmarole about "favourites" in great dynastic families.'

'*Eh?*' Noakes clearly felt out of his depth.

Burton pursed her lips. 'She called them *mignons*—'

'Gangs of pretty boys that the aristos liked to have dancing attendance,' Doyle interrupted eagerly. 'Nobody was ever sure if things got sexual . . . The French were into it big style, but it caught on over here too.' He turned to Burton. 'Didn't you say James I was always slobbering over some young bloke or other, ma'am?'

'That's right. The Overbury poisoning involved one of James's favourites.'

'Do you think Stella was suggesting the intimacy between Mr Larrain and Richard Twiss was all about *image*, Kate?' Markham asked. 'An affectation to whip up interest in them and the Artisan Centre . . . ramp up the bohemian vibe?'

'Yes, guv, I reckon that could be it. She and Gerard seemed pretty strait-laced . . . It was obvious they knew what I was driving at when I asked about Richard's close friendship with Larrain. That's why Stella tried to distract us with the historical flim-flam.'

Doyle was struck by a thought. 'There was *one* thing, though.'

His colleagues waited expectantly.

'When I was outside with Gerard, he implied that Lady Twiss always saw off anyone who threatened her relationship with Richard . . . He said something like, "My sister-in-law likes to rule the roost. Gets rid of hangers-on in double quick time."'

'Interesting.' Markham was thoughtful. 'But nothing explicit?'

'Well, underneath all the fruity harrumphing, I had the feeling he didn't like Edith,' Doyle replied. 'But maybe it's the *women* who didn't hit it off and the husbands got drawn in.'

'Anything new from Dimples, sir?' Burton asked.

As Markham updated them on the toxicology, Doyle's brow puckered.

'It's weird when you think about it . . . If the murderer wanted to finish Larrain off at the hall, they couldn't have been sure he wouldn't have a vape or swig from the hip flask while he was still at work . . .'

'They definitely wanted it to happen up *here*,' Noakes pronounced with conviction. 'Wanted him choking an' jerking an' whatnot in that creepy effigy room . . . they were *staging* it, see,' he added surprisingly.

'I think you're right, Sergeant,' Markham concurred. 'It fits with the sexual sadism that Dimples talked about . . . the warped egotism of a truly complex criminal.'

His wingman tried not to preen but failed entirely.

'So, how'd it pan out then?' Doyle tried to picture the scenario. 'Did the killer arrange to meet Larrain up here . . . then tamper with the vape kit and hip flask just before he headed out? Or did they hold off until he was at the hall and then somehow manage to doctor the stuff behind his back?'

'They couldn't be sure Larrain would leave his things lying around once he were at the Hall,' Noakes declared with conviction. 'So my money's on 'em doing the dirty *right before* he left the centre.'

Doyle considered the case from all angles. 'But what was to stop Larrain vaping or having a nip from his flask on his way here? I mean, the murderer couldn't necessarily *count* on him collapsing bang on cue in the effigies room like that . . .'

'Maybe they walked up to the hall with him,' Burton surmised. 'Kept Larrain under observation the whole time.'

'Surely that would be too risky, Kate,' Markham said. 'There was always the chance of being spotted.'

'Gerard Twiss said Larrain was always round here,' Doyle commented thoughtfully. '"Mooching round the place", was how he put it.'

'Only nobody saw him that night,' Burton said exasperatedly. 'And there's no CCTV or anything like that to go on . . . So we're pretty much stuffed.'

'If Mr Larrain's habits were well known, then the murderer must have been confident that he wouldn't vape or resort to his hip flask until he was at the hall,' Markham reasoned slowly.

'Mebbe they knew he liked to save it for that room with the weirdy statues . . . cos it spiced things up,' Noakes suggested. 'Kind of like a *ritual*. If Aznavour were a bit kinky that way an' the murderer knew his routine, then *well* . . .' There was a wealth of meaning in the DS's expansive gesture.

'Do you know, I think you're on to something there, sergeant,' Markham said thoughtfully, revolving the picture in his mind. 'From what we've learned about Mr Larrain, I believe he may indeed have resorted to nicotine and alcohol when he visited the waxworks . . . The killer must have been familiar with his habits, knew it was what he liked to do.'

'Like Harold Shipman.' This being Noakes's lodestar when it came to necrophiliac dysfunction. 'When the old folk were dead in their armchairs, he sat an' watched 'em an' *gloated* cos he got off on it being like some creepy picture show.'

'Don't forget, Larrain's the *victim* here,' Burton protested.

'True, Kate. But at least it gives us a working hypothesis for his death,' Markham told her gently.

'At least with Shipman they didn't die in agony,' she said weakly. 'Strychnine's a horrible way to go,'

'Mercury ain't a bundle of laughs neither,' Noakes pointed out morosely.

'I know . . . But,' her complexion acquired a rosy glow, 'Nathan and I were talking about it last night.'

Probably what passes for foreplay with those two, Noakes thought sardonically.

'Larrain would've had violent convulsions,' she said. 'It's called *tetanus* . . . Your body thrusts into an arch while your head and heels stay on the floor and your eyes practically come out of their sockets . . . There's this Joker-type grimace — *risus sardonicus* . . . You lose complete control of your body and it's like someone's sitting on your chest crushing the breath out of you . . .'

'Not counting the burned throat,' Doyle put in faintly.

Markham preferred not to imagine the oesophageal trauma. Privately, he was thankful it had been Noakes and not Kate Burton who attended in the immediate aftermath of the discovery at Carton Hall. Backward and chauvinistic no doubt, but he had this desire to shield her from the worst depredations that humans inflicted on each other. Strange, seeing as she was now a seasoned detective inspector, but there it was . . .

He suspected that Noakes entertained similar sentiments.

'That heart attack were prob'ly the best thing,' the DS said gruffly. 'Put the poor sod out of his misery.'

But not before the killer had enjoyed the spectacle of Larrain being ushered into eternity with strychnine twisting every joint of his body.

Now Doyle asked, 'Would the strychnine have been enough to do for Larrain without the mercury?'

'Dimples said you get paraesthesia with about forty milligrams of mercury vapour,' Markham replied. 'The burning sensation would've made him thirsty. And thus the more inclined to reach for a drink.'

A grim silence fell. Eventually, Markham broke it.

'Did you visit Lady Edith's sister at the Dower Cottage?' he asked Burton.

Burton pulled herself together with a visible effort, the neat bob swinging as she sat up straighter on the matching Hepplewhite to Doyle's.

'I did, sir. Isobel Farquhar . . . Big-boned horsey lady with pudding bowl haircut, red cheeks and a booming voice.' A wry smile. 'No great harm in her, though.'

'Loud and bossy,' Doyle qualified. 'Broad, dyed hair and this shiny blue dress. Like some kind of throwback to Queen Victoria or a pantomime dame. You could see the daughter had a rough time of it.'

'When we called, they were on their way out to the Artisan Centre,' Burton took over the narrative. 'Shopping trip followed by some homeopathic appointment for the old lady . . . There wasn't much to be gleaned from them. It didn't sound like they were regulars at the hall and only saw Charles Larrain at the centre . . . his workshop or studio or whatever they call it is a few doors down from the alternative medicine centre.'

'How come a dotty old bat like that were into alternative medicine?' Noakes's pug nose wrinkled in a way that suggested he had no very high opinion of complementary remedies.

'The daughter, Frances, talked her into it,' Burton explained. 'Some treatment or other for rheumatoid arthritis apparently . . . Isobel was on to her fifth session and seemed to think it had helped with the symptoms.'

'What do you reckon to Frances then?' Noakes sounded resigned. 'Any chance of *her* being involved with Larrain?' He thought of Muriel's library books with their blurbs about dried-up spinsters turning out to be dark horses. 'Still waters an' all that . . .'

'Don't see it, sarge,' Burton answered promptly. 'Retired teacher, quiet and sensible.'

'Not totally past it, mind,' Doyle said condescendingly. 'Some decent clobber and war paint would work wonders.'

Burton shot him a quelling look at this casual misogyny.

'I had the impression her life was just the way she wanted it,' she said. 'Sure, the old lady's cantankerous, but it's a comfortable set-up . . . living there at a peppercorn rent and plenty of money between them.'

'How about alibis?' Noakes grunted.

'They turn in early,' Doyle said in an ironic tone, declining to be squelched. 'Cocoa followed by a good book. Didn't stir from the cottage till church the next day.'

'So we've got sweet FA. Again,' the older man grumbled. 'Jus' crocodile tears all round an' everyone making the right noises . . . but all of 'em secretly glad that Aznavour's copped it.'

'Something of a sweeping generalisation, Sergeant,' Markham said austerely. 'Shock takes people in different ways, remember, and Richard Twiss looked pretty traumatised from where I was standing.'

'Yeah, guv, but *what have we got?*' Noakes began ticking them off on his pudgy fingers. 'There's Sir Simon an' Lady Edith . . . He comes over like Colonel Blimp an' she's this stuck-up prune-face, with summat iffy going on between her an' Ricardo,' he added darkly.

Markham sensed that Burton was exercising heroic restraint as she listened to the lurid summing up.

'Then there's the in-laws at Cold Comfort Farm down the road.' Noakes produced this literary pearl with a flourish, proud of having remembered it from a conversation with Olivia. 'Sounds like Gerard's more on the ball than Baron Hard-up. Auntie Stella's cosy with Margaret Twiss an' the runty younger brother, plus she an' Mags have bonded over history an' all that jazz . . . But neither of 'em came up with owt useful 'cept for Ger saying Lady Edith's dead possessive about Ricky.' He scowled. 'No dice with the Dower whatchamacallit . . . Izzy Wizzy might be Lady Edith's sister, but it don' look like they're great chums. As for Frances, she's under the old bat's thumb an' wouldn't say boo to a goose. So no chance of getting owt from *her*.'

As the DS paused to get his second wind, Markham observed drily, 'You've forgotten Michael. The son and heir.'

'Thass cos *he* looked like a bleeding waxwork,' Noakes retorted. 'Ready to go in a glass case like all them other effigies. Hardly said a word an' looked like he wanted a lie-down.'

Markham smiled. 'Not exactly a power-house,' he agreed. Remembering Margaret Twiss's full mouth and cloud of dark hair, he added, 'His sister, on the other hand, was most striking . . . very enigmatic.'

Noakes didn't know what 'enigmatic' meant, but he wasn't sure he liked the sound of it, one of his quirks being jealousy on Olivia's behalf whenever Markham's beauty-loving gaze alighted on another woman.

Perfectly aware of this idiosyncrasy (and secretly liking the quixotic loyalty it displayed), Markham continued levelly, 'Her curatorship of "The Power of Poison" exhibition is most impressive.'

'That bloke Hassett prob'ly did most of it.' Noakes shot back, clearly reluctant to relinquish his prejudice against the glamorous chatelaine.

Burton's mind was running along a different track. 'Come to think of it,' she mused, 'the Twisses are a bit like the Valois dynasty.'

'*Come again?*' Noakes gaped at her.

The DI looked embarrassed, as though she hadn't realised she had spoken aloud. 'That was the name of Catherine de Medici's family,' she told them. 'When her favourite son died, the line died out with him.'

'Wasn't there another son?' Noakes enquired beadily. 'The hunchbacked one with terminal acne? Shouldn't *he* have become king when big bro snuffed it?'

'He was the youngest . . . died of tuberculosis before his brother.' Burton could never resist a pedagogic opportunity, a trait she shared with Olivia Mullen. 'They were always at each other's throats and plotting. But being the youngest, he got the worst of it . . . pretty much a pawn in Catherine's plans for French domination. Catherine even tried to marry him off to Elizabeth I when he was fifteen and she was thirty-seven. She'd already tried to get the older boy — her favourite son — married off to Elizabeth, but he wasn't having it.'

'*Gross.*' Doyle couldn't help being intrigued. 'Wasn't the other one — the favourite son — *that way inclined?*'

'Most likely, yes,' Burton replied cheerfully. 'But personal preferences didn't count for anything back then — especially with the nobility.'

'And you think that the Twisses resemble the Valois clan, Kate?' Markham asked curiously.

'Sort of, guv,' she replied with a faint blush. 'There's the same kind of hothouse repressed emotions . . . strong matriarch fixated on the sons and ignoring her daughter.'

'When you put it like that . . .' Markham nodded thoughtfully.

Noakes was not to be gainsaid. 'Not to mention perviness . . . *favourites* an' stuff going on behind closed doors.' He smacked his lips lubriciously. There was nothing better calculated to get the Noakesian juices flowing than scandal in high places. 'If Aznavour an' Tricky Dicky had summat going, then *that* could've caused all kinds of problems . . .'

'Not so much *The Waltons* then, Sergeant,' Markham said, recalling his wingman's previous epithet. 'What we've got here is potentially far murkier than that.'

'Makes Princess Di an' the royals look like Enid Blyton,' the other agreed happily. 'Mebbe Aznavour were blackmailing 'em . . . Mebbe—'

'*Whoa*, Sergeant,' Markham interrupted. 'Let's not get ahead of ourselves.' A quick glance at his watch. 'Let's get Sir Simon's PA in followed by the lady from the shop. After that, I want to check out the Artisan Centre.'

* * *

By the time they had finished interviewing staff, the weather had turned increasingly raw, with sleet as sharp as needles coming down in blustery squalls. Although only early-afternoon, it was growing dark, the remaining light fading as twilight encroached.

Mrs Irene Clark, Sir Simon's widowed PA, turned out to be an eminently presentable woman with handsome features and silvery hair that fell in waves to her shoulders. Markham guessed that she was in her late fifties and from higher up the social scale than the housekeeper, the latter's rounded vowels softened in this case to a barely perceptible northern accent. Like the family, she gave little away, so that Markham once again felt he was up against a conspiracy of silence. There was a warmth about the woman's manner when she spoke of Sir Simon that did not extend to his wife or sons, though she was animated when praising Margaret Twiss's achievements in putting Carton Hall on the map. Competent and efficient, she talked them through the running of the hall and staff responsibilities. When it came to her own alibi, it was the old story: safely abed in her terraced house at Old Carton Clough.

'I'm sick of these old family retainers an' their blasted discretion,' Noakes muttered when she was gone.

Markham suspected the disenchantment was mutual, having registered the PA's startled surprise at the big barrelsome detective whose regimental tie as the day wore on came to resemble some sort of noose round the neck of a convict about to mount the scaffold or a would-be suicide unsure whether to go through with it.

Kindly Miss Evans from the shop yielded nothing useful, though at least she offered the first viable alibi, having stayed with her married nephew on Saturday night. More garrulous than the rest, like Annette Sullivan she seemed somewhat star-struck by Richard Twiss, Charles Larrain and the 'celebrities' who occasionally appeared on the premises, though Noakes declined to be impressed. 'Two-bit C listers,' he muttered, as she chunnered on happily about *Strictly Come Dancing* and 'that *lovely* Mister Du Beke.'

'Christ, you don' reckon we'll have to interview a load of dancers, do you?' Noakes said afterwards to Doyle as they huddled over the fire. 'Margot Fonteyn over there can do that,' he added, jerking his head towards Kate Burton as she earnestly made notes.

Doyle grinned as he recalled their colleague's raptures during the investigation of a ballet company some

Christmases previously. 'Hey, here's a joke for you, sarge . . . What kind of train is a ballerina? *Tutu!* Geddit?'

As Noakes chuckled conspiratorially, Doyle took advantage of his good humour to ask curiously, 'Why d'you have such a down on *Strictly* and dancers, sarge? I mean, seeing as you're no mean shakes at the ballroom dancing.'

'I jus' don' like all the commercialisation,' the older man replied. 'The missus says it's turning into a three-ring circus. Making ballroom *cheap*.'

Clearly the Oracle had spoken.

As the other two chatted, Markham and Burton drifted across to the window, mirror images of discouragement.

Markham was surprised when his fellow DI leaned her forehead against the cold pane, eyes shut as though summoning up the spirits of the hall.

'Do you ever think old buildings and gardens are like stoppered bottles, sir?' she said wistfully. 'With all these strange fragrances from the past inside . . . as if the place doesn't really belong to the people who live here now.'

Suddenly aware of his wondering gaze, she caught herself up with an apologetic laugh.

'Sorry, sir.' She rubbed her eyes. 'I'm maundering.'

'Not at all, Kate.' A wry smile. 'The DCI would say I've infected you with my "feyness".'

Their eyes met as they enjoyed a moment of amused complicity.

But not for long. As though scenting danger, Noakes lumbered over. 'What next, boss?'

'Well, we need to get this place,' the DI gestured at their incongruously genteel surroundings, 'set up as our incident room.'

Burton glanced at her watch. 'We're waiting for the tech guys and some uniforms,' she said. Moving away from the window, she reached for her mobile. 'I'll see where they've got to.'

A knock at the door heralded the arrival of sandwiches and more drinks wheeled in on a trolley by two overalled girls who sidled in with downcast eyes, hardly daring to look at the CID hotshots.

'There was some problem back at base, guv, but the techies are sorted now,' Burton announced. 'They said to give them an hour or so.'

'Fine.' Markham noticed Noakes circling the refreshments. 'We can break for lunch, though after those elevenses it feels like overkill.'

'You don' know when we'll manage to snatch a bite later, boss,' the DS asserted cannily.

The DI looked at this walking antithesis of a Lean Mean Fighting Machine.

'Somehow I think you'll always manage to improve the shining hour, Noakesy,' he said drily, 'one way or another.'

* * *

With lunch long over and the support team in situ, the detectives — who had lingered awhile, engrossed in their various theories — were preparing to depart when the door crashed open and Christopher Hassett confronted them, all urbanity fled.

'What is it, Mr Hassett?' Even as he asked the question, Markham felt a sinking dread.

'Something's happened at the Artisan Centre . . . an accident. It's Isobel Farquhar.'

Burton stared at the curator. 'What?' she demanded. 'We were with Mrs Farquhar just earlier today and she was fine.'

'I don't have any details . . . but the local police need you down there.'

'Tell them we're on our way, Mr Hassett,' Markham rapped.

And with that they were out into the brumous dusk, sleet having given way to soft wet flakes of snow which swirled about them like frozen tears dropping from the skies.

5. INVISIBLE HAND

Old Carton Artisan Centre being just a quarter of a mile from the hall, they were there in a matter of minutes, drawing up next to an ambulance in the carpark at the front.

The centre consisted of a converted stable block, with workshops and units arranged around two cobbled court-yards. Antique Victorian lamp posts cast a sulphurous glow over the various outlets and the frightened faces of late-after-noon shoppers huddled uncertainly in doorways.

'Get rid of 'em,' Noakes growled to a pimply young constable who was ineffectually trying to herd onlookers towards the exit. Hearing the note of menace in his voice, two hard-bitten older colleagues hastily went to assist, and in a matter of minutes the area was clear.

Police tape outside a corner unit in the main courtyard indicated the crime scene. A discreet brass plaque on the wall announced that this was the Ideal Clinic.

Ducking beneath it, the detectives found themselves in a comfortable pine-floored sanctum with fashionably exposed stone walls and an agreeable aroma of eucalyptus. To the rear were French doors that looked out on to the smaller of the two courtyards. What looked like specialist massage chairs and other ergonomic furniture were arranged in clusters round the stone walls, the various zones partitioned off with mobile dividers in soothing pastel hues. Despite the bitter winter weather, it was a warm and cosy space, presumably benefiting from underfloor heating.

A uniformed sergeant and two paramedics stood next to a booth with frosted windows talking to a dark-haired young woman in white lab coat and disposable gloves whose laminated badge proclaimed her to be 'Ms Connolly, Senior Practitioner'.

'Where's Mrs Farquhar?' Markham asked without preamble making his way over to her.

'In there.' She gestured towards the booth which appeared to be firmly shut.

'What's in there?' Noakes demanded, thinking that it looked like a spray tan cubicle.

'It's for craniosacral therapy,' she stuttered.

The DS was baffled. 'Why do they need a Tardis?'

'Our senior ladies prefer a more *private* experience. It's soundproofed . . . they can read during treatment . . . or there are headphones for easy listening if they want to relax.'

Noakes's expression was sceptical. *A bleeding gimmick, in other words.*

'Please tell us what happened,' Markham instructed quietly.

'Mrs Farquhar was scheduled for her treatment today. She and her daughter did some shopping first and came in at quarter to four. Miss Farquhar went off to have a coffee . . . said she'd come back in half an hour when the session was finished.'

'Was that their usual routine?' Burton asked, thinking that if this was the case, then the killer would have known when to strike.

'Yes.' And now the woman looked uncertain. 'But the appointment book is on my desk,' she said, pointing to a workstation next to the entrance. 'I'm on my own today, so if I was busy with a client or doing the three o'clock stocktake,' she gestured to a door in the far corner, 'I suppose someone could have nipped in and checked to see who was booked for a treatment. Mrs Farquhar was the only one down for craniosacral therapy today.'

Seeing that Burton looked somewhat askance, she added defensively. 'The cash register's locked in the bottom drawer, so there's nothing for anyone to steal.'

'Go on,' Markham encouraged.

'Well, I settled Mrs F with magazines, then shut the door once I'd got her started . . . There's a range of vibrating settings with shiatsu heat options.' The woman's evident pride in the salon's amenities struck Markham as tragi-comic. 'I offered her tea or coffee, but she said water was fine . . . I always put a jug and glass out first thing when I know a client's booked in. It's important to watch out for dehydration — we're very particular about that . . . making sure clients know to drink plenty of water.'

Noakes's look of scepticism deepened, but he held his peace.

'Then what happened?' the DI prompted gently.

The beautician looked distressed. 'I was over at the desk when I heard this sort of weird screeching noise.' Her voice shook. 'I thought maybe she was having a stroke or something . . . When I opened the door, she was half crumpled over, beating the arm rests with her head flopping all over the place like she was on fire or something.'

'Did you touch her?' Burton asked.

'I was worried in case I might make things worse . . . she was jerking uncontrollably and thrashing about, so I might have hurt her. There's a control panel on the desk which means we can override the motors in case of an emergency. I switched everything off and phoned 999.' Her voice broke. 'When I went back to Mrs F, she sort of jack-knifed and then went still. There was a gurgling noise and then nothing.' An audible gulp. 'I could see she was dead. After that, I just waited for someone to come.'

'The pathologist's on his way, sir,' the taller of the paramedics, a burly middle-aged man, told Markham. 'With it looking like some kind of toxic response, we just did a visual confirmation. Nothing's been touched.'

'Where's Mrs Farquhar's daughter now?' Doyle asked.

The woman looked around distractedly. 'With the vicar Mr Harte . . . He and his wife help out part-time in the bookshop two units along. They took her in there, got her a cup of tea . . .' Her voice trailed off.

Markham turned to Doyle. 'I want you to check up on Miss Farquhar, Doyle, and please arrange a hot drink for Ms Connolly while you're at it.'

The DI forced reassurance into his voice.

'One last thing, Ms Connolly. You mentioned doing the three o'clock stocktake. Is that your usual practice?' Silently, he added to himself, *And if so, how many people know about it?*

A tremulous smile. 'Sounds a bit OCD doesn't it?'

That's one way of putting it, Noakes thought.

'Me and the other girls always do our run-through then — see that everything's in order with supplements and vitamins. It usually takes half an hour. People in the other units have a tea break around the same time . . . Sometimes we bake and swap treats . . . It's more friendly, see.'

Only too well. So everyone knew little Miss Muffet was playing nurse out back leaving the treatment area unattended. Noakes's beefy face was inscrutable, but he could have wept.

'What about the shop door an' the cubicle thingy?' he asked. 'D'you keep 'em locked when you're not out front?'

She turned a bewildered face to him. 'Well, no . . . there's no need. It's not like we get people messing around, vandals or anyone like that . . .'

Just a bleeding murderer, the DS thought savagely.

Once Doyle had escorted the beautician away, he growled, 'What happened to health an' safety then? With staff skiving round the back an' no one watching the shop . . .'

'Let's have a look in the stockroom while we're waiting for Dimples to show,' Markham said placatingly. He nodded to the paramedics. 'If there's something toxic in that booth, you did well to stay clear.'

They nodded. 'We'll sort a stretcher, sir.' And with that, they disappeared.

The stockroom was perfectly standard, with boxes on steel racks and a folding ladder so that staff could reach the top shelves. To the right was a tiny galley kitchen and off that an equally minuscule staff cloakroom with two folding chairs and a toilet cubicle in the corner.

Coming back into the main treatment area, Markham could see that everything was expensive and high-spec, with tasteful artwork — mainly local landscapes, including Carton Hall — on the stone walls and an impressive aquarium next to the water cooler. Opening another door marked 'Customer Restroom', he was greeted by the scent of bergamot. Observing the up-to-the-minute fixtures and fittings, he reflected that business must be good.

At that moment, Dimples Davidson bustled in. Already suited up, he greeted them cordially, looking more than ever like a country vet on his way to a lambing or some equally bucolic pursuit.

Pulling on a paper mask, he said, 'I'll check her over and then fill you in.' Then more soberly, the bushy eyebrows contracting, 'Looks like your poisoner's got a taste for killing.'

And Mrs Farquhar knew something that made her a threat, Markham thought grimly.

The detectives retreated to the French doors, contemplating the twilight as it stole over the snow-filled courtyard, where more lamp posts illumined the enclosure with an eerie blue-black glow.

'This one's a confident bugger alright,' Noakes muttered, looming against the glass like an old bull. 'Knew the lass's movements, so must've sneaked in while she were out the back . . . straight in an' out.'

They stood in silence for some minutes digesting this. Eventually, recalling their previous investigation in a beauty clinic, Noakes said, 'Wonder if they keep that Botox stuff in here . . . It's gotta be poisonous, yeah?'

'Botulinum can be fatal,' Burton said thoughtfully. 'But not straightaway . . . I think it takes a couple of days for symptoms to show.'

'So what else could do the job that quickly?' the DS demanded.

'Strychnine in the water jug,' the pathologist said heavily behind them. They all turned quickly to face him. 'And a hefty slug of chloroquine for good measure. They use the stuff to clean fish tanks.' He waved a hand at the aquarium. 'It's readily available.' Peeling off his gloves, he sat down heavily on a nearby cushioned box seat, looking ludicrously bulky and out of place.

'The lass who runs the place said they always make sure the customers drink plenty of water,' Noakes groaned. 'She puts a fresh jug out first thing.'

The medic's shoulders slumped. 'A push-button stainless-steel jug and tumbler were on the floor next to the body.' He heaved a sigh that seemed to travel up from his well-polished brogues. 'Basically, their good practice signed that lady's death warrant.'

'No, it was the *murderer* that did that,' Doyle countered with unusual vehemence.

The pathologist looked surprised, but Markham knew the young detective was thinking of the grandmother to whom he was close.

'Well, with a woman in her early eighties — no doubt on medication of various kinds, Statins and the like — there was only ever going to be one outcome. Chronic respiratory failure and shock.'

'You're sure about the strychnine an' other stuff, doc?' Noakes asked intently.

'She presented the same way as the other poor soul down at the hall — hyperreflexia, frothing and so forth. There's a crystalline powder on the carpet which looks to me like chloroquine, or there could be other drugs in the mix . . . maybe flurazepam . . . lorazepam . . . Look, I can't tell you anything for sure until I've got her down at the morgue, but I'll put a rush on it.'

Dimples then looked around curiously.

'What kind of outfit is it here, then?' he asked. 'The lady wife shops up this end now and again.' He grimaced. 'She says it's mainly overpriced scented candles and knick-knacks, but there's a couple of good delis . . . I don't recall her mentioning this place.'

Given the redoubtable Mrs Davidson's outdoorsy credentials and the fact that she was very much a 'dog person', Markham somehow couldn't envisage her as a patron of the Ideal Clinic. Mind you, Isobel Farquhar seemed an equally unlikely candidate for new age holistic ministrations but had presumably been converted somewhere along the line.

Davidson lumbered to his feet. 'I'll get the paramedics to move her now.' He gestured to the stretcher-bearers who came forward with a body bag.

The detectives averted their gaze from the flurry of movement in the cubicle, only turning back when the shuffling of feet heralded Mrs Farquhar's departure, the dreadful boomerang shape that distended the heavy duty canvas a gruesome reminder of her death throes.

Paper-suited SOCOs had arrived and were busy about their work, flitting around Markham's team like a species of giant moth.

Now it was Noakes who sank down on an outsize pouffe as though winded.

'They knew the receptionist lass's routine,' he said glumly. 'Sounds like you could set your watch by her. An' she were on her own here today . . . disappears into the back at three, prob'ly on her mobile, texting the boyfriend or her mates . . .'

'Which is when they were able to check out that booth and spike the water jug,' Doyle concluded.

'The killer needed to be sure Mrs Farquhar was booked in for the craniosacral treatment,' Burton joined in.

'Someone who knew her, then,' Noakes said. 'Cos this were premeditated. I mean, it's not like you jus' happen to have the gear handy.'

'What about that bloke, Graham Young?' Doyle objected. 'Didn't you say he always had some of the stuff on him so he could feel powerful?'

Markham smothered a smile at his wingman's expression. *Hoist by his own petard*, he thought.

'Yeah, but that were a freaky sexual hang-up,' Noakes countered. 'Plus, Young were always looking to get his end away . . . We're talking about an' eighty-year-old woman here.'

'But what about Shipman?' Doyle persisted stubbornly. '*He* had a thing for grannies, sarge.'

Burton came unexpectedly to Noakes's rescue. 'Shipman was a *doctor*,' she pointed out. 'Took his medical bag everywhere, so it wasn't just an impulse spree.'

Doyle knew when he was beaten. 'Okay, like you say, it must be someone close to her . . . starting with the daughter cos let's face it, she was closest of all.'

'We'll get a statement from Miss Farquhar now,' Markham said levelly. 'But *kid gloves* . . . We make no assumptions.' He looked round thoughtfully. 'Someone close to her,' he mused, 'or someone who knew her routine, knew about her appointment in here and saw their opportunity . . .'

'The killer took *pleasure* from Mr Larrain's death,' Burton said slowly, cutting in. 'But this was different . . . There wasn't the chance to watch it . . .'

'Maybe that points to Frances,' Doyle suggested. 'Couldn't face watching her mum suffer, so she made sure she wasn't there for the main event.'

'*Possibly*,' Burton conceded, 'but it seems more like a question of *expediency*. Isobel Farquhar had to be eliminated for some reason. Something she knew or suspected . . . and this killer already had poisons available.'

'They could've got a thrill just from imagining how she died, like Larrain all over again,' Doyle speculated. 'If they've got a thing for poison, perhaps it was mixed motives. They had to get rid of the old lady and the stuff was available . . . but they also *liked* the idea of her dying like that.'

Noakes sagged. '*Jesus.*'

Despite being a famous frowner on blasphemy, Markham let this pass. There was something deeply troubling to him too in the spectre of a killer for whom cruelty acted as an aphrodisiac.

'Come on,' he said. 'Miss Connolly said they were looking after Frances in the bookshop. We need to hear what she has to say.'

* * *

In normal circumstances, Markham would have delighted in the charmingly old-fashioned little bookshop with its rickety shelves, curios in china and wood crouching like the guardians of the place, wonky handmade signs and the pervasive musty odour of camphor that was catnip to bookworms. But not today.

The vicar introduced himself as the Reverend Frank Harte. Lean and rumpled with tousled brown hair, fine hazel eyes and a hint of five o'clock shadow, he had the boyish good looks of a young man, though he had been the incumbent of Old Carton Parish Church for several years. His wife Anna was a slight woman with delicate features and ash-blonde hair swept simply into a side-fringe and plait over one shoulder. A musical voice, calm manner and steady blue eyes made it no surprise to learn that she was a part-time health and wellbeing adviser at Bromgrove University. She was beautiful but her rather unexciting combination of fawn jumper and long black skirt disguised it. Clearly solicitous of Frances, she had obviously exerted a calming influence, so the detectives were able to get her account without too much difficulty.

Somewhat dough-faced, though with a fine complexion and well-cut thick auburn hair, the victim's daughter appeared dazed.

Markham carefully avoided any reference to murder in favour of 'unexplained death', though he could tell that the Hartes were not deceived.

'Who knew about your plans for today?' the DI asked finally.

'Just about everybody,' she replied raising her hands helplessly. 'Mum felt such an improvement from her treatments at the clinic that she was full of it. I heard her talking about it on the phone . . .'

'So they would have known up at the hall?' Markham asked quickly.

'Well, we're not in and out of each other's pockets,' Frances re-joined with some hauteur, 'but I know Mum mentioned it to Aunt Edith. I'm pretty sure she would've told Gerard and Stella as well . . . he suffers with sciatica, and Stella wondered if alternative medicine might help.'

'You don't recall anything out of the ordinary happening when you visited the centre today?' Burton asked. 'Didn't notice anyone unusual?'

'We had a bit of a walkabout first and then a snack in the tearoom. I think Catherine Metcalfe put her head round the door . . . I don't know about the rest of them . . . We didn't really pay much heed,' she faltered. 'Mum wanted some fabric for new cushions and planned on getting the sofa reupholstered, so we were talking about that.' The woman's face crumpled. 'Her arthritis was so much better, she said it was like she'd been given a new lease of energy.'

And then Frances Farquhar began to cry. But she was not one of those women who looked beautiful in grief, and the harsh, hacking sobs held a self-accusatory undertone as though to lament a life half lived.

Frank Harte leaned forward, his expression concerned.

'Look, Inspector, couldn't this wait? Frances has had a terrible shock. She's coming home with us for the time being . . . It might be better if you interviewed her tomorrow once you know more about what happened.'

Anna Harte laid a slim hand on her husband's arm.

'They're just doing their job, Frank.' Her candid blue gaze met Markham's. The colour of forget-me-nots, he thought appreciatively, struck by the novelty of such a woman showing up as the vicar's wife when he had expected a more prosaic specimen of humanity. 'But Francie may be able to remember more for you once she's had a decent rest.'

'Well, if *Francie*'s our killer, all I can say is she deserves a bleeding Oscar,' was Noakes's verdict after the trio had departed for the vicarage. 'Sounded like our neighbour's dog with all that caterwauling.' He bit his lip in compunction. 'Seemed fond of her mum, though.'

Doyle's mind was running in less elevated channels. 'The padre's wife is a bit of alright,' he declared. 'Shame about the clothes. I mean, why do they have to go all Kate Humble just cos it's the countryside . . .'

'I suppose you think they should all look like the Yorkshire Shepherdess,' Burton observed tartly. 'Herding the sheep in a mini-skirt and full makeup.'

'Well at least that one hasn't let herself go,' Doyle retorted, stung. 'It's a question of self-respect. No reason to give up and not bother anymore.'

'I wouldn't say Mrs Harte has exactly "given up", Doyle,' Markham said in a tone of reproof. 'A certain conservatism is in order when you're the vicar's wife . . . And don't forget, she works part-time at the university. The pastoral team aren't exactly noted for, er, rocking the latest high street look.'

The young detective laughed shamefacedly. 'Fair enough, sir.'

'An' anyway,' Noakes rumbled indignantly. 'There's nowt wrong with Kate Humble. Nice natural-looking lass if you ask me . . . Don' spend all her time filing her nails an' worrying about split ends.'

Unlike dear Natalie. For a terrible moment, Markham was afraid he had said it out loud.

Kate Burton's eyes carefully slid away from his.

'When we've quite finished our debate about standards of feminine beauty, perhaps we should take a look round the centre, including Charles Larrain's aromatherapy shop?' he suggested.

His fellow DI practically clicked her heels.

'I'll get one of the local uniforms to take us round,' she said, disappearing into the courtyard.

Her colleagues mused for a time as they waited at the bookshop counter, perched on the tall stools which served as office furniture.

'Assuming the killer spiked the water when wossername the beautician girl were off on her tea break — *sorry*,' Noakes smirked, '*doing the stocktake* — then any of 'em could've done it.'

Doyle nodded. 'Yeah, we finished interviewing around half one or two and then hung on for the techies till about quarter past four which was when Hassett came to tell us about Mrs Farquhar . . . The hall's practically next door to the centre, then you've got the farm a bit further down the road . . . could drive it in minutes . . . a bit longer on foot. So you're right,' he nodded again decisively, 'they *all* had opportunity.'

'Frances said she saw Catherine Metcalfe, but she an' her mum were yakking about cushions an' fabric an' stuff, so God knows who else they didn't notice.' Noakes looked as though he didn't have any great faith in Frances Farquhar's powers of observation. 'An' they were stuffing their faces too, so prob'ly wouldn't have noticed if Catherine Bleeding Medici had showed up.'

Markham's lips twitched at the bizarre scenario his wingman had conjured.

'We haven't got a handle on our first victim,' he said. '*Charles Larrain*. He's the key to it all, remember . . . Maybe his studio will shed some light.'

But when a self-conscious young constable escorted them to the aromatherapy shop, it proved to be something of a let-down.

'It's just like *The White Company* in the town centre,' Burton murmured as they took in the stripped back wood floor along with minimalist cube display stands sporting fragrances, diffusers and scented candles from the luxury *Larrain Brand*.

'What's with them herb thingies or dried flowers or whatever they are hanging from the ceiling?' Noakes asked. 'S'like a garden centre or summat.'

Doyle grinned.

'It's all about *authenticity*, sarge . . . You know, make the punters feel it's all dead rustic so they get the idea Charlie boy goes foraging in meadows and along the riverbank for his rose petals and wild basil . . . The back to nature vibe. River Cottage and all that.'

'It's a bleeding con,' the other grunted, squinting at the prices on the chichi packaging. 'Aznavour probably just ponced about sniffing an' going into raptures like he'd mixed the stuff himself, when it all came from somewhere else in the first place.' He scowled ferociously, trying to recall Muriel's favourite perfumier. *Bingo*! His expression cleared. 'Yeah, Jo Malone or one of that lot.'

'I doubt he would get away with counterfeit produce, Sergeant,' Markham interjected. 'But I expect you're right about the labour being imported from elsewhere.'

'Smells wonderful, at any rate,' Burton conceded, and indeed the unit was pervaded throughout with the most incredible scents. Citrus and sandalwood, Markham thought inhaling appreciatively.

'The pong's giving me a headache,' Noakes grunted, the observation eliciting a snigger from their escort.

A utilitarian backroom contained sinks, worktops and shelves with various flasks, but there was no office equipment or stationery visible. 'As blank and streamlined as the rest,' Markham commented.

In the end, slightly befuddled from the perfume, it was a relief to come back out into the freezing air of the courtyard, feeling it slice into their lungs as they huddled under an awning next to the Old Carton Tearoom.

Markham dismissed the uniform with a courteous thanks for his services then turned to Burton.

'What about Larrain's home?' he asked wearily. 'Has that been processed yet?'

Burton frowned. 'Bachelor pad in town, guv, just off Faulkner Street. It's like a show flat . . . *immaculate*. Almost as though no one lived there.'

'Mebbe he didn't,' Noakes said. 'Out and about with his—' seeing Burton stiffen, he had a swift rethink of the term he was about to use — 'lovers.'

'Like in that Paul Young song,' Doyle added philosophically, '"Wherever I Lay My Hat (That's My Home)".' He saucily whistled a few bars before subsiding as he registered his mentor's scowl deepen.

'No computer, paperwork, diaries . . . ?' Markham persisted.

Burton shook her head. 'Nada, sir.'

'Must mean someone got there before us,' Doyle suggested. 'As in cleaned Larrain's place out once they knew he was dead . . . before Annette found his body and raised the alarm on Sunday morning.'

'Or maybe he avoided his flat cos he didn't feel safe there? Almost like he were on the run . . .' Noakes pondered.

Markham raised a quizzical eyebrow at his sergeant.

'Larrain's not in the system, guv,' Burton cut in. 'Clean as a whistle from that point of view.'

Standing there with nothing to report, she felt absurdly disappointed at having built up Charles Larrain in her imagination to the point where he loomed like some shadowy necromancer and specialist in the dark arts. Having Noakes's sceptical eye rest on her made her feel even more foolish.

It was the fact that Larrain had died where he did, she thought ruefully. Choking his guts out in that sinister antechamber surrounded by wax statues, right next door to an exhibition about poisoning and skulduggery in the Renaissance. Small wonder if he had become as real to her as Cosimo Ruggieri or any of those Florentine magicians.

But she felt in her bones that a fascination with poison and suffering was something Larrain and his killer *shared*. And that once they tracked the killer's obsession to its *source*

— whether at the hall or elsewhere — they would find the clue to the mystery . . .

In the meantime, soggy and disconsolate, she was miserably aware that the investigation had got off to a sluggish start.

'Time to call it a day,' Markham said quietly as though aware of her depressed spirits. 'Briefing 8am sharp in the morning—'

'At the hall, guv?' Doyle put in.

The DI smiled. 'Where else?' Like Kate Burton, he felt powerfully drawn to the place for reasons he barely understood.

Of one thing he was certain, though.

Carton held the key.

6. THE BOTTOM OF THE GLASS

Wednesday morning dawned cold and crisp under clear skies, which served as an antidote to Markham's low spirits of the previous evening. There was no sign of a thaw, so the view from his apartment windows exerted its now familiar blue-and-white allure, quietening gnawing anxieties that the Carton investigation had already stalled.

As it was a 'wellbeing day', allowing staff and students at Hope a holiday for their Christmas shopping, Olivia and Markham enjoyed a rare opportunity to breakfast together.

'I don't suppose you'll manage to snatch any time off,' she said wistfully as they gulped down toast and coffee.

'There's a memorial service for Charles Larrain at Old Carton Parish Church, two o'clock, if you're up for it,' he said hesitantly. 'Though it hardly seems fair to steal part of your day like that.'

Olivia smiled at him. 'No really, Gil, I'd like to go with you. By this afternoon, I'll have had my fill of browsing tinsel-land in the town centre.' She threw him a saucy look. 'The worst of it is, I'll just end up running into all the kids and their parents . . . won't dare stock up on anything from Victoria's Secret, otherwise it'll be all round school like wildfire.'

He grinned. 'Victoria's Secret, eh? That sounds promising.' Then a less pleasing thought occurred to him. 'You could always give the Artisan Centre a whirl. Get away from the madding crowd and all that.'

'Hey, that's not a bad idea.' She buttered herself some more toast, enjoying her breakfast with a gusto that was at odds with her willowy frame. 'What's it like up there?'

'Pretty much your standard craft and design outlet.' He chuckled. 'Selling what Noakesy would call overpriced tat.'

'The kind of stuff Muriel loves, though,' she said mischievously with her head on one side.

He grimaced. 'Indeed . . . And Natalie is in and out of there by the minute apparently. Very much in demand.'

'When she's not interfering like billy-o at the Harmony Spa.' This being the health clinic owned by the mother of Natalie's fiancé.

'Well, according to Noakes, "Our Nat" likes to take a hands-off approach at Harmony.'

Oliva gave a snort of derision. 'You mean ma-in-law's got the measure of her and won't stand for any interference.'

'That's one way of looking at it, though it does sound as though she's less sharp-elbowed these days . . . I'm looking forward to hearing her impressions of the set-up at the centre.'

'*Oh no*, don't tell me,' Olivia groaned. 'Muriel's suckered you into going round there for lunch.'

'The *two of us*, Liv,' he said ruefully. 'She suggested Sunday after the carol service at the cathedral. You know you always like *that*,' he said with a mock-wheedling expression. 'And once you get a schooner of sherry inside you, lunch won't be so bad.'

She laughed. 'You make me sound like an alcoholic, Gil!'

But he could tell the battle was won.

'And anyway,' he added, 'this could be Noakesy's last Christmas in CID. So, it's a special occasion.'

'Any news on his leaving plans?'

'Well, he taps the side of his nose and looks mysterious whenever I mention it . . . I don't think he's had any luck recruiting Doyle, even though there's a hardboiled girlfriend who's set her heart on him leaving the force. Feels he's "selling himself short", or words to that effect.'

'*Really?*' Olivia wrinkled her nose. 'But isn't he wedded to his CID career? Dead set on going far, was what he said the last time I saw him.'

'Seems the girlfriend's some civil service hot shot . . . A will of steel according to Noakes . . .'

She laughed. 'I bet he said "ball-breaker".'

'He didn't hold back, but I'm trying to be genteel seeing as it's so early in the morning.' Markham sighed. 'I have detected a certain dejection in Doyle, so it's possible his remaining in CID may be a romantic deal-breaker.'

'Hmm.' Olivia said nothing more, but privately she wondered if there might be a more personal source of resentment against the police . . . That sense of it always being a third wheel in the relationship, like bloody Kate Burton.

Almost as though he had intuited the direction of his partner's thoughts, Markham said, 'Kate's got Nathan helping with a profile of our killer.'

'Oh yes?' There was an edge to her tone.

'According to Nathan, the murder of Charles Larrain points to what's called a "process-focused" killer . . . someone who wants to prolong the experience of the victim's agony because they derive pleasure from their suffering.'

Despite herself, she was gripped. 'You mean a sadist?'

'Essentially, yes,' he replied. 'They often take trophies, like photos of the victim or a piece of clothing as a reminder of what they've done. Apparently, Larrain always wore a designer cashmere scarf and had one on at work the day he died . . . but it wasn't found with his body.'

'So that ties in with wanting him to die vomiting up his guts surrounded by those effigies and death masks he liked looking at.'

'Correct . . . An "act-focused" killer would just want to achieve the death of their victim — get it over quickly and without any fuss . . . But the way Larrain died suggests some kind of emotional investment.'

Now Olivia was crumbling up her toast as though she had suddenly lost her appetite. 'What about that poor woman who died in the massage booth? Did the killer have some kind of vendetta against her too?'

'It's possible . . . But I think it's more likely Isobel Farquhar knew or suspected something that made her a threat to the killer, so she had to be disposed of . . . Inflicting ghastly pain and suffering would have been a fringe benefit, if you like.'

'Something to savour in their imagination.' Olivia shivered. 'God!' she burst out. 'How could a weirdo like that not stand out?'

'Psychopaths usually don't, Liv. And never forget, in a village community folk respect each other's space. They don't necessarily like to poke their noses into other people's business.'

She was struck by this. 'It's the perfect camouflage, isn't it . . . ? *Nothing to see here, move along*! When all the time someone's *grooming* the locals to ignore what's really happening right underneath their noses.'

'Maybe that was why Isobel Farquhar had to die,' he said sombrely. 'Maybe she was someone they *couldn't* hoodwink.'

'Imagine,' she breathed, 'you've probably met them already, walking round Carton . . . playing the part of the grieving neighbour when all the time . . .'

Markham eyed the percolator and decided he could risk another black coffee. 'Well, I'm not sure too many tears were shed for Larrain . . . Sounds like he was the kind of character who snake-talked his way into people's lives—'

'Sounds parasitic?'

'Something like that. Half-French with well-practised charm . . . He had certainly got his feet under the table at the hall. I ran into the housekeeper's son last night when I checked in there before coming home. He wasn't as discreet as his mother . . . said Richard Twiss wouldn't stir a foot without Larrain's say-so, and the rest of them hated him.'

'What was this bloke like, the housekeeper's son?' Olivia enquired curiously.

'Hmm. Patrick Scarron, a sort of disreputable Heathcliff lookalike, helps out as a groundsman at the hall. Probably gives his mother the run-around. Lives in a shared house on Bromgrove Rise with a couple of students from the university, but no one can vouch for him on Saturday night. Says he doesn't actually recall much about that evening,' he added wryly.

'Ah, off his face then?'

'That's *his* story,' Markham shrugged, 'but who's to say this isn't our process-killer.' He took a sip of coffee. 'On the other hand, apart from the events manager, he was really the only one I felt was being honest about Larrain.' Collecting their plates, he crossed the galley kitchen to the sink. 'To be frank, Liv, this case makes me feel there's something toxic about Middle England and the whole "well that's their business" mentality.'

'Wasn't the vicar able to fill you in on Larrain?' she asked.

Markham shook his head. 'Too busy comforting Isobel Farquhar's daughter, but maybe he'll open up today.'

'If he's doing this prayer service for Larrain, the man can't have been *all* bad,' Olivia suggested.

'Or maybe it's all about maintaining appearances and a service being the "done thing" . . . part of the institutional cover-up that's allowed someone to get away with murder.'

She walked over to the sink and leaned into him. Looking anxiously into his face, she said gently, 'It's not like you to be cynical about religion, Gil.' She squeezed his hand. 'You always say it gives suffering a meaning, remember.'

He looked down affectionately into the luminous green eyes that were suddenly full of concern. Recently he had begun to lose faith in the strength of their relationship, Olivia's scathing comments about Kate Burton in particular having cast a shadow. But in that instant, he felt less despondent about the future.

'That's true,' he murmured. 'I've always felt religion carries the whole human story within it . . . which makes it so much more than anything a single individual could come up with, no matter how great they are. The only true reality.'

There was a faint flush on the high cheekbones as he added, '"Once a Catholic", you know.'

Olivia's own unflashy Anglicanism lacked the emotional fervour of Markham's religious faith, but like Noakes she was moved by the sense he gave of reaching for a hand which would lift him out of the deepest darkness and make pain comprehensible.

Now all she said lightly was, 'I've never been inside Old Carton Parish Church, but I believe it's a real jewel . . . Somehow it got overlooked by Cromwell's thugs and escaped being pillaged and ransacked during the Reformation.'

'In that case, I look forward to clouds of incense, smells, bells, votive panels, the whole nine yards,' he laughed.

Relieved to hear him sounding brighter, she said, 'Are there eats after the service? George is bound to be disappointed otherwise.'

Markham cast his eyes to heaven.

'I believe there'll be refreshments up at the hall afterwards . . . Proximity to Borgia-style artefacts hasn't affected Noakesy's appetite in the slightest, but hopefully Kate and Doyle will be able to rein him in. The last thing I need is Sidney and the Twisses looking on aghast as my sergeant hoovers up every last vol-au-vent in sight like it's an all you can eat buffet.'

She chuckled, then her face fell. 'Is Muriel coming?'

'No, you're safe for today. But,' he teased, 'who knows, she might take it into her head to show up for Isobel Farquhar's interment on Friday.'

Momentarily distracted, Olivia asked, '*Interment?*' How've they managed that seeing as she's only just died? That's indecently quick.'

'Sir Simon Twiss is a former senior coroner, which I suspect oiled the wheels,' Markham said with heavy irony. 'But Dimples has taken all the necessary tissue samples and there's no doubt about cause of death. Poisoning with a mixture of strychnine, chloroquine and flubromazolam.'

'I think I've heard of that last one,' she said. 'It's anti-anxiety medication.'

'Yes, but even 0.5 milligrams can be lethal . . . by decreasing the level of consciousness and damaging the airways.'

Olivia shook her head wonderingly. 'They really weren't taking any chances, were they?' she said. 'Threw everything at the poor woman.'

'I'm hoping the buffet or whatever they're laying on at the hall after the service will give us the chance to take a closer look at our suspects—'

'You hope that someone will be indiscreet?' she finished.

'In my experience people always know more than they think they do . . . Things lie dormant beneath the surface of their minds, like spawn drifting around the bottom of a muddy pond. Somehow,' he said quietly, almost to himself now, 'we've got to make it float to the top.'

'Yuk . . . *pond life!*'

'Well, I'm certainly beginning to feel like some kind of naturalist looking for a particularly dangerous specimen.' He smiled at her. 'Some cleric or other — I can't remember who — said a first drink from the glass of natural science makes you atheistic, but then at the bottom of the glass, God is waiting to make everything clear.'

She leaned up and kissed him. 'You'll nail them in the end, Gil. You know you always do. Now, I have to gird my loins for some serious retail therapy . . . I'll meet you at the church later.'

After she had left, Markham stood a while longer looking out of the window at the trees in the landscaped gardens outside, bare and still, their branches etched stark black against the duck-egg blue of the sky.

Spawn in a muddy pond, he had told Olivia.

Could these fish be made to swim up to the surface?

* * *

At the morning briefing, Kate Burton contributed some colourful shading to the team's picture of the Twisses.

'Nathan's friend Mike at the university knows them a bit through Margaret Twiss,' she said before admitting, 'I tracked down some stuff she'd written too.'

'Oh aye?' The look Noakes threw at Doyle screamed *Boffin Alert*!

Burton was quick to notice. 'Relax, sarge,' she grinned. 'It's just really strange the way the Twisses mirror the Valois dynasty—'

'You mean creepy Catherine de Medici an' that lot?' Despite himself, Noakes could not help being fascinated by the Italian Jezebel and had hugely enjoyed imparting the gorier details to Muriel over toad in the hole and apple crumble the previous night. Even Natalie ended up being drawn in, particularly when he got on to stories about primitive Renaissance hygiene, which meant even pets had to be sprinkled with perfume, and poisonous beautifiers like lead skin whitener that were just left on the face and added to until they had to be chiselled off and reapplied.

'You should think about doing a history degree, Dad,' she told him, at which Noakes felt absurdly pleased.

'Well, the whole tribe are *beyond odd*,' Burton said now. 'Mike told Nathan he thinks that's why Margaret Twiss got hung up on Catherine de Medici and her family in the first place — because they were so like the set-up at home . . . quite uncanny really.' Gratified at having her colleagues' full attention, she continued, 'Richard Twiss is his mother's favourite, just like Catherine's middle son—'

'The one she said she wanted to be buried alive with?' Noakes interrupted eagerly.

'Yes. And Richard comes across as a dandy just like Edouard Alexandre,' Burton rolled her Rs most impressively. 'He later became Henri the Third and was known for wearing earrings and bracelets and being so obsessed with women's fashion that his wedding had to be put back from daytime to the evening because he took forever doing his wife's hair.'

Doyle frowned. 'How come he got married to a woman if he was homosexual?'

'Oh, that didn't make any difference in those days because love didn't usually come into it,' she said airily. 'But Henri got serious crushes on women, though everyone assumed it had to be platonic . . . not a heterosexual thing . . . more like they were film idols or something like that.' It was clear Burton was relishing the impromptu lecture, but nobody objected. 'When one of his crushes died, Henri had all his clothes embroidered with death's heads and got them to decorate his shoes with tiny silk skulls.'

'King of the Hermaphrodites then,' Doyle chuckled. Seeing the DI bristle, he added contritely, 'Sorry, ma'am, but, like you said, it's beyond weird.'

'I remember you saying that there were also these *mignons* hanging about,' Markham said smoothly. 'Male favourites.'

'That's right, sir.' Burton was recalled to the historical narrative. 'They were always making mischief between Henri and his mother and sister.'

'Hmm.' Markham was struck by the potential parallels. 'And you think Richard Twiss's relationship with Charles Larrain may have caused similar problems with his family.'

'Well, Mike seemed to think Larrain had caused no end of trouble, though he didn't know the details.'

'Mebbe Mags is our poisoner,' Noakes ruminated. 'Seeing as she's got an obsession with Queen Catherine an' her freaky family . . . That's how she got the idea to pay Larrain back for being a troublemaker. But then she had to kill Izzy cos the old bat got wind somehow.' He scratched the bristles which, try as he might, never mutated into sleek five o'clock shadow. 'But then Ricardo's gotta be up there, lover's tiff with Aznavour . . . or Aznavour could've gone too far with upsetting his mum . . .'

'Lady Edith looked the ruthless type to me,' Doyle commented. 'I reckon she'd have got off on making Larrain suffer if he came between her and Richard. Farmer Gerard said she had to be top dog, remember? Didn't like competition.'

'There were definitely tensions in the family because of Larrain,' Markham said before bringing them up to date on his conversation with Patrick Scarron.

'So *everyone* hated Aznavour,' Noakes concluded glumly. 'Including that weedy eldest son who looks like he can't tie his own shoelaces without help.'

'The staff weren't keen on him either,' Doyle pointed out. 'Catherine Metcalfe came right out and admitted it, while Sir Simon's PA and the housekeeper just looked cagey.'

'An' the curator bloke, Hassett . . . He kept shtum as well. I dunno, like Aznavour were infectious or summat,' Noakes said, resorting to this surprising metaphor as he struggled with the riddle.

Markham thought back to their encounters with Irene Clark and Carmel Scarron. 'They were certainly on their guard,' he agreed, 'though with Christopher Hassett, I think it was a case of natural reserve.'

He wandered across to his poky office window, smiling as he watched the local youngsters aiming snowballs at the station's downstairs windows. God help them if that feisty PCSO on duty downstairs took it into her head to return fire . . .

He turned back towards the team, relishing the fact that for once his radiator appeared to be emitting heat.

'Carmel Scarron was uneasy about something,' he said. 'It was when I mentioned the poison exhibition . . . She looked almost, well, *sly* suddenly.'

'Prob'ly a trick of the light, guv.' Noakes spoke up stoutly, having been favourably impressed by the housekeeper's promptitude with food and drink. 'Or she's jus' creeped out by them statues an' masks an' the rest of it . . . can't imagine her going in there with a feather duster or whatnot by herself.'

Mischievously, Burton said, 'The exhibition isn't *all* death and poisons, sarge . . . There's lots of quirky historical stuff.' Markham could almost have sworn she winked at him. 'I mean, did you know that it was really Catherine de Medici who invented knickers?'

Noakes's lower jaw sagged.

'Yes, *really*.' Burton was now impenetrably solemn. 'She liked riding side-saddle but didn't want anyone looking up her skirt when she got on and off her horse . . . So she got these underpants designed to sort the problem. Gold and silver cloth, obviously.'

Doyle winced. 'Sounds uncomfortable.'

Knowing Noakes's prudish streak, Burton moved on from lingerie. 'She was quite the innovator . . . used tobacco for headaches . . . invented the folding fan . . . all sorts.'

'When she weren't busy bumping folk off.' As ever, her grizzled colleague was determined to have the last word.

'She was a fanatically protective mother living in a dangerous age,' Burton countered reasonably. 'She did what she had to.'

'If Margaret sees Lady Edith that way, then it could be she thinks her mother's capable of murder,' Doyle volunteered.

'It could be the brother,' Noakes mused, 'the youngest one . . . Philip . . . He came across like a mummy's boy too.' Now the DS looked energised. 'For all we know, *he* could be the same as Richard . . .'

'In what sense?' Burton regarded him with a jaundiced eye.

'Well, homosexual . . . Him an' Ricky could have had a fight over Aznavour.'

'We're getting ahead of ourselves here,' Markham interposed firmly. 'As things stand, there's nothing to suggest any sort of love triangle between Mr Larrain and the Twiss brothers.'

'There's the vicar,' Doyle speculated, though not with any real conviction. 'Perhaps he was the one involved with Larrain.'

'*Knock it off!*' Noakes exclaimed scornfully. 'Look what he's got waiting for him at home . . . I mean, who'd cheat on *her*?'

'It's not unheard of,' Markham observed mildly. Then, 'Did Nathan's friend have any intel on the Hartes, seeing as Mrs Harte works at the university, Kate?'

'They're a rock-solid couple according to Mike. He said they're friendly with Philip Twiss . . . not so much with the rest of the family. Apparently, Anna Harte mopped up the mess after an ex-girlfriend of Richard Twiss tried to kill herself . . . pretty much saved her life.'

'How come Ricardo had girlfriends? Seeing as he were like that Frenchy you said pranced around wearing earrings an' bracelets an' stuff?' Noakes enquired beadily.

Burton suppressed a sigh. At least, she supposed, the absorption of historical anecdotes represented a kind of progress.

'Yes, but the "Frenchy",' she tried to keep the sarcasm out of her voice, 'also had involvements with women, sarge. Remember, I mentioned there were platonic relationships, crushes, stuff like that . . . and nobody could be sure how far they went?'

Noakes looked as though it was all beyond him, and Markham felt a wave of affectionate sympathy for his burly, bewildered wingman.

'Why did this woman and Richard Twiss break up, Kate?' he asked. 'Was it something to do with Charles Larrain?'

'Mike didn't say, but I wouldn't be surprised boss.' The DI riffled through her notebook. 'Her name's Claire Mawdsley . . . No answer from her mobile yet, but I'll keep trying.'

'Thanks, Kate.' Markham stretched, enjoying the unfamiliar sensation of warmth at his back. 'In the meantime, I want you to check in with Frances Farquhar at the vicarage—'

'You don' see *her* for this do you, guv?' Noakes interrupted. 'I mean, finishing off her mum like that . . . ? An' she looked proper wrecked afterwards. She were in a right old state.'

'We can't rule anyone out at this stage, Sergeant. Let's see if Kate can pin down her movements at the centre . . . find out if there's any time unaccounted for which gave her an opportunity to doctor that jug of water at the Ideal Clinic.' Impatiently, he raked a hand through his thick wavy hair in the manner which had led susceptible civilian staff to christen him 'DI Dreamboat' and Noakes to reflect gloomily on the unfairness of life.

'We also need to find out where people were in relation to the Artisan Centre yesterday,' Markham continued. 'Its proximity to the hall means that potentially everyone's in the frame.'

Noakes's scowl on hearing this was prodigious, but the DI continued briskly, 'Doyle, while Kate's following up with Frances Farquhar and the Hartes, I want you to speak to the stallholders and staff at the centre.' Recalling what he had said to Olivia earlier about fish swimming up from the depths of a murky pond, he added with more conviction than he felt, 'Try to jog their minds . . . Somebody must've seen *something*.'

'What about you an' me, guv?' Noakes demanded.

'We'll go back to the hall. Now the incident room's set up there, we can take stock and prepare some briefing notes for the DCI.'

The DS tugged at the extraordinary maroon jerkin which Markham could only assume had been plucked from his wardrobe with a view to wiping the eyes of the gentry but which, along with the rust-coloured ribbed sweater underneath, was at least two sizes too small. *Hope springs eternal*, he thought, suppressing a grin at the disjunction between Noakes's self-image and the distinctly less flattering reality.

'Happen Mrs Thing'll sort us a fry up,' his wingman said hopefully.

'You don't want to turn up to the memorial service smelling of grease, Noakes,' his boss said austerely.

'Oh, there'll be time for a wash and brush-up before then,' came the reply happily.

The DI resigned himself to the inevitable. At least Noakes's appreciation of the Carton commissariat was bound to be well-received and might loosen tongues. As things stood, they had few other cards to play . . .

* * *

The exterior of Old Carton Parish Church belied Olivia's description of it as a 'jewel', the red sandstone rubble masonry, white limestone dressings, crenelated tower and gabled roof of bell cast tiles striking Markham as nothing special.

The interior, however, was different and as they explored it before the memorial service, Markham immediately fell under the spell of its atmosphere.

Long and narrow with a three-bay North aisle, his attention was immediately drawn to a full-length icon of the resurrected Christ casting off his shroud hanging next to a pointed wooden arcade through which was the altar. Behind the altar, an arched stained-glass window continued the resurrection theme with a bearded God the Father bestowing the crown of eternal life on a mitred figure surrounded by haloed spectators. A railed-off marble tomb to the right, with a recumbent nobleman in doublet, hose and huge cartwheel ruff, denoted the presence of a crypt.

'I dunno about that picture,' Noakes muttered as he contemplated the icon. 'Jesus follows you with his eyes like he's really come back to life.'

'That's rather the point of it, Noakesy,' Markham told him, admiring the mixture of stern majesty and benignity.

Olivia drew the DS's arm through hers.

'Look at these pillars,' she urged, pointing to wonderfully engraved dragons and knights in chain mail, armed with sword and shield, ready to fight against the snarling beasts. One knight's foot even rested in a dragon's jaw.

Predictably, these were more to Noakes's taste. 'They're even better than the ones we saw in that mouldy crypt down in London,' he grunted, referring to a recent investigation which had taken them down into the catacombs beneath a religious institute. 'But what's with the woman waving them palms in the air . . . Is she meant to be a princess or summat? The one St George had to rescue?' He peered closer. 'Or mebbe it's Mary cos the Bible says a dragon comes to get her . . . yeah, that's in *Revelation*.' He looked distinctly pleased with himself at producing this nugget of information.

'Could be,' Olivia murmured. 'Or maybe she's meant to symbolise the Church's victory over evil.' With a slight shiver, she thought of the unknown killer in Old Carton masquerading every Sunday as a devout worshiper while all on the time they were on the side of the Devil.

Noakes noticed her shudder and in a trice, the dreadful jerkin had been unzipped and draped over Olivia's shoulders. 'Should've known the sky pilots wouldn't stump up for some decent heating,' he grumbled to cover his self-consciousness. 'It's colder than a witch's tit in here.' Remembering where he was, the piggy eyes slid apprehensively sideways towards the Risen Jesus as though he expected immediate reprisals for such irreverence.

Olivia laughed. 'You're right about that,' she said, drawing the cardigan about her as though it was the softest cashmere. 'I should've worn my thermals instead of this lightweight trouser suit. But I might've known my very own knight would come to the rescue.' She smiled at him.

Stop flirting, Liv, Markham thought indulgently, watching as a tide of red rose up his wingman's beefy neck. *Much more of that and I won't be able to bring Noakesy back down to earth.*

As though she read his mind, Olivia moved away towards the sanctuary and the stained-glass window with its panoply of resurrection splendour, Noakes padding after her like a giant St Bernard following its mistress.

'That fella in the window getting the crown thingy must be one of them Twisses . . . some bishop or bigwig,' he pronounced gazing intently at the richly coloured spectacle. 'The missus says in medieval times rich folk got thesselves painted into holy pictures . . . posing with saints an' angels an' what have you. She heard it in a lecture at the WI.' He aimed a kick at one of the octagonal pillars before thinking better of it. 'I call it chuffing big-headed. Like they're so special they get to rub shoulders with Jesus an',' he gestured vaguely, 'the rest of 'em up there straightaway, no questions asked.' A portentous scowl. 'Anyway, what about Purgatory an' us having to be *cleansed* an' stuff?'

Olivia chuckled. 'I think it's like airports, George . . . The Twisses presumably see themselves as being on the VIP track, you know, the *Premier Lounge* and all that.'

He looked anything but pacified at hearing this. 'Bloody cheek, thass what I call it.'

Suddenly they heard the sound of voices in the porch and the squeaky wooden door opening.

'It sounds as though the congregation is arriving,' Markham said briskly. 'Let's find somewhere at the back.' He glanced at his watch. 'Kate and Doyle should be along any minute.'

And then it's Curtain Up.

7. UNHOLY NIGHT

As it turned out, the memorial service for Charles Larrain felt muted, the mourners cutting a dark swathe in the church's gloomy interior that was only relieved by the stained-glass coronation of a deceased Twiss ancestor and the purple vestments of Frank Harte whose dignified gravitas suited the simplicity of the occasion.

'Them county poshos all look the same,' Noakes muttered crossly as he scanned the congregation, ignoring a reproachful look from Kate Burton who had arrived pink-cheeked and somewhat out of breath with a contingent from the village, followed by Doyle who had lingered to admire Anna Harte as she greeted worshipers in the porch. Watching as the woman took her place in a pew at the front, Markham was struck afresh by the grace which not even her drab black ensemble could dim.

Aware of Olivia following his gaze, he murmured, 'The vicar's wife,' to which she retorted ironically, 'You never mentioned she looked like *that*.' Markham smiled at the barely detectable undertone of jealousy.

'What were you expecting?'

'Something along the lines of a Barbara Pym character,' she shot back. 'As in worthy and plain.'

Noakes was bang on the money about everyone looking the same, the DI thought ruefully as the opening hymn *Abide With Me* swelled from the organ loft. But although initially the mourners seemed indistinguishable, absorbed into one black smudge, gradually individuals became distinct.

Gerard and Stella Twiss flanked Frances Farquhar in a manner uncomfortably reminiscent of prison warders. In the circumstances, Markham was impressed that Frances had decided to attend, though her unsteady gait, untidy hair and unfocused expression suggested she was medicated up to the eyeballs. Anxious looks exchanged over her head by the couple from the farm reinforced that impression.

Interestingly, Gerard and Stella didn't bestow a single glance on the other side of the family, who stood together in a pew on the opposite aisle. Sir Simon, in hacking jacket and pink chinos (*pink*! Noakes hissed), and Lady Edith, wearing a black trench coat and faux fur Cossack hat, gave the appearance of exercising rigid self-control in order to get through the proceedings. The sons Michael, Richard and Philip could have modelled for Burberry in their expensive wool and herringbone, while daughter Margaret in the row behind sported an elegant black coatdress, its restrained simplicity set off to perfection by pearl earrings and a black velvet barrette clip securing the abundant dark hair.

Markham felt, rather than saw, Olivia's gaze alight on the undoubted beauty of the family.

Like a snowy dove trooping with crows, he thought admiringly, before turning his attention to the other mourners.

Well, 'mourners' was pushing it really, seeing as how Richard Twiss was probably the only person there with a strong personal connection to the deceased. Red-eyed but composed, he turned round just once to shoot a venomous glance at his sister who stared stonily ahead.

Catherine Metcalfe stood next to Christopher Hassett. Smartly turned out in a black cashmere coat and a striking — if somewhat over the top — black fascinator, she whispered animatedly to the curator, repeatedly laying long red fingernails on his arm in a markedly proprietorial manner. Cynically, the DI wondered if the events manager was holding him in reserve in case she didn't manage to extract a proposal from Michael Twiss.

Hassett certainly scrubbed up well, his lean greyhound looks and velvet-collared Crombie coat imparting an air of distinction à la Jacob Rees-Mogg. Markham had the impression he was embarrassed by Metcalfe's incessant fidgeting. It also struck him as interesting that the woman did not sit with the family despite being Michael's girlfriend.

Irene Clark, trim in a black car coat and mauve silk scarf, Carmel Scarron and a smattering of staff from the hall stood together, the housekeeper keeping a motherly eye on Annette Sullivan whose periodic snuffles punctured the sostenuto of the organ music. Carmel's son, Patrick Scarron was nowhere to be seen.

Likewise, there was no sign of DCI Sidney, which definitely counted as a bonus given that the savage power of Noakes's lusty vocals had already caused one or two heads to swivel and provoked an outbreak of nervous tittering among the younger hall staff, which was only quelled by a glare from Irene Clark.

Olivia had returned Noakes's horrible jerkin, so that he was now once more resplendent and unmissable. At least her bell-like tones took some of the harm from the way he murdered *The Lord's My Shepherd*. Even Kate Burton and Doyle — decidedly unproficient in choral skills — felt impelled to try and obliterate their colleague's bravura performance.

Although the air of the church was chill, so that his breath drifted upwards like a cloud of incense, Markham was overcome by a curious sense of lethargy, his eyes wandering to the memorial brasses and plaques and then back to the stained-glass window with its vainglorious depiction of a Twiss magnate receiving his eternal reward . . .

A gentle tug on his sleeve from Olivia alerted him to the fact that the vicar had invited the congregation to sit down, a stifled groan from Noakes heralding the eulogy.

In the event, however, Harte merely delivered a five-minute homily which made no mention of Charles Larrain or Isobel Farquhar beyond what appeared to be a sincerely uttered prayer 'for all the faithful departed, together with our recently deceased brother and sister'. Markham wasn't sure what to make of this reticence and wondered whether Harte had refrained from delivering a more detailed remembrance speech at the family's behest. In light of Charles Larrain's tempestuous relationship with the Twisses, at least it avoided hypocrisy.

In his pleasant baritone, Harte concluded with what was obviously a quotation. Markham couldn't place it but found comfort in the sentiment:

'In this season of Advent,' intoned the vicar, 'we are reminded that between the two births of Christ — the first in Bethlehem and the last at the end of time — the Saviour will continually be born in us and change this world's unholy night into the holy night of his birth.'

Suddenly, comfort was replaced by the pangs of self-doubt.

Could his team restore light and hope to Old Carton after the unholy night of these murders?

Could they overcome evil like those dragon-slayers on the church's engraved pillars?

Did a murderer even now stand among them, exulting in the evasion of justice?

Markham took a deep breath in an attempt to calm his fears.

Finally, they were back on their feet again for the closing hymn, and Markham had a strange sense that the little church was impatient for them to leave so that its ancient damp-threatened walls could once more wrap the chilly precincts and vaults in silence.

At last it was over and a straggling procession wound its way towards the hall, the prospect of refreshments very welcome on a freezing afternoon with snow lying thick underfoot. As the mourners left the parish church, a starved looking thrush hopped disconsolately along the stone wall which separated it from the pocket handkerchief-sized graveyard next door. Noakes clearly wished there were some breadcrumbs to give the little visitor, rummaging fruitlessly in his cardigan as though in hopes that its pockets might yield some stray remnants of a McDonald's snack. Then, to Markham's amusement, he ducked his head shyly by way of apology for having come unprepared. The bird seemed to understand, regarding the beefy policeman steadily with its head on one side before disappearing among the neighbouring tombstones.

Olivia linked her arm through Noakes's. 'Come on, George,' she urged. 'Otherwise we'll be last in the queue.'

The reminder worked like a charm and in no time at all the hall rose before them in all its lacy winter tracery.

* * *

Refreshments were served in Lady Mary's Drawing Room on the first floor.

'Milking that ruddy ghost for all they're worth,' Noakes hissed balefully, but he was nonetheless impressed with the watered silk walls in blush rose, venerable mahogany sideboards, portraits of distinguished-looking Elizabethans and magnificent Tudor hammerbeam ceiling. Aubusson carpets in faded aquamarine tints covered the floors while tapestry frames displayed samplers and richly embroidered textiles to best advantage. The occasional tables and comfortable walnut armchairs with velvet covered seats were of more recent vintage but harmonised well with the other furnishings. A roaring fire crackled in the vast inglenook hearth which occupied practically the whole of one wall, while the other was taken up by a stained-glass window showing stylised medieval lovers whose conjoined hands clasped a golden goblet. In the dying afternoon light, it seemed to Markham that the lovers' faces had a lurid cast.

Noakes turned to him. 'At least it ain't Catherine de Medici, so we get a break from all that chuffing poison.'

Anna Harte's musical contralto observed from behind them, 'Sorry, Sergeant, but it's meant to show Tristan and Iseult drinking the love potion.'

Registering his blank expression, she added, 'It's an old legend . . . Tristan is sent by King Mark to fetch Iseult from across the sea to be his bride. Iseult's mother has prepared a love potion for her daughter to take to the king, but Iseult and Tristan drink it by mistake on the voyage and end up falling madly in love.'

The DS stared beadily at the stained-glass couple as though to say, *I might have known.*

Markham liked the woman for her uncondescending manner towards his sergeant. Olivia, too, unbent as the vicar's wife chatted about the history of the hall and its various artefacts. Eventually, as though remembering her position, Anna Harte excused herself to mingle with the other visitors, their stiffness thawing as she moved among the various groups.

Sandwiches and canapés, along with hot drinks and frangipane mince pies duly making their appearance on trolleys, Noakes tucked in with his usual gusto.

'The DCI isn't going to get here, guv,' Kate Burton murmured discreetly to Markham. 'I checked with the station on our way up . . . He's stuck in that meeting at Division.'

Markham felt some of the tension leave his body. The last thing Sidney needed was a reminder of Noakes's virtuosity when it came to putting away rations. If anything was guaranteed to hasten his wingman's retirement, it was his unabashed enthusiasm for free hospitality. Out of the corner of his eye, the DI noticed Gerard and Stella Twiss watching Noakes with the stealthy fascination of anthropologists encountering a primitive tribesman. Burton obviously had seen it too, given that she made a beeline for the couple, standing so as to obscure their view of her happily oblivious colleague. As for Doyle, baulked of the chance to monopolise Anna Harte by Gerard Twiss, he settled for Catherine Metcalfe who while equally easy on the eye lacked the other woman's refinement. Olivia, Markham noted wryly, was soon locked in animated conversation with Christopher Hassett and Margaret Twiss, but the latter broke off when the rest of her family entered the room.

Sir Simon, Lady Edith and their sons made no particular effort to engage with their guests other than producing rictus smiles for the vicar who flogged away at polite conversation for several minutes before retiring from the fray with an expression of intense relief. *Duty done*, he telegraphed to his wife.

Markham would have liked to sink into one of the walnut armchairs, but instead courteously circulated among the villagers before endeavouring to engage Frances Farquhar in conversation. Unsurprisingly, it was tough going. As Doyle observed sotto voce, the poor woman appeared 'zonked' as though she hardly knew where she was. No doubt it was the senior Twisses who had pulled strings in organising her mother's interment, as she was clearly in no fit state to object to anything. Eventually Irene Clark volunteered to drive her to the vicarage where she was staying for the time being, and shortly after that the remaining guests drifted away, Olivia hitching a lift into Bromgrove with Miss Evans from the shop.

Doyle yawned. 'Anyone learn anything?' he enquired languidly before answering his own question as he took in the others' weary expressions. 'Thought not.'

'They're not buying "unexplained death" for Izzy,' Noakes grunted. 'They know it's gotta be connected to Aznavour.'

'Let's get back to our incident room and take stock,' Markham told them.

''S much warmer in here,' his wingman grumbled. 'An' there's proper chairs, not like them itty-bitty museum things . . . *dead uncomfortable they are* . . .'

'*Nevertheless*,' the DI re-joined firmly in a tone that brooked no argument.

Somehow they managed to get lost, blundering along a corridor in the east wing, weaving between sightless alabaster busts interspersed with suits of armour and random curios.

They were about to retrace their steps when suddenly they heard angry voices coming from behind a door at the far end.

'Sounds like they're having a right old ding-dong,' Noakes observed laconically with his gift for stating the obvious.

At that moment, Christopher Hassett emerged from a room further along the passage. Visibly flustered at encountering the detectives, he nonetheless said nothing as he escorted them to their incident room.

'Can you shed some light on what that was all that about, Mr Hassett?' Markham asked quietly.

'Cos it's clear as mud to us,' Noakes added belligerently.

The curator waited until they had drawn their chairs up to the fire which wasn't doing much to impart warmth. 'I'll arrange to get you a heater,' Hassett murmured distractedly, shooting his cuffs and smoothing his surprisingly flamboyant ruby waistcoat which Noakes eyed suspiciously as they awaited his explanation.

'It's a complicated family,' Hassett said at last.

'*You don' say,*' Noakes retorted with heavy sarcasm before subsiding at a sharp look from his boss.

'There was bad feeling after the last exhibition,' Hassett continued. 'I suppose it never really went away.'

'When was that, sir?' the DI prompted, aware of the other's acute discomfort but keen for more background information.

'Christmas last year,' came the reply. Again, that nervous adjustment of his clothing before the curator resumed. 'It wasn't one of Margaret's better ideas,' he said finally. 'But she was fed up of Larrain . . . figured he was making her family a laughingstock, so she might as well go the whole hog, twist the knife and make *him* suffer for a change.'

'Go on,' the DI prompted.

'She arranged an exhibition about King Henri — Henri III, Catherine de Medici's favourite son who, among other things, enjoyed appearing *en travesti,*' was the unexpected answer.

'*Come again?*' Noakes wasn't disposed to make this any easier.

'He liked dressing up as a woman — hair tinted with violet powder . . . stunningly brocaded dresses, lapdogs in little jew-elled baskets hung round his neck, doublets worn over corsets. Done up to the nines . . . So much so, that no one took any notice of the woman he'd married because all eyes were fixed on him.'

'A perv then,' Noakes said trenchantly, ignoring Markham's warning frown.

'Certainly a very complex character and given to wild extremes of behaviour, Sergeant,' the curator replied. 'At one point, he underwent some sort of religious experience which had disturbingly morbid, even necromantic, overtones. He engaged in extreme practices of self-mortification such as flag-ellation and built a sinister oratory which he swathed in black crepe and festooned with skulls and bones taken from a local cemetery . . . all the while being egged on by a group of monks he had taken up with. They even held a barefoot procession a week before Christmas in deep snow, which resulted in the Cardinal of Lorraine dying of pneumonia.'

Noakes's jaw dropped.

'How did Henri,' he pronounced it Henry, 'square the religious oojah with prancing around in jewellery an' all the rest of it?'

'As I say, he was a troubled exhibitionist, but no one saw fit to question his behaviour, not even his mother . . . It was all part of the divine right of kings. In those days, lèse-majesté was punishable by death.'

'Thank chuff for Prince Charles,' Noakes said fervently. 'No chance of *him* hitting the dressing up box or digging up skulls. *He* jus' talks to plants . . .'

Hassett's lips twitched. 'There was almost certainly an erotic dimension to the religious zealotry. Some of the young courtiers whipped themselves into a sort of ecstatic frenzy following Henri's example.'

'An' you mean to say his old mum went along with all the nuttiness?' Noakes demanded in bafflement.

Hassett gave a non-committal shrug. 'Up to a point. However, she undoubtedly had a deep-rooted hatred of the *mignons* — the court favourites — she felt had corrupted her son.'

'She didn't mind him being into women, though?' Doyle liked to have things clear in his own mind.

'Oh no, not at all. As far as she was concerned, women were much less trouble . . . more easily controlled. She practically threw them at him — any young girl with a thirteen-inch waist was guaranteed an introduction.'

'*Thirteen inches.*' Doyle was suitably impressed. 'Blimey.'

Hassett smiled. 'Not that it did much good. Henri was a sucker for any male gallant who crossed his path in padded breeches slashed with fashionable colours . . . They even called it the "slashing style" because of his obsession with it.'

Normally Burton would have enjoyed the history lesson, but she was impatient to see where it led. 'Okay, but this is all *true*, right?' she piped up earnestly. 'I mean, historically speaking it's all kosher?' Her expression thoughtful, she added, 'I remember a film with Cate Blanchette as Elizabeth I . . . There's this scene where she catches some French prince camping it up in lace and diamonds . . . frizzed hair, low *décolleté*, the works—'

'*Ah*, that was Henri's brother who undertook an abortive courtship of Elizabeth.'

Noakes stared at the curator. 'So *he* were a freaky crossdresser an' all?'

Markham braced himself to apologise for the pejorative description, but Hassett merely laughed.

'The brothers had certain traits in common, Sergeant . . . Rumours of a dissolute lifestyle — maybe even including incest with their sister Marguerite — swirled around them from their youth.' Another grim chuckle. 'All highly ironic given that the French monarch was traditionally called "The Most Christian King" and supposed to be a pillar of morality.' The curator smiled at Noakes whose fascination with the topic far outstripped that of the average visitor to Carton. 'Preachers over here were so panicked at the thought of one of the French royals laying profane hands on their beloved

Virgin Queen, that they denounced them as sorcerers and instruments of uncleanness . . . Oh yes, no one was in any doubt about the sons of Catherine de Medici.'

Markham was thoughtful.

'But from what you say, all these facts about French royalty are well known,' the DI returned to Burton's earlier point. 'Academically speaking, there's nothing contentious about any of it . . . Margaret Twiss is a Renaissance specialist after all, and with Henri III being so spectacularly decadent it's hardly surprising she wanted to use him for an exhibition.'

'Yeah, folk always want to know about high-ups perving,' Noakes chimed in. '*Kerching*! Bound to get the punters flocking . . . pay for a new roof or decent heating.' The DS glanced around appraisingly, his eyes narrowing as they rested on the decidedly meagre fire. 'It must take *gazillions* to keep this gaff going.'

'You're right about that, Sergeant,' Hassett agreed. 'The hall's overheads are astronomical.' He hesitated, weighing his words. 'The problem wasn't so much that Margaret arranged an exhibition about the Valois dynasty. They're always good value, the gift that keeps on giving . . . No, it was more that the family disliked the . . . *slant* she put on things—'

'How d'you mean?' Noakes interrupted impatiently.

'The choice of Henri III . . . his effeminacy . . . the morbid obsessions . . .'

'And the male favourites,' Markham finished quietly. 'Too reminiscent of Richard Twiss's association with Charles Larrain, perhaps?'

The curator exhaled deeply as though grateful Markham had said it. 'Some of the pictures and stories could have seemed like a sly commentary on Richard and Charles Larrain,' he acknowledged.

'Were *they* into cross-dressing an' whipping thesselves too, then?' Noakes enquired eagerly.

Markham glanced swiftly at his fellow DI, well aware that such debate was definitely not the kind of spectator sport Burton relished, though he suspected Doyle enjoyed it. At least Noakes hadn't referred to 'Aznavour', which was some comfort.

'There was an element of self-display which set tongues wagging,' the curator replied carefully. 'And their shared interest in the more macabre aspects of funerary practice — effigies, death masks, memento mori — also attracted a certain amount of unfavourable comment. Plus, they veered from sensualism to a weird sort of ostentatious piety . . . hung out with the High-Church crowd . . . even had a plan for refurbishing the parish church, but the vicar put his foot down when people started muttering about Popery.'

At least *someone* had their priorities right, Noakes thought sardonically. Next thing you knew, they'd all be genuflecting to Rome.

Despite his own recent dabbling at the fringes of Catholicism, the DS didn't at all like the sound of Tricky Dicky, whose ponytail coiffure that day had put him in mind of a dancer from *Strictly*. Not that he had anything against ball-room dancing, but Muriel felt that kind of thing was the thin end of the wedge and *totally* unsuitable for family television.

Still less was Noakes comfortable with Dicky's creepy parfumier chum. He had a feeling cross-dressing was the least of it . . .

Markham's voice broke across these reflections.

'I think I see, Mr Hassett,' the DI said. 'There was food for mischief in that exhibition.'

'The family certainly thought so,' the other replied. Sensing that Noakes's thoughts still ran on the French royals' taste for transvestism, he continued, 'Look, by the standards of his time, King Henri III was not so unusual, because his contemporaries often wore fantastically elaborate costumes . . . It was only in Spain under King Philip that fashions were far more austere. Henri's father would have cured his excesses by sending him off hunting or jousting, something warlike at any rate. But he died when Henri was young, and anyway it wasn't Henri's kind of thing. He preferred staying indoors, out of the cold.'

This elicited a snort from Noakes.

'Sounds a right big girl's blouse!' he scoffed.

Burton winced, but Hassett was obviously getting used to the plain-spoken sergeant and continued, 'Well, given the country's religious divisions and the endless cabals, Henri had an unenviable task . . . more or less relied on his mother to bump off his enemies—'

'But she didn't stop at that,' Noakes interrupted eagerly. 'Cos you said she had it in for Henri's boyfriends . . . didn't like 'em moving into *her* territory. A bit like Lady E,' he added insinuatingly.

'*Exactly*, Sergeant.' Again, there was the sense of Hassett weighing his words. 'As I say, Henri — and his brother — were fairly standard Renaissance courtiers . . . But the parallels with Richard Twiss and Charles Larrain struck too close to home as far as Sir Simon and Lady Edith were concerned. Philip freaked out about the whole homosexual Oedipal thing — it didn't help that he and Richard were dead ringers for the Valois brothers — while Michael got on his high horse about the family honour being at stake.'

'How explicit *was* the innuendo, Mr Hassett?' Markham asked. 'Presumably your average punter wouldn't have made the connection with the Twisses.'

'True, but you see those in the know *did* . . . And it was the humiliation in front of their own intimate circle which stung.'

Noakes frowned. 'Couldn't they have ridden it out? Sounds like Ricardo an' Larrain were pretty brazen — didn't care about gossip or folk having a go — so the family could've carried on like it were all perfectly normal . . . you know, *Nowt to see here, move along.*'

Hassett's expression was shadowed. 'There'd been no end of rows about Larrain worming his way into the family, so they were all massively sensitive about it turning into a local joke.'

'And how did Mr Larrain react to the exhibition?' Markham asked. 'If he was an attention-seeker, it must have gratified his ego at some level.'

'Perhaps it would have done if Margaret's commentary hadn't made him look contemptible . . . She was very clever about it, but he would have no doubt recognised himself in the descriptions of the *mignons* who fawned over the Valois brothers and fought their mother for the top spot.' The curator flicked an invisible speck of dust from his ruby waistcoat as though to buy himself time before continuing, 'She did a pen-picture of one of the male favourites — d'Épernon — which incorporated some of Larrain's mannerisms . . . his habit of calling everyone "darling boy", for example, and sort of pirouetting on the balls of his feet like a ballet dancer about to perform a jeté. Little pretentious affectations that were instantly identifiable . . .'

'Do you know if Mr Larrain tackled her?' Markham pressed.

'Margaret said not but apparently he gave Richard hell about it, so Richard bawled her out . . . and after that, they pretty much didn't speak.'

'Must've made the parentals happy that she took Larrain down a peg or two though,' Doyle observed.

'Oh, they didn't see it like that at all.' Hassett shook his head. 'Felt the whole thing was undignified and exposed them to ridicule. It was the same down at the Farm and Dower Cottage.'

Mother of God, what a freaky family. Noakes wasn't up to any of this. What with pervy noblemen, cross-dressing, feuds and all the rest of it, his head felt like it was going to explode . . . He could see the guvnor and Burton were lapping it up, but he couldn't for the life of him see how it moved the investigation on any further.

After the curator had left them with a promise to email proofs of last year's exhibition brochure, the DS said as much to Markham.

'Okay, so they all hated Aznavour. An' they weren't too keen on Little Sis after she used that exhibition thingy to settle scores.' The DS tugged his hair fiercely. 'Margaret were having a go at her mum, too, for playing favourites an' being .

. . creepy with Tricky Dicky.' Noakes instinctively shied away from any mention of incest. 'But in the end, all she did was get up everyone's nose, 'xactly the same as Larrain. *Hey*,' a thought struck him, 'mebbe she'll be the next one to cop it.'

'I devoutly hope not, Sergeant,' was the dry response. 'Two victims are more than enough to be going along with.'

'At least none of them asked if Isobel Farquhar was murdered,' Doyle murmured.

'Not the "done thing" in the circumstances,' Markham sighed.

''S a bit rum worrying about the "done thing" when you look at the state of them,' Noakes protested. 'I mean they're seriously screwy what with all those hang ups about being like some family from the olden times.'

Restlessly, Markham got up and began to pace the room.

'Somehow I can't get a handle on the Twisses,' he said after several turns. 'It's weird, but the Valois dynasty seem real and vital despite the fact of them being long dead, while this lot might as well be ghosts for all we really know about them.'

'Hiding behind their masks,' Doyle concluded. 'Just like the spooky waxworks in that chamber of horrors.'

It struck Markham as an astute observation. He was just about to say so when the young detective continued unexpectedly:

'When you think about it, there's all kinds of weirdos out there,' he said. 'Walking the streets . . . managing companies . . . even running academic seminars.' Seeing Burton frown at this, he added hastily. 'I read somewhere that half the CEOs in this country have sociopathic traits and that's why they're so successful.'

'Proper little ray of sunshine you are,' Noakes scowled. 'Saying we're all psychos.'

Undeterred, his protégé went on, 'It's like it says in that Shakespeare play, "All the world's a stage". Everyone's playing a part.' He flashed a grin. ''Cept you, sarge. You're the real deal.'

He's got that right, Markham thought suppressing a chuckle. Whatever failings could be attributed to Noakes, inauthenticity was not among them.

Suddenly a cloud passed over Doyle's frank, open face. 'Paula doesn't like it when I come out with stuff like that,' he said diffidently. 'She says it's creepy and peculiar and that being in CID is making me morbid.'

'Knock it off, lad,' Noakes replied gruffly. 'Being a mixed-up bastard's part of the job description . . . Shippers'll tell you the same all day long.' The DS glared at Burton as though defying her to contradict him.

Kate looked uncomfortable on hearing this, as though reluctant to associate her level-headed fiancé with anything so messy.

Markham made a mental note to quiz Burton about Doyle's partner, since this change from the youngster's usual cheerful optimism suggested that some sort of pastoral strategy might be in order, over and above whatever advice Noakes saw fit to dispense during the pair's weekly drinkathon.

Bringing himself back to the investigation, he said slowly, 'It's most likely our murderer was playing a part today . . . playing it so convincingly as to pass unnoticed.'

He glanced out of the window. Outside it was dark with a crescent moon visible in the pale cold sky.

Christmas is coming and we've got sweet FA.

He became aware the others were waiting expectantly. 'Right,' he said. 'Kate, I want you to try and get hold of Richard Twiss's ex—'

She was reaching for her mobile before the words were out of his mouth. 'Claire Mawdsley . . . I'm on it, guv,' she said retreating into the corridor.

He turned to the other two. 'We need to pad out those notes for the DCI,' he instructed. 'Give him some more background detail.'

Noakes guffawed. 'You mean all that stuff about what Henri the Quatorze got up to?'

The DI smiled wearily. 'I doubt DCI Sidney will care for too much information about the Valois clan, but we could include something about that exhibition last year . . . It shows the level of resentment against Charles Larrain if nothing else.'

They lapsed into silence, pondering what the curator had disclosed.

Then Burton was back, swiftly hanging up the call.

'Bingo! Ms Mawdsley said she can meet up tomorrow, guv. I suggested lunchtime at the Grapes.'

Noakes looked hopeful.

'I need you and Doyle here to recheck statements and alibis for both Charles Larrain and Isobel Farquhar,' Markham said to him firmly. It wasn't that he didn't trust his wingman — Noakes's interview approach could be surprisingly sensitive at times. Still, something told him Burton's gentle touch would be better suited to this particular interviewee, in light of what he suspected would turn out to be a complex sexual background. And besides, it was only fair to give his fellow DI a fair crack of the whip.

'Righto,' his wingman said philosophically thinking that there was always Mrs Scarron and her frangipane mince pies to fall back on.

'Come on,' Markham instructed. 'The computers are up and running. Let's see what's on the system. I want to take a look at the PM report for Isobel Farquhar.' He realised with a guilty pang that they were in danger of forgetting the second victim in their fascination with the family at the hall.

As the team scattered to their various tasks, he wondered what light the elusive Claire Mawdsley might shed on the Twisses.

Maybe *she* would be the one to stir up this murder investigation and bring their quarry up from the depths.

8. THE TOILS OF PASSION

The Grapes was the team's favourite pub in Bromgrove, despite being resolutely unfashionable with its array of brasses and knick-knacks and décor that had somehow stayed stuck in the 1970s, not to mention swirling patterned carpets and psychedelic motifs that seemed almost calculated to make visitors feel that they were coming down from an acid trip.

Not that the owner Denise, with an embonpoint and beehive to make Bet Lynch proud, would have any truck with shenanigans of *that* sort. She ran a tight ship — quite literally, given the predominance of nautical instruments and seafaring paraphernalia among the curios crammed into every available space — and was proud to count Markham's gang of four among her favoured patrons for whom a booth in the cosy back parlour was always readily available. Although the uneven wooden floor imparted a flavour of seasickness and the crimson flock wallpaper dotted with Prince of Wales feathers (Denise being a huge fan of royalty) clashed horribly with the dark oak wainscoting, Markham had always relished the pub's quirky charm and its motherly proprietor who, Olivia griped, 'spoiled him shamelessly'.

The DI suggested to Kate Burton that they should enjoy a coffee before Claire Mawdsley joined them so Thursday afternoon saw the two colleagues nursing cappuccinos in the back room over a plate of home-made cookies which, in Denise's words, would 'put them on till lunchtime'.

Kate enjoyed the glow of the crackling wood fire and, even more, the feeling that her boss found it soothing to sit like this with her away from the controlled chaos of the incident room at Carton Hall and out of reach of their superiors back at the station.

Out of reach only up to a point, of course, since DCI Sidney had announced his intention of attending Isobel Farquhar's interment the following day 'when they could bring him up to speed on developments'. That word 'developments' as delivered by Sidney invariably carried a menacing undertone . . .

But for now, this was her idea of heaven.

Increasingly secure in her relationship with Nathan Finlayson, she no longer hankered for the moon with mad fantasies of seducing Markham away from Olivia Mullen. But she knew there existed a special affinity between herself and the man she still thought of as her boss. She still held him dear — and maybe the feeling was mutual. Maybe one of the chambers in *his* heart had her name above the door; a place totally distinct from the rooms that belonged to others — maybe even just an attic room tucked out of the way — but reserved for her alone. Burton knew her handsome, melancholic guvnor had to draw a prize in life's lottery — in this case, willowy, witty Olivia rather than her plain, dumpy self — and therefore had the common sense to keep a tight rein over her behaviour where he was concerned. Nonetheless, she relished the unspoken sympathy and undercurrents of feeling that flowed between them. There was always an element of caution in her relationship with Markham, as though she hardly dared trust herself in case it threatened to cross the border into something stronger.

She wondered if Olivia was aware of this, since it seemed to her that the DI's partner regarded her with increasingly hostile eyes.

Well, Burton told herself with a sudden flare of defiance, Olivia Mullen could think whatever she chose. Meanwhile, it was up to her to spell out the covert message that *she* had no designs on Markham.

She felt keenly that there was something almost ridiculous in these feelings for her boss . . . something Lady of Shalott-like in her attitude towards this man who dominated her emotional horizons like a knight riding by to some mythical Camelot. Doyle was in the habit of joking about how Noakes regarded himself as Olivia's 'knight in shining armour', but her own attitude towards Markham was hardly less quixotic and equally unrealistic.

She could only be thankful that Nathan had no clue about how she felt.

And anyway, was there anything *really* so very bad about it?

She wasn't asking for anything. Not love. Nothing romantic. She knew she couldn't afford to expose herself to false hopes. She just wanted Markham to keep a fraction of himself for *her* and allow no one to meddle with it or spoil their understanding . . . It was only a crumb but she required it to keep her going . . .

'Penny for them, Kate,' came the pleasant baritone from across the table.

'I was just thinking about Christmas,' she lied smoothly, pulling herself together. 'It'll be very different this year without Dad.'

The tenderness in the dark features at this reference to her father's death earlier in the year almost undid her, so she gabbled on.

'Mum didn't know where to put his ashes, so in the end she settled on the hen house — it's where he liked to sit and think — but now she's terrified they might get mixed up with the birds' feed.'

He burst out laughing at this unexpected confidence from his sober colleague. 'Is that really likely, Kate?'

And now she was laughing too.

'No, they're in a special urn up on the wall, but she's got this obsession that it's not, well, *seemly* . . . convinced herself that it's bound to be a disaster, so I'm in and out of there by the minute checking for her.' She grinned. 'Dad would laugh his socks off at how ridiculous it all is, but that's my mum for you.'

Markham recalled her telling him during a previous investigation how she used to sit with her father in his hen house and make up stories about a riotous student social life so that he wouldn't imagine she was 'Billy No Mates' and be disappointed that university wasn't living up to expectations. It had almost made him want to cry as he heard about her holding forth to Mr Burton and an audience of poultry like some kind of latter-day Scheherazade.

She was remembering it too, but there was no treacherous wobble in her voice as she asked politely, 'What about you, sir? Are you and Olivia doing anything special for Christmas?'

'If Liv has her way, we'll be indolent couch-potatoes watching weepies and rom coms till we're square eyed.' He gave a fake grimace then paused. 'Are you and Nathan going to your mum's?'

He could not say why, but something in him still couldn't accept the idea of Kate Burton and Nathan Finlayson as a *couple*. Some shameful inner voice had persisted in whispering that Kate Burton couldn't commit to anyone because of *him*, and now he reproached himself for the sheer chauvinism of such a dog-in-the-manger response. Burton had just as much right as anyone to take happiness where she could find it . . . and besides, Finlayson was a decent man and a good fit . . .

'Yes,' Kate replied, 'and Mum even trusts Nathan to do the cooking . . . I'll just get quietly sloshed while he's on sprout peeling duty.'

Somehow Markham couldn't imagine Kate Burton getting 'sloshed' but smiled at this picture of domestic bliss.

Suddenly he remembered he had meant to ask his fellow DI about Doyle. 'By the by, Kate, what's up with DS Doyle these days? He seems a bit down in the mouth.'

She flashed a mischievous grin that illuminated her earnest face, giving it a puckish charm that was very endearing.

'Don't you worry, guv. I'll bet that right now Sergeant Noakes is telling him to *prenez un grip*.'

Markham chuckled. 'I take it the current girlfriend wants him out of CID,' he said.

'It's pretty serious, sir . . . Doyle reckons she's *The One*.' Burton wrinkled her snub nose. 'She wants him to have a "proper job".'

'Would joining Noakesy as a private investigator count as one?'

'Don't know about that . . . she doesn't really approve of DS Noakes, sir.'

No surprises there. Markham didn't care to imagine how his wingman would go down with some 'PC Guardianista'.

'So, who do you reckon is likely to win this, er, tug of war over Doyle?'

'Well, he's pretty far gone on Paula, sir.'

Markham suppressed a smile at Burton's tone. She and Doyle were the same age, but at this moment she sounded infinitely older and wiser.

'I reckon she'll wear him down in the end, guv.' It was pretty clear who Burton had pegged as the ultimate victor in this war of attrition. 'He's got a great CV,' she continued magnanimously. 'So, he'll most likely have his pick of jobs if he decides to leave CID.' She frowned and was thoughtful for a moment. 'But he really *likes* policing . . . likes being at the sharp end, sir. And he's good at it. Knows his own mind too.' Not a pen-pushing apparatchik in other words.

'Right, Kate, I'll leave it to you to bring him round and keep him in the force,' Markham told her, only half joking. 'It's obvious he respects you. If anyone can "turn" our boy, it's you.'

Burton coloured up in an intriguing metamorphosis so that she looked positively pretty.

What was it about his fellow DI that tugged at his heartstrings? Markham wondered. It came down to innocence, he decided. Kate's naked *vulnerability* — an implicit appeal for his protection — that Olivia lacked.

Did that make him the worst kind of male chauvinist? he asked himself uneasily.

Was it possible to love two women at the same time? Or was he misconstruing the tranquil sense of wellbeing he experienced when with Kate Burton as something more passionate?

He had an electric connection with spiky, clever Olivia. And the sex was stunning. But there were times when he craved something more *restful*, and he had become wary of her jealous reaction to the other women he encountered, Kate Burton in particular. Since he'd never raised the subject of Olivia's particular dislike for Kate, Olivia clearly thought she had successfully concealed her feelings from him. A fact which somehow made it even harder to clear the air — as though bringing her jealousy into the open would humiliate Olivia when she was at her most vulnerable.

Olivia's jealousy paradoxically had the effect of making him feel even closer to his colleague, as though his partner saw something in Kate Burton that he had *missed* . . . the pearl of great price . . .

Markham knew that Olivia was tormented by her inability ever to give him a child because of an earlier abortion. Sometimes he wondered if subconsciously she believed that he kept her at arm's length on that account . . . as a punishment for having done something that, deep down, she felt was unforgiveable.

But it just wasn't so. His was a reserved nature — made more so by his experiences in early life — and that had nothing to do with anything his partner had or hadn't done. He had asked Olivia to marry him, only for her to accuse him of humouring her. The problem was, at some level, he suspected that this might be true . . .

The DI became aware that Burton was watching him with a puzzled expression.

'Sorry, Kate,' he shrugged. 'I was wool-gathering.'

'That's alright, sir.' A shy smile. 'It feels good to get away from the investigation for a bit.' She gestured round the room which was beginning to fill up. 'Pretend we're Christmas shoppers, like normal folk.'

Suddenly he was curious to know more about Burton's plans for the holidays.

'I take it you normally enjoy this time of year,' he said.

To his surprise, she became confidential. 'That young girl who found Charles Larrain's body, Annette Sullivan . . . she got a bit emotional when we were talking up at the hall. Her dad died a few months back and she started on about him loving Christmas, quoted me his favourite poem . . . Oddly enough, I remember having to learn it when I was in the Juniors.'

Folding her hands primly in front of her like the schoolgirl she once was, Burton duly recited 'Christmas' by John Betjeman.

Tears stung her eyes suddenly. 'Dad was always working when I was little, and there was never any money going spare for posh hotels . . . But,' her chin went up, 'I reckon *he's* one of the shining ones now.'

Too moved to reply, Markham simply stared as Burton began to blush, smoothing down her bob in an agony of embarrassment and fidgeting furiously with the lapels of her trouser suit as though she feared having made an almighty fool of herself.

Careful, careful. He knew he must give no inkling of his instinctive response to this display of vulnerability.

'D'you know, *I* seem to recall that poem too,' he said lightly, finally managing to speak, stirring his coffee thoughtfully as Burton surreptitiously rubbed her eyes before remembering (too late) that she was wearing eye makeup and hastily withdrawing her hands. 'Stuff about Christmas being all about bath salts and cheap scent and hideous ties . . .'

She laughed shakily. 'That's what sarge calls it . . . "Ugly Christmas Sweater Time", same as in the *Bridget Jones* film.'

'He needs to watch out . . . Olivia tells me there's such a thing as the "so-hideous-it's-almost-chic" craze . . . Noakesy might end up a follower of fashion in spite of himself!'

The easy banter helped, and Burton was once more in command of her emotions.

'I think Mrs Noakes . . . er, Muriel . . . takes Christmas pretty seriously.' Clearly, she didn't feel first-name informality was quite right when referring to her colleague's formidable spouse. 'Apparently, she's big on giving hospitality and all that.'

'Unlike Olivia then,' Markham replied drily. 'Liv has developed a repertoire of what she calls "discarding techniques" for getting rid of importunate visitors. Her latest ploy is to ask very loudly if they would like a cup of tea, by way of letting them know they've outstayed their welcome.'

Burton gulped uncertainly as though uncertain what to make of such rudeness.

'And does it work, sir?'

'Oh yes, every time.'

His fellow DI looked momentarily nonplussed, then said brightly, 'Well, unless we get a result with this Carton case, sarge may be able to dodge *all* the parties by saying he's got to work.'

Typical of Burton to see the silver lining in such a scenario.

'*Ugh, Kate,*' he emitted a mock-groan. 'Don't even go there! We've *got* to get a result . . . There's the prospect of Sidney at tomorrow's interment to concentrate our minds.'

At that moment, Denise bustled over to them. 'I've got a young woman name of Claire Mawdsley out front asking for you, Inspector. Okay if she joins you?'

'Absolutely, Denise, and if you could send some menus over . . .'

Burton sat up straighter, like a subaltern eager to go into battle with all flags flying thought Markham in amusement.

'Perhaps this is it,' his fellow DI whispered urgently. 'Being Richard Twiss's ex, she's *bound* to give us something.'

But forty minutes later, Burton's excitement had evaporated.

'Not much joy there, guv,' she lamented toying with her excellent chicken pie. 'I thought it'd relax her coming in here, but she was even more uptight than the rest of them.'

'Hmm. You made the right call, Kate. I think it was more a case of her not wanting to revisit painful memories as opposed to the venue . . . At least it confirms that Charles Larrain was an unguarded missile, wreaking havoc among the Twisses . . . and one Twiss in particular. Come on, eat up,' he told her. 'We've got a clearer idea now of just what a time bomb Larrain was.'

As they finished eating, he thought about the woman who had just left them . . .

Claire Mawdsley was very attractive, with long wavy Pre-Raphaelite locks of a shade somewhere between auburn and chestnut and striking grey-green eyes. Her figure was slightly mannish, but the black belted sweater dress subtly emphasised her waist and hips while high heels completed a stylish ensemble.

'Charles Larrain was very handsome,' she told them. 'Like a young Kirk Douglas, only dark.' She looked Markham up and down in frank appraisal. 'Tall, slim and glamorous like you, Inspector.'

As she said this, the DI had a flashback to the foam-flecked face of the corpse they had discovered at Carton Hall. Thank God, Richard Twiss's ex didn't have to live with *that* particular image, he thought.

'The Gallic charm was all a bit put on,' she told them. 'A bit phoney. But he was clever and seductive and *such fun* . . . had everyone grovelling at his feet. To be honest, I could see why Rick fell so hard for him. The whole family did at first. He wrapped Rick's mother round his little finger, so *she* ended up in love with him as well as Rick.'

This was certainly news to the detectives and cast Lady Edith in a new and interesting light.

'But as time went on, he managed to cut Rick off from everyone . . .' she added before falling silent.

For love, all love of other sights controls, And makes one little room an everywhere, Markham thought to himself, intrigued by the scenario she conjured up.

'It hurt like hell losing Rick, but little by little he drew away until one day I woke up and found our relationship was over. I wasn't even sure *how* it had happened . . . just knew that it was somehow all down to Charles.'

Markham very much doubted the breakup had been as clinical and bloodless as she tried to convey, and he suspected her feelings towards Larrain were decidedly ambivalent — a mixture of love and hate.

Perhaps sensing his scepticism, she went on, 'I fell apart after we split . . . ended up in the Newman for a while.' This being the psychiatric hospital behind Bromgrove General. 'Frank and Anna Harte helped patch me up and I got through it . . . But it was bad while it lasted. I cut ties with pretty much everyone at Carton, which was a shame because I was good friends with Margaret and Pip.' Markham was glad Noakes wasn't there to hear *Pip*, his wingman being all too fond of mocking posh diminutives. His fellow DI, on the other hand, radiated quiet empathy and elicited the woman's alibi for Charles Larrain's murder in no time . . .

Now, laying down her knife and fork, Burton said, 'If she's telling the truth about staying over in Birmingham, then she's in the clear for Larrain, boss.'

'Certainly looks like it,' he agreed, knowing that his colleague would meticulously follow up what they had been told with Claire Mawdsley's hosts for that night.

'She didn't seem to think Richard Twiss had it in him to subject Larrain to such a painful, lingering death,' Burton continued with obvious disappointment. 'As she tells it, he was more into mind games than physical cruelty.'

'Yes, but who knows what might have happened if Richard's relationship with Larrain hit the rocks and he fell apart at the seams? Especially if his mother was somehow involved in the fallout,' Markham countered. 'An experience like that could have unleashed all kinds of demons. Don't forget, Ms Mawdsley admitted herself that she had a mental breakdown that required hospital treatment and for her to be "patched up" by her friends the Hartes.'

Burton considered this.

'She certainly implied that there was something odd going on between Richard and his mother . . . but that could just have been spite, guv . . . a woman scorned and all that.' She frowned. 'On the other hand, Hassett kind of confirmed it when he talked about the family getting the hump over that Valois exhibition because of all the innuendo. Plus, there was something off about the sons' body language towards Lady Edith . . .' She sighed. 'A right hornet's nest.' Her shoulders slumped despondently as she declined pudding. 'Nothing else for me thanks, guv. It doesn't look like Claire Mawdsley gave us the breakthrough we need.'

Markham didn't like seeing her look so downcast.

'Oh, I don't know about that, Kate. I'm getting a sense of something intensely *sexual* behind the murder of Charles Larrain.'

'Really, sir?'

'Yes . . . You see, he had an effect on women and men—'

'Evidently not Sir Simon and Gerard Twiss,' she objected.

'I'm not sure anyone was entirely immune.' He paused. 'And then there's the way he was murdered. "Each man kills the thing he loves . . . The coward does it with a kiss . . ." The poisoning was a kind of making love, a kind of possession . . . Our killer turned Larrain into an object for their own twisted pleasure and savoured every minute of it.'

Burton shivered at the conviction in his voice, remembering the macabre artistry of the Tapestry Room.

'What next, guv?' she asked.

'Back to the hall . . . and then a brainstorm, so we're ready for the DCI tomorrow.' Looking at the suddenly wan little face opposite, he cajoled, 'Are you *sure* about pudding, Kate? I can't imagine a certain DS not too far from here passing up Denise's Christmas trifle.'

This produced a flicker of merriment. 'Better not tell sarge I wimped out . . . the way him and Doyle are, I'll never hear the end of it.'

'Not if Mrs Scarron has been assiduous in her attentions,' he told her, and the meal ended in laughter.

* * *

Isobel Farquhar's interment next day took place in driving sleet at the Twiss family mausoleum. Known as the Pavilion, it stood in a small beech grove where branches tossed and writhed relentlessly overhead as the dowager was laid to rest.

The small, classically symmetrical building with strikingly tall pyramidal roof had a pseudo-Greek aspect, featuring a laurel wreath on the triangular pediment and two Corinthian-style pillars on either side of a bas-relief doorway.

Seeing Noakes peer at the doorway, Christopher Hassett kindly explained, 'That's a phoenix on one side and St Benedict of Nursia on the other.'

'Why's the old geezer standing on a snake?' the DS wanted to know.

'He's the patron saint of healing.' And now the curator looked self-conscious. 'Various monks tried to poison him because he was too strict . . . The serpent symbolises the powers of evil.'

'Chuffing Nora, they're bleeding well *obsessed* with the stuff,' Noakes muttered. 'No getting away from it, even when you pop your clogs.' Eyeing the prominent roof, he added balefully, 'An' trust them to want summat that looks like the Pharaohs built it.'

At a sharp dig in the ribs from Doyle, who spied Sidney hovering, Noakes shut up, though not without many an ironical eyeroll at the pretentiousness of it all.

The interment being strictly private, only family, senior staff and the detectives were present in the chilly stone rotunda lined with coffin shelves, two stained-glass fanlights depicting doves with olive branches (presumably emblems of the Holy Spirit) as the only embellishment. The team felt a collective sense of relief that the caskets appeared to be in a decent state of repair, with no sign of long-dead Twisses to discompose the gathering.

As with the memorial service at the parish church, Frank Harte did the honours.

Markham gave him credit for keeping the proceedings brief but sincere, with a simple eulogy that clearly gave comfort to Frances Farquhar as she stood arm-in-arm with the vicar's wife.

'Sounds like Izzy were a decent sort,' Noakes observed as they followed the mourners back to the hall. 'Kind to folk who were down on their luck — even if she didn't want the neighbours to know owt about it.' He gave the brim of his oilskin sou'wester hat an irritable tug, before adding with typically idiosyncratic piety, 'Let's hope the ones she helped put in a word for her on the other side.'

After Sidney had proffered his official condolences ('with the usual taradiddle an' bootlicking,' as Noakes complained afterwards), the family promptly disappeared, though Irene Clark was properly deferential and attended the detectives to their incident room with the promise of refreshments to follow shortly. Markham was relieved to see that Christopher Hassett had been as good as his word, providing an electric heater to supplement the picturesque, but not especially efficient, fire. With nose still blue with cold and his bald dome looking clammy as though from condensation, the DCI's visibly dour mood was unlikely to be improved by an arctic freeze indoors.

'Well, Markham,' he began with trademark nasal honk more than usually suggestive of catarrh, 'suppose you bring me up to date.'

And away they went . . .

Though fair play to Sidney, the DI thought as they waded through the background and dramatis personae, despite being taken aback by the peculiar historical antecedents and unusual family dynamic, he *did* appear to be genuinely absorbing and computing it all. Even Noakes's 'marginalia' on the subject of the Renaissance and poisoners in general — subjects on which the DS was almost touchingly keen to demonstrate his proficiency — were met with respectful attention.

The DI knew that Sidney was bound to be thinking about his own post-retirement options. Perhaps he was even slated for a prominent role with the force on the civilian side — though Olivia, only half joking, persistently maintained that he really wanted to be a TV pundit, a suggestion that had Noakes and Doyle shuddering with mirth. In which case, it wasn't unfeasible to suggest that his Cold War with Markham might give way to a more productive working relationship. In the fullness of time, it wasn't beyond the bounds of possibility that some sort of friendship might even be possible . . . once Sidney had got off the career treadmill and was freed from the shackles of jealousy.

As he toyed with these agreeable fantasies of glasnost, the door to their sanctum suddenly swung open, but instead of the anticipated tea trolley, Irene Clark stood there gazing round wildly at them.

In an instant, the DI was on his feet. 'What is it, Mrs Clark, what's the matter?'

'It's Carmel,' the PA said. 'She's dead.'

9. A MURDERER'S PALETTE

'*Bug spray?*'

Noakes stared at Dimples Davidson as though the pathologist had lost his marbles.

'I believe so, yes,' the other replied calmly. 'We had a case of accidental inhalation recently . . . I recognised the smell.'

'. . . only this weren't accidental,' the DS pointed out.

The bluff medic pursed his lips, determined not to be steamrolled. 'She was the housekeeper, right? Well, looks like she had something of an obsession with vermin, so there was plenty of insecticide in her kitchen cupboard . . . huge place like this, you can see why.' Eyes narrowed in concentration, Dimples pursued his scenario. 'My guess is she went mad with the stuff — chucked it round without realising she'd left the gas stove on . . . had trouble breathing and became disorientated. Managed to turn the stove off but passed out, hitting her head on the kitchen table . . . hence all that blood under the head. Sir Simon's PA said the woman was a severe asthmatic and never went anywhere without her Ventolin inhaler, but it wasn't on the shelf where she usually kept it, otherwise she might have stayed upright long enough to get out of there.' He whistled. 'It's a miracle she didn't blow the whole place to kingdom come.'

Markham contemplated Dimples steadily.

'How about this for an idea,' the DI said. 'Mrs Scarron was busy organising refreshments for us following Isobel Farquhar's interment in the family mausoleum. She was interrupted by someone who knew she had a thing about insects in the kitchen, they said something calculated to make her reach for the Rentokil can, and either she was in such a tizzy that she forgot about the stove, or her visitor turned on the gas while she was distracted after having already pocketed her inhaler. The combination of insecticide and gas was dangerously toxic, which led Mrs Scarron to collapse and sustain massive trauma to her head as a result of concussion. Satisfied that the outcome was fatal, her attacker then turned off the gas.'

The pathologist thought intently. 'Yes,' he agreed finally. 'I'd say that's feasible. It would have been obvious the poor soul was a goner, so no need to risk leaving the gas on or hang around . . .'

'But that's what this creep gets off on,' Doyle interjected. '*Hanging around* to watch them throttling to death. That's how they get their jollies.'

'Not this time,' Markham said decisively. 'This was an *act-focused murder*, like Isobel Farquhar's. A matter of expediency because Mrs Scarron posed a threat.'

Kate Burton was thinking hard. 'If you're right about how it happened, guv, then even if the killer was found in the kitchen, they had a ready-made excuse. They could say they wandered in for a drink or a chat and found her like that on the floor. The set-up's pretty informal . . . Mrs Scarron being almost one of the family, a long-standing servant and salt of the earth kind of thing, so people were free to pop their head round the door.'

Noakes, who had been pacing up and down like a caged animal, cautiously lowered his great bulk into one of the spindly chairs as though he had good reason to fear that it might go to pieces under him. As ever, he looked far too big and weighty for the elegant room. His piggy eyes stared across at the window to the leaden sky and opaque clouds before returning to his colleagues.

'I don' see old mother Twiss calling Scarron one of the family,' he rumbled, having formed no very favourable opinion of Lady Edith. 'She's a twenty-four-carat snob that one.'

Markham held his ground. 'I agree she'd be quick to freeze someone out for over-familiarity — probably goes from nice to nasty in seconds — but it'd be different when it comes to staff because *she's* the one in the driving seat . . . No need to throw her weight around with *them*.'

'Hmm.' Noakes looked unconvinced, but Doyle saw the logic.

'Yeah, she probably saves the Queen Mum routine for the public side but lays off in private,' he said. 'Sir Simon seems pretty easy-going . . . can't imagine him cracking the whip or insisting on the whole *Downton Abbey* palaver. To be fair, all of them looked pretty poleaxed about Scarron, even prune-face.' Seeing Burton stiffen, Doyle added apologetically. 'Sorry, ma'am, but I can see what sarge means about Lady Edith being a snob. The way she looks at us, it's like she's scraped us off her shoe or something.'

The pathologist being securely ensconced with the 'county set' and not remotely in awe of them, said, 'It's nothing personal, lad. She divides the world into Us and Them. There's probably members of the royal family she dismisses as common.'

'Yeah, as in Harry an' Meghan,' Noakes muttered.

The medic smiled with the imperturbable ease of a man totally comfortable in his own skin and remarkably tolerant of the foibles of others. 'The snobbery and aloofness are a defence mechanism,' he pointed out. 'You see, she's morbidly self-conscious about her own family coming from "trade". It's the kind of thing that matters to her.' His tone made it abundantly clear that he personally couldn't give two hoots about pedigree, acres and all the rest of it. But then, Markham reflected wryly, as a man at the top of his profession and possessed of comfortable private means, this prickly awareness of class and status had never formed part of Dimples's psyche. A swift glance at Kate Burton's intent, absorbed expression confirmed that his fellow DI, by contrast with this comfortable complacency, *was* acutely sensitive to such nuances and secretly compassionated the chatelaine of Carton Hall. Markham liked Burton all the better for her reaction.

Noakes was growing impatient with the psychoanalysis.

'Okay, so it could've been freaking *any* of 'em,' he growled. 'She were there for the Pavilion wotsit, then after that she were slaving away back at base sorting the sausage rolls or whatever. So, the killer had a chance to nab her in the kitchen once the coast was clear an' the family had buggered off.' The DS shot Dimples a baleful glare. 'Can't you give us a time of death, doc?'

'Only that it was some time in the last hour, as rigor hadn't set in and the blood was still sticky.'

Noakes scowled. 'What about her dodgy son . . . Patrick? We know *he's* got form.' And indeed, it was true, the data trawl having turned up a caution and a suspended sentence for assault. 'That lass who found Aznavour's body . . . Annie wossername—'

'Annette Sullivan,' Burton said heavily.

'Well, I got chatting to her downstairs while you an' the guvnor were buttering up Lord an' Lady Muck,' the DS continued truculently. 'She said Aznavour an' Patrick had a bit of a slanging match a while back.'

'What about?' Doyle asked.

'She couldn't say — most likely didn't want to be caught earwigging — but according to her, it were a fair old ding-dong an' Pat called him a jumped-up tosser.'

'Sounds about right to me,' Doyle observed earning himself a reproving frown from Burton. 'Come on, let's face it,' he went on hastily, 'the man was an arrogant poser who had Richard Twiss by the short and curlies. No wonder everyone hated him.' Slyly, he added, 'You could see the DCI likes Patrick Scarron for Larrain's murder better than any of the poshos, that's for sure. And now he's done a runner . . . At any rate, there's been no sign of him since before that prayer service for Larrain.'

Markham sighed. There was no doubt that Sidney would prefer the murderer to come from 'below stairs', but nothing pointed to Patrick Scarron other than this vague report of an argument with Charles Larrain and the fact that he had a record.

'If Mrs Scarron's son is a bad lot, then maybe this death's got nothing to do with Charles Larrain's murder,' Dimples mused. 'If he'd fallen out with his mother, *that* could've triggered the attack . . . He might even have pulled that stunt with the insecticide to make it look like there's a serial poisoner on the rampage.'

'Nothing to say we wouldn't look at *him* for the poisoner,' Doyle observed.

'True, but it'd still be throwing sand in your eyes,' Dimples came back. 'Sort of a double bluff.'

'I don't think Mrs Scarron's death was down to her son,' Burton said slowly. 'It's too much of a coincidence. It feels to me like she was attacked by the same person who killed Larrain and Isobel Farquhar. It was natural for them to reach for poison, because they *like* using the stuff . . . *like* what it does to people.'

Dimples was reluctant to relinquish his hypothesis. 'Scarron could be your poisoner, only somehow his mother found out and threatened to go to the police,' he suggested.

Burton found an unexpected ally in Noakes who now seemed less keen on the idea of Patrick Scarron as prime suspect.

'*Nah*, Pat's more your common or garden thug,' he said consideringly. 'Trouble with a capital T alright, but not the type to have a thing for death masks an' creepy statues . . . Whoever killed Aznavour had some sort of kink . . .'

'A necrophiliac streak perhaps?' Dimples said. Then he added, 'Or maybe they've used poison before, so it was always going to be their weapon of choice.'

'You may be on to something there, doc.' Noakes seized on the idea eagerly. 'Shippers thinks Aznavour was offed by someone who's into sadism big style.'

The pathologist was puzzled. '*Shippers?*'

'Professor Nathan Finlayson,' Burton explained with a resigned expression. 'Sarge says he's the spit of Harold Shipman.'

'But isn't he your fiancé, m'dear?' Dimples sounded mildly scandalised as her colleagues smirked.

As if that was ever going to stop DS Noakes's fun! Burton's expression implied, but she didn't say it.

Alert to her discomfort, Markham intervened. 'That's an interesting idea,' he said. 'Though I don't believe there are too many poisoners on our database.' He turned interrogatively to Burton who had quickly recovered her self-possession.

'I ran cross-checks for the last ten years, sir,' she told him. 'There was nothing even vaguely like the Larrain modus operandi, though obviously I'm going to widen the parameters.'

'Good, Kate.' The DI shot a quelling look at his wingman. 'Noakes can help you with that.'

The DS blew a silent raspberry. But at the same time, an idea had lodged in his mind. *A previous poisoning somewhere on their patch . . . one that went unsolved for some reason . . . and now the killer was back . . .*

Dimples also shook himself as though his mind was busy with similar dark thoughts.

'I'll leave you to it,' he said briskly. 'You'll have my report asap, Markham.' Slyly, he added, 'At least these days you leave me in peace to get on with the PM.' With a glint in his eye, he addressed Burton, 'Time was when you never missed one. S'pose these days you're too grand for that side of things.'

Before she could launch into protestations to the contrary, Markham interposed smoothly, 'Stop winding us up, Dimples. You're so damn thorough, we don't need to be there while you get to work with the Stryker.'

The pathologist looked pleased at that. It was undoubtedly true that their partnership had settled into such a well-established groove that Markham no longer felt the need to dispatch members of the team to observe. An inner voice whispered that he disliked inflicting the gorier aspects of an investigation on them — not from any want of concern for victims but from a strange inexplicable urge to shield his colleagues, particularly Kate Burton, from graphic illustrations of human depravity. He doubted that his fellow DI would thank him for such paternalism, and he knew his attitude to be condescending as well as anti-feminist, but there it was . . .

When Dimples winked at him, he had an uneasy feeling that the other intuited the nature of his dilemma. Had Dimples somehow picked up on the conflicted emotions he was experiencing for his colleague? All Markham's instincts told him so. The doctor, however, merely headed for the door with a cheery, 'Be seeing you.'

Markham's colleagues huddled round the electric heater.

'Christ, it's cold in here,' Doyle muttered.

Burton cleared her throat reprovingly and the young detective flushed, remembering that his boss found blasphemy offensive. 'Sorry, sir,' he mumbled.

But in fact, Markham wasn't listening having wandered over to the window from where he contemplated the darkening grounds, increasingly aware of the stillness, the bleakness and chill of the late winter afternoon.

At least the DCI had left them in peace to 'get on with it', he reflected, though not without making it abundantly clear that he favoured the idea of their killer originating from behind the green baize door as opposed to coming from the ranks of the Twisses and their intimate circle. This was vintage Sidney, they'd seen it countless times before, but at least he had been prepared to entertain other possibilities which represented a turn-around.

It was true that, as Doyle pointed out, the Twisses had appeared genuinely distraught at the discovery of Carmel Scarron's body. Philip and Margaret, in particular, had pretty much gone to pieces, the latter appearing to be glued to her brother's chest as she shuddered and sobbed. Judging by the dirty looks Richard and Michael shot their siblings, they obviously resented Philip being her hero on a white horse, but they appeared equally shaken along with their parents who stood as though frozen to the spot. Gerard and Stella Twiss, as at the memorial service for Charles Larrain, made no effort to reach out to the other branch of the family beyond Stella squeezing her niece's arm while Gerard awkwardly patted Philip's back. It had seemed an age before the Hartes, who had been invited to stay for a drink after the interment, murmured that they should be getting back to Frances whom they had left in Lady Edith's private sitting room when Irene Clark raised the alarm.

'Bloody bad aura round that crowd,' Noakes had commented as Burton shepherded the family away. Despite his lumbering uncouthness, Markham's wingman was sensitive to atmosphere and like the DI had sensed an unsettling dynamic which seemed to embrace Catherine Metcalfe and Christopher Hassett as they hovered on the fringes of the group. The DI agreed with his sergeant's verdict but wasn't clear about the source of the discomfort or whether it even had any relevance to these crimes . . .

Now Noakes came up alongside him.

'Don' look like we'll be getting a bite to eat any time soon,' he grunted.

'Not with the kitchen being a crime scene, no,' Markham said with a thin smile.

'Mebbe we should go into town an' get summat,' the DS suggested hopefully.

Markham gave a grim laugh. 'Not even murder takes away your appetite does it, Sergeant?'

'We've gotta keep our strength up, boss . . . An' anyway,' Noakes added cunningly, 'It's brass monkeys in here, even with that poxy heater Hassett gave us . . . Can't think straight when I'm cold.'

Markham resigned himself to the inevitable.

Once outside, as though by common assent, they turned to look back at the hall. No lights showed at the front of the building and the black windows had a jagged empty look, like so many blank-eyed basking sharks thought Markham, startling himself with the monstrous analogy.

'Freaking creepy place,' Doyle muttered uneasily. 'Looking at it now, I almost believe that stuff about ghosts and Lady Mary or whoever she is. The one who makes the light change when she comes calling.'

Burton's face was stern. 'Don't forget, there's a chapel, and Mr Hassett told me the vicar held a service of blessing a few years back after the *Gazette* did some sensationalist piece about the Tapestry Room and people saying the place was haunted.'

Doyle was fascinated. 'You mean like an *exorcism*?'

Markham sensed that Paula the ball-breaker was unlikely to indulge this kind of psychic speculation. His fellow DI also seemed uncomfortable with the notion of demonic infiltration.

'I think it was more just reassurance for staff and a way of putting the lid on daft rumours,' she said repressively. 'The legends and stories were great for business, but the Twisses felt some of the coverage was getting out of hand and they didn't want to alienate the more conservative elements of the community.'

There it was again, thought Markham, that preoccupation with putting up a front so that no one got to see what lay behind the mask.

'What did the padre do then?' Noakes asked curiously, temporarily diverted from thoughts of Costa and triple chocolate muffins. 'I mean prayers ain't enough, right? He'd have to chuck some holy water about an' go round making the sign of the cross over everything.'

Burton blinked. 'I don't think it was anything on those lines, sarge. Just a few prayers for the souls of the dead, that kind of thing.'

'Oh.' The DS looked disappointed, clearly rather taken with the idea of the Reverend Frank Harte as some sort of clerical ghostbuster.

Markham chuckled at his expression. 'I'd say Harte's too down to earth for anything flashy,' he said. 'And his wife works at the university, remember. Something as dramatic as a full-blown exorcism would only set the rumour mill turning and create quite the wrong impression.'

'Yeah, I guess.' Noakes was loath to relinquish his fantasy scenario. 'Reckon Baron Hard-up an' his missus wouldn't go in for stuff like that.'

'Well, Mr Hassett told me that Sir Simon was quite interested in Spiritualism at one time,' Burton said.

Noakes stared. 'As in Ouija boards an' séances an' things?'

Doyle, too, was intrigued. 'He doesn't look the type.'

Burton grimaced. 'It was just a passing fad apparently . . . Lady Edith saw to that.'

'Well, living here with all them weirdy bits an' bobs, you can kind of understand it,' Noakes concluded.

The hall's black windows began to glitter as the setting sun gilded it from a new angle, the lurid glow creating the illusion that bloodshot eyes were trained on them.

Noakes shivered. 'Let's get out of here,' he muttered.

Crunching across the snow-covered gravel, despite the freezing cold, Markham's throat was suddenly tight and his eyes hot. It flashed upon him with the force of a settled conviction that the death of Carmel Scarron was merely the forerunner to another disaster waiting in the wings.

* * *

Later that night, back at the Sweepstakes, Markham brought Olivia up to date with developments over toast and coffee. Her protests that they should really have 'a proper supper' were only half-hearted, making him suspect she felt as wrung out as he did.

'School's a nightmare right now,' she sighed. 'I feel like the Grinch for complaining, but the kids have been high as kites since the beginning of December and the staff aren't much better . . . brandishing boxes of Roses and mince pies at you every five minutes.'

He chuckled. 'That'd be Noakesy's idea of heaven.'

A brittle smile greeted this riposte. 'Call-Me-Tony makes lots of noise about the importance of "delivering challenging lessons" right to the bitter end, but in reality, he turns a blind eye while the lazybones brigade just put on DVDs and pretend there's some kind of educational benefit to showing *Nativity 3*!'

'They'd do better with *Oliver Twist* or something Dickens-related,' he remarked.

'Well, I'm throwing in the towel tomorrow,' she admitted with a grimace. 'I'm going to show them *A Christmas Carol*. Definitely *not* the awful one with the Muppets and Michael Caine, but the version with George C. Scott . . . it's only average, but they'd turn up their noses at Alastair Sim or anything in black and white.'

'Didn't Henry Winkler star in a film version?'

She giggled. 'Just imagine . . . the Fonz playing Scrooge.'

He was pleased to see she had cheered up. 'I think there's a controversial remake starring Guy Pearce—'

'That's the guy from *Neighbours*, isn't it . . . ? Not sure I could take him seriously.'

'Oh, he's done some interesting stuff. But more to the point, the critics raved about it being downbeat and radical . . . "Dickens for people who don't much like Dickens".'

'That'd suit my lot down to a T.'

Mischievously, he added, 'Apparently Scrooge even tries it on with Mrs Cratchit — money in return for sexual favours or getting her into prostitution, something like that. So there's plenty for your right-on feminist brigade at Hope to get their teeth into.'

She grinned at this.

'C'mon,' she said. 'Let's move next door.'

They carried their mugs into the living room where she closed the heavy damask curtains and turned on the lamps, their trusty wood burner enhancing the cosy ambience.

Markham settled back in his favourite high-backed armchair facing the wood burner while Olivia sat cross-legged on the deep pile Axminster. By rights, the colour scheme — crimson and maroon — should have been a no-no given the sanguinary associations, but Markham loved the richness and the sense that this was his safe retreat where none could touch him. Noakes, predictably, had been less impressed. 'S'like you're going back to the womb or summat,' he had sniffed, reducing Olivia to paroxysms of laughter.

Sensing her partner's need to keep off the subject of Carton Hall for a while, she said inconsequentially, 'I read somewhere that Ian Brady always made a point of revisiting *A Christmas Carol* every year.'

He was instantly diverted. 'The Moors Murderer?'

'The very same . . . Apparently, he had a fetish about it. Took him back to childhood and reminded him of innocence.'

'Blimey,' Markham took this in. 'I must remember to tell Noakesy. He's like a magpie for hoovering up details about serial killers.'

'It's a strange book,' Olivia said thoughtfully. 'John Ruskin said it's all mistletoe and Christmas pudding, but actually Dickens was writing about the resurrection.'

'Maybe that's why Brady liked it,' Markham surmised. 'Perhaps it held out the promise of hope even for him.'

'Well, at least Dickens wore his Christianity lightly. In his will, he told his children to stick to the New Testament and they wouldn't go far wrong . . . the broader spirit of the Gospels, though, not the narrow construction.'

It occurred to Markham that Noakes would warm to the celebrated author on hearing that.

'I remember my old English teacher inveighing against the idea of its just being a fairy tale. He talked about the three ghosts being like the three kings, and said Tiny Tim was meant to be a modern-day Christ Child—'

'But ever since it was published, people feel compelled to dash round buying up turkeys,' she reminded him caustically.

'I suppose we've Mister Dickens to thank for the whole festive razzamatazz,' he mused.

'*Bah humbug!*' she chuckled. 'Oh, I reckon he understood anti-Christmas syndrome alright — you know, folk resenting the idea of enforced jollity . . . Let's be honest, there's a bit of Scrooge in *all* of us. That whole good versus evil thing.' Then, more seriously, 'But you're right . . . In the early nineteenth century, Christmas was just some old rural feast associated with manor houses and baronial goings on. Then Dickens brought it into the city — made it an *urban* celebration and ramped up the darkness — wind howling outside, snow coming down, poverty stalking the streets — to make the cosiness all the greater.' She rolled her eyes theatrically. 'Christmas is a middle-class knees-up really.'

Markham felt himself starting to relax, the tensions of the day gradually leaving his body as he willingly allowed himself to be distracted. Noakes had a point about the apartment being womb-like. The living room, in particular, soothed him as he savoured its elegant simplicity, his eyes wandering over the fitted bookshelves on either side of the hearth and Olivia's collection of delicate Meissen ballerinas on the top shelves. There was another wing-backed armchair, also upholstered in crimson velvet, facing his own next to the round Pembroke dining table, but Olivia invariably preferred to lounge on the carpet like some elegant Siamese.

'The book's got its dark side,' she went on. 'At one level, it's about psychic trauma—'

'Ah yes, Dickens was trying to exorcise the ghosts of his deprived childhood, wasn't he . . . the disgrace of his father being imprisoned for debt and him having to drudge in the blacking factory when he should have been getting an education.' Markham recalled being intrigued by the autobiographical resonances, as though the famous author had been on the psychiatrist's couch.

'Yep, you see, Scrooge represses what happened to him as a lonely child at school — there's even a glimmer of abuse

— and it's only by replaying the painful memories that he's able to move on . . .'

As he heard these words, Markham felt a depth-charge go off in his subconscious mind as though this was somehow important. He tried to give it more thought, to explore what that charge meant . . . but then the moment had passed, and his partner was chattering away with renewed animation.

'Actually, just talking about it, I'm starting to feel quite enthusiastic, Gil. Maybe the end of term needn't be such an intellectual desert after all.'

He smiled down at her upturned face.

'You can sell it to your, what do they call themselves . . . oh yes, your Senior Leadership Team, as an attack on wicked capitalism, sweetheart. They're *bound* to like that. Or if all else fails, try the, er, *alternative* version with Scrooge trying to get Mrs Cratchit on the game.'

Olivia looked shamefaced. 'To be honest, though I might rail against Lipscombe and her "inclusive" agenda, I quite like alternative interpretations . . . Wouldn't want to risk Scrooge the Pimp with my Year 7s but sounds like the sixth form might go for it.' Her lovely vibrant face was flushed and eager, green eyes starry and alight with enthusiasm. 'Besides, the old curmudgeon can be *fun* . . . got a sense of humour.'

'Can't say I remember *that*,' Markham observed wryly.

'Oh yes, when his business partner Jacob Marley returns from the dead to tell him he's going to be visited by three ghosts on successive nights, Scrooge asks if he can't have them all at once to get it over with. And there's the bit when he says the whole thing's down to indigestion and having eaten cheese for supper . . . he even tells the first ghost, "There's more of gravy than of grave about you." He's quite droll in a grumpy sort of way.'

'*Ah*,' Markham grinned broadly. 'He's beginning to remind me of someone not a million miles from here.'

Olivia grinned back. 'You mean George . . . Yes, now you mention it, I can see the resemblance.'

After a companionable silence, Olivia said hesitantly, 'How about the case, Gil? Or would you rather we talked about something else?'

He sighed. 'No, my love, that's alright . . . I only spoke to Carmel Scarron at any length just the once, but she struck me as a decent soul . . . Oh, she played up to the caricature of the old family retainer, but she'd obviously settled into her role over the years, and I got the impression she was the beating heart of that weird family . . . insofar as it *had* a heart.' A gulp of his coffee and Markham continued, 'I'd forgotten about it until now — we were so wrapped up in theories about how she died — but when we interviewed Mrs Scarron, I had the impression she was holding something back . . . as though she'd remembered something important.' Sadly, he concluded, 'I think she may have decided to parlay what she knew into hard cash.'

'Even though she was fundamentally decent?'

'She was devoted to her ne'er-do-well son . . . I think if she was tempted to try blackmail, it was on *his* account and not her own.'

Markham's face was downcast. Olivia wondered if he was thinking of his own brother whose downward slide he had been unable to halt.

'And now Patrick Scarron has done a bunk,' he wound up. 'Needless to say, Sidney sees it as an answer to prayer.' Then, with a touch of compunction, he added, 'In fairness to Sidney, appearances are certainly *against* Mr Scarron.'

'God Gil, you're *always* so charitable!' Olivia's tone left no doubt that she regarded this as being a major handicap in the battle of life. 'You know perfectly well Judas Iscariot is gagging for the peasantry to take the rap!'

'Actually no, Liv,' he countered, 'I think in this case Sidney's genuinely trying his best to be objective about it . . . And God knows, there's no one else in the frame right now.'

She got up and padded into the kitchen to fetch more coffee, biting her lip to avoid spewing more anti-Sidney invective.

'It's odd the way the killer chose to finish off Mrs Scarron,' she said after replenishing their mugs and setting them down carefully on the lacquered antique side-table at his elbow. 'I mean, why couldn't they just stab her or strangle her? It'd only have taken seconds. That whole business with the insecticide seems . . . oh, I don't know . . . a bit *peculiar* and unnecessary . . .'

'I see what you mean, Liv, but I don't think they could be sure of not being interrupted. And besides, Mrs Scarron was wiry, a fighter. They couldn't be confident of overpowering her.'

'Wouldn't a *man* manage it?'

'They'd have had more chance than a woman, sure, but this killer is cautious and calculating. They wanted a get-out in the event that someone walked in on them. It's less risky saying they'd come across her flat out on the kitchen floor . . . And anyway,' he thought back to the earlier team meeting, 'this is someone with an *affinity* for poison.'

'Who was it found her?'

'Sir Simon's PA, Mrs Irene Clark.'

'Shouldn't *she* be top of your shit-list then . . . isn't that what George calls it?'

'Sometimes, Liv, I wonder if you and Noakesy aren't twins separated at birth . . .' He shook his head, exasperated and amused. 'It's only in books that the one who finds the body is CID's prime suspect.' He stared into the depths of his mug. 'And anyway, Mrs Clark is as respectable as they come. At the risk of sounding like Sidney, her character is impeccable, and she's been with Sir Simon coming up to twenty years.'

'Stranger things, Gil . . .'

'I know, I *know*.'

Suddenly, she couldn't bear the battered, defeated look in his eyes.

'What are you up to tomorrow?' she asked without much hope that they would have any time together on Saturday.

'Full case review back at the station,' was the weary reply. 'Nathan Finlayson is going to draw up a profile for us.'

'And how's it going with him and Kate these days?' She endeavoured to sound casual, but her voice was tight.

'Well, she's managed to wriggle out of Muriel's festive bunfight on Sunday on the basis that they're going to some party at the university.'

Olivia rolled her eyes. 'Betcha she made that up.'

'No, Kate's too straight for tricks. It'll be kosher.'

He didn't see Olivia dig her nails of her right hand into the palm of the other as she registered the frank admiration in his voice.

Suddenly she felt sick and cold and empty.

But, she reasoned, at least Markham's fellow DI wasn't coming to the Noakeses. That was *something*. Where Kate Burton was concerned, she felt unsure of Markham — she didn't know what he was thinking, though she never had this difficulty in relation to anyone else.

Her depression was all to do with its being mid-winter, she told herself firmly . . . the lowest time of the year, with everything shrouded in snow and fog. No more talk of ghostly tales and murder, she decided. Instead, she was going to focus on Christmas as a return of light and warmth . . .

'Nearly time to put our tree up,' she said as lightly as possible.

Markham grinned. 'Sure you don't want to wait and check out Muriel's first? She's bound to have some tasteful tips for you.'

Picking up a cushion, Olivia biffed him with it.

'No thank you,' she said lifting her chin. 'While you're at your case review tomorrow, I am going to channel my inner Mrs Claus and produce something stupendous to knock the socks off everyone.'

As they adjourned to their big squashy Chesterfield to watch television, Markham once again had that nagging feeling that something significant had been said . . . and he had missed it.

That night, he dreamed of Scrooge. But in his dream, there was no redemption and the miser retreated to a gothic belfry whose spire cut the air like the tapering blade of a knife.

10. CHINK OF LIGHT

Saturday 18 December passed uneventfully, with the team holed up in CID thrashing out various hypotheses with Nathan Finlayson, fuelled by pizza from the local Domino's.

Markham felt curiously relieved to be away from Carton Hall, despite being officially based there for the duration. For all its sprawling grandeur, he had come to find the mansion oppressive and sinister, as though nowhere was free from the killer's hate-filled gaze.

Finlayson was fluent and interesting as always, but at the end of it all Markham still felt the investigation was stuck in a cul-de-sac going nowhere.

When it came to the motivation behind Charles Larrain's murder, the professor was unequivocal. Sexual jealousy was the trigger, he told them, with the staging in the Tapestry Room evidence of pseudo-necrophiliac impulses that had their roots in early-life trauma.

'You mean like Dennis Nilsen?' Noakes said eagerly. 'He claimed that seeing his grandad's corpse when he were five sent him round the twist.'

'Psychiatrists today view Nilsen as a self-serving narcissist, but I think there's something in that story,' Finlayson agreed. 'Certainly his childhood experiences, including possible abuse, were the key to it all.'

'What do you mean by "pseudo-necrophiliac"?' Doyle wanted to know.

'That this isn't someone wanting to have sex with corpses,' Finlayson replied simply. 'I suppose you could call it a lighter shade on the necrophiliac spectrum . . . It might include someone who obtains sexual gratification or satisfaction from proximity to death.' He looked at Kate Burton who was listening intently 'like Shippers were the bleeding Messiah', as Noakes commented acidly afterwards to Doyle. 'Catherine de Medici's daughter Marguerite was a case in point,' the academic told them.

Despite himself, Noakes was hooked. 'How come?'

'She and her lady-in-waiting got involved with two noblemen who were later executed for plotting against the royal family. After they were quartered and beheaded, the women arranged for the embalmed heads to be sent to them as keepsakes.'

Doyle was revolted. 'That's *disgusting*,' he burst out. 'Bloody *perverse*.'

'Not really, Sergeant,' Finlayson replied mildly. 'Not for those times. Catherine de Medici is reputed to have had an enemy's decapitated head embalmed and sent as a gift to the pope. In Marguerite's case, it's what we call an extreme example of "magical thinking" . . . Just as some people can't bear to get rid of a loved one's clothes or shoes, she and her friend needed to find a way of keeping their lovers close.'

'Are you saying the killer needed to murder Charles Larrain in that particular way because of an earlier bereavement?' Markham asked.

'Not necessarily an *actual* bereavement, but I would say there was some fragmentation of personality resulting from an experience of loss or separation. It might even be that they brought the separation on themselves, resulting in serious undermining of the psychic constitution, so that some sort of appalling upheaval took place with the result that there was an inner rent which did not mend.'

Aware that Noakes was boggling, he added, 'I'm resorting to technical supposition here in the absence of tangible evidence . . . Wasn't it Goethe who said, "In every great separation lies a germ of madness"?' Seeing that the DS looked deeply under-whelmed, he continued hastily. 'One of my colleagues recently treated an adolescent girl for a psychogenic disorder — a type of hysteria that produces physical symptoms — after her mother died of cancer and her elder sister was killed in a car accident when taking her to school. Later, her father went to pieces, and she somehow internalised his grief so that it became *her* responsibility. One manifestation of the disorder was that she became morbidly obsessed with violent death and fixated on the idea that other family members wanted to poison her. She was referred for treatment after her uncle became alarmed by weird drawings of coffins and dead animals. At one point, she insisted that big, charred fingers were reaching out to strangle her.'

'Chuffing Nora,' Noakes blustered. 'Did your mate manage to fix her?'

Finlayson smiled at Noakes's blunt query.

'She's still in therapy, but her treatment appears to be going well so he's quietly optimistic.'

'Did her dad get a grip, seeing as the lass needed him?' As a father himself, this was important to Noakes.

'Yes . . . he was so wrapped up in his own grief, that he never noticed what was happening. It took the daughter's breakdown to snap him out of his self-absorption.'

'Selfish git,' was Doyle's succinct judgement.

But there was one particular aspect of the tale that had caught Markham's attention. 'You say you think the killer might have brought the separation or loss on themselves,' he remarked thoughtfully. 'Could this encompass some form of criminal behaviour?'

'Quite possibly,' came the calm reply. 'If they inadvert-ently or deliberately caused injury or loss of life and were never brought to account for what happened, then the repressed consciousness of what had happened might lead them to repeat that behaviour if stressors arose similar to those which activated the earlier crisis.'

'Look, are we talking some teen psycho who went tonto an' got away with it?' Noakes demanded irritably.

'It's a legitimate line of enquiry,' Finlayson answered with Spock-like inscrutability.

'Talk about hedging your bleeding bets,' Noakes complained later after having listened none too patiently to a discussion of DSM paraphilias which held Burton enthralled. 'The way things are going, sounds like we should be rounding up pervs with a thing for funeral parlours an' morgues . . . mebbe we should ask Dimples if any of his teccies have been hanging round the fridges!'

'Take it easy, Sergeant,' Markham admonished him as two red spots burned on Burton's cheeks. 'Professor Finlayson was just setting out the general parameters.'

'Yeah, well I say we need to forget about that an' start getting *specific* before this sicko has another go.' Gobbling his pepperoni slices twice as fast as the others had made Noakes dyspeptic, his large florid face darkening with heartburn as well as wrath.

The previous night's discussion of *A Christmas Carol* with Olivia came back to Markham.

'I wonder,' he said slowly, 'if we need to be looking at historical cases involving children which may or may not have resulted in criminal proceedings . . . incidents which had the potential to generate the type of psychogenic disorder Nathan was talking about.'

'Something serious,' Burton murmured, 'which was papered over at the time or never found out, so they didn't work through what had happened . . . just buried it instead.'

'Only it wouldn't stay buried,' Doyle put in. 'When Charles Larrain crossed their path, it brought back all the old feelings . . . and because of the past they had this weird *compulsion* to poison him up at the hall.'

'But why *there*?' Noakes demanded. 'I mean, what's so special about them death masks an' freaky statues?'

'Nathan talked about "petrification of the object—"' Markham began.

Burton interrupted eagerly. 'That's right, agalmatophilia . . . It's in the *DSM* under fetishistic disorders.'

Noakes shot a meaningful glance at Doyle. *And she's off! Buckle your seatbelt, Dorothy.*

But sensing their restiveness, she kept it simple. 'An attraction to statues and mannequins, maybe incorporating the desire to transform another into the preferred object.'

'So, what're you saying' Noakes was keen to cut through all the psychiatric BS, 'is that the killer had some fantasy about turning Aznavour into their very own Living Doll?' Winking at Doyle, he launched into an execrable off-key rendition of the sixties classic.

'No offence, sarge, but I reckon I prefer Cliff Richard,' was Burton's deadpan response, eliciting a snigger from Doyle. Noakes shot him a deadly look of the whose-side-are-you-on variety before returning to the attack.

'Are you serious about it being some whack job with a thing for dolls an' dummies?' he demanded.

'You know, those lyrics you belted out just now were interesting, Sergeant,' Markham said. 'Especially the bit about locking the loved one up so no one else can get at them . . . there's the idea of intense possessiveness and sexual jealousy bordering on the pathological . . .'

'Plus keeping stuff locked up in a box,' Doyle added unexpectedly. 'Lots of people keep things from the past shut up in boxes, kind of like hoarding.'

'And there's dangerous memories as well,' Markham observed quietly. 'You put them in a box and throw away the key.'

'*Jesus wept* . . . Sorry guv,' Noakes apologised automatically, though without sounding very contrite. 'So now we're looking for some sort of rapey hoarder who likes getting kinky with statues!'

'That's a somewhat extreme formulation, Sergeant,' Markham sighed. 'However, I don't think it's too far-fetched to hypothesise that we could be looking at someone whose early-life trauma triggered a psychological disorder with sexually morbid elements.' The DI steepled his elegant musician's fingers together. 'Remember what you told us about the killer Graham Young always keeping poison to hand because it made him feel powerful? Well, I believe *our* murderer has a similar irresistible attraction to the stuff which could be tied up with that early-life experience.'

At that moment the sound of carol singers came floating up from the pavement down below.

'*God no*,' Noakes groaned. 'Thass all we need . . . twenty-three choruses of 'Good King Wenceslas' cos that soppy git on the desk gets all sentimental and won't move 'em on. Any minute now, he'll be out there with a tin of Quality Street an' we'll be stuck with that godawful racket for the next hour.'

Doyle laughed. 'Don't be such a Scrooge, sarge.'

Markham started slightly at the reference. There it was again: the damaged man crippled by the legacy of childhood neglect and abuse, ultimately set free from his demons in Dickens's parable of redemption.

But this was real life as opposed to a fairy tale. As things stood, the killer's demons currently had the upper hand . . .

'Let's keep going with the data trawl,' he said. 'Based on what Nathan said, I want to include cases involving juveniles . . . anything we've got for minors, whether it ended up going to court or not. If we draw a blank, then let's try the Council and Social Services.'

Noakes looked decidedly down in the mouth on hearing this, having repeatedly clashed with the 'do-gooders' in previous investigations.

However, he was 'saved by the bell' when a member of the civilian staff disturbed their conference.

'Sorry to interrupt, sir,' she said to Markham. 'Patrick Scarron's just arrived downstairs with his solicitor.'

Noakes, halfway out of his chair at the summons, was visibly awash with relief at the prospect of ducking out of computer duties.

'Yes, Noakesy,' his boss said with an ironic inflection. 'I can see you're eager to have a crack at Mr Scarron, so let's get it over with.' He turned to Burton. 'I'll leave you and Sergeant Doyle to divvy up the data download between you. But then you can get off. It *is* Christmas after all.'

And with that, the two men disappeared.

Doyle was pleased by Markham's parting words. Maybe there'd be time to get that expensive perfume Paula had said she liked. At least it might soften her up before yet another discussion of his future prospects.

Tomorrow being Sunday, they'd get a break from Carton Hall and that creepy family. He grinned at the thought of the boss and Noakes taking in the carol service at the cathedral before lunch with Muriel. Poor old Olivia would no doubt get dragged along too. He'd had his own excuses off pat. That Natalie was a man-eater; he still shuddered at the memory of her moving in for the kill one Christmas when they were both still single.

His mouth twisted. *Moving in for the kill* . . . not the happiest analogy in the circumstances.

Burton's voice cut across his thoughts.

'Look lively, Sergeant,' she said crisply. 'I've drawn up a spreadsheet.'

He suppressed a groan. Trust Noakesy to dodge the grunt work. That interview with Scarron would most likely be over in double quick time. The man would hardly have come to the station all lawyered up unless he was confident of getting off . . .

Markham reached pretty much the same conclusion as he and Noakes sat opposite Patrick Scarron in dreary interview room one on the ground floor. Scarron's solicitor, a David Niven lookalike wearing a decidedly pinched expression, had clearly prepared a script to which he intended his client should adhere come hell or high water.

'I took off because I panicked, Inspector. What with having a record, I was afraid you'd finger me for Larrain,' Scarron told them hoarsely. 'But then when I heard about Mum's accident, I knew I had to come in.'

'How'd you find out?' Noakes demanded.

'A mate texted me.'

The news outlets had indeed been briefed that Carmel Scarron died in an accident. Markham was adamant about that, though it was belied by reporters' knowing reference to 'tragic events' following the murder of Charles Larrain, one pert madam laying on the innuendo as she talked about the 'unexplained death' of Isobel Farquhar and — opening her Bambi eyes to their widest — raised the possibility of Carton Hall lying under a curse.

It seemed to Markham as he scrutinised Patrick Scarron that the man was genuinely distressed about his mother and had no idea of the actual circumstances of her death. There was real bitterness in his voice as he declared that he'd known she was heading for a stroke or heart attack given the way she worked her fingers to the bone 'for that sodding family'. A dry cough from the solicitor warned him: *stick to the script.*

Even though Scarron had no alibi for his mother's death, having 'gone on the batter' and lacking anyone to vouch for him, the DI felt increasingly sure that this was not their man.

Noakes thrust his face forward. 'A little bird told us you an' Azna— I mean, Charles Larrain — had a bust up. What were that about?'

Scarron shoved an unruly lock of shaggy black hair behind his ear. 'He kept playing lord of the manor and coming the big man . . . though no one's the boss of me 'cept the Twisses. If you ask me, Richard an' me got on too well for his nibs's liking.'

Another warning cough.

Noakes glared at the solicitor who, to his credit, shrank back in his chair.

'As in you had summat going between you, as in *boyfriends*?' the DS demanded belligerently.

'*Get out of it!*' The reaction struck Markham as genuinely indignant. 'I've got birds queuing up . . . have to fight them off.'

'Arrogant little shit thinking he's God's gift,' the DS exploded afterwards.

'But not our man, Noakesy.'

'He's got no alibi for any of 'em,' the other growled stubbornly. 'Well, nothing worth diddly squat seeing as his old mum ain't around to vouch for him . . .'

Markham sighed. 'As you may have noticed, alibis are noticeably thin on the ground in this investigation.'

'An' the forensics ain't likely to be a fat lot of help neither,' Noakes said glumly. 'I mean, the whole lot of 'em could've been in an' out of that kitchen . . . The same applies to the weirdy statue room an' the beauty salon place where Izzy snuffed it. Makes you wonder what's the point of having SOCOs swarming all over the show when there's nowt to show for it.'

'Let's not get hung up on cross-contamination and secondary evidence now, Noakesy,' Markham said calmly. 'Once we get our man . . . or woman . . . *then* we can start worrying about whether we're able to make it stick.'

'Well, *that one's* Tefloned his way out of it,' the DS groused, watching as Scarron and his solicitor headed for the station exit, reflecting with savage satisfaction that no way was Mister Hoity Toity Lawman going to offer the dishevelled groundsman a lift in his swanky Mercedes. 'Hey, don' you think it's a bit odd when he said that Michael Twiss arranged the brief for him? Mikey didn't exactly strike me as the caring sort.'

'You should know better than anyone that appearances are deceptive, Sergeant,' Markham said wryly. 'And anyway, stands to reason the family might want to head off any more scandal at the pass.' *They probably had the David Niven doppelganger on permanent standby.*

'So, what now, boss?' It was only too obvious that Noakes feared being put on spreadsheet duty.

Markham was suddenly desperate to exchange the station's stale fug for the needle-sharp clean air of St Chad's next door. If he could only meditate in peace on his favourite bench, then recent events might form some kind of coherent pattern. As it was, he felt sluggish and despondent.

'Let's call it a day for now, Sergeant,' he said. 'I think we can safely leave Burton and Doyle to handle the data.' The austere features relaxed making him look much younger. 'Besides, we need to gird our loins for the carol service tomorrow.'

'An' dinner at ours,' his wingman added, touchingly anxious lest the guvnor forget the main event. 'The missus is doing Jamie Oliver's beef wellington with chocolate log for afters.' It occurred to him that he probably shouldn't be giving Markham a preview of Muriel's menu, thereby stealing her thunder, but no harm letting him and Olivia know she was pulling out all the stops.

'Chocolate log, my favourite,' the DI murmured diplomatically. 'So sophisticated, putting her own twist on traditional fare.'

Noakes looked deeply gratified on hearing this. As the missus always said, she and his boss were 'kindred spirits', and here was positive proof.

'I'll be on my mobile if anything comes up,' was Markham's parting injunction. 'Maybe some time away from the case will help things come into focus.' He spoke with considerably more confidence than he felt.

* * *

St Mary's Cathedral dated from 1861 and was popularly known as the 'jewel in Bromgrove's crown'. Although mid-Victorian, the architecture somehow ended up as what Olivia called 'Byzantine revival with gothic twiddles'. Noakes — by his own admission 'a church-at-Christmas-and-Easter kind of bloke' — said it was totally OTT. Despite the garishness of the blue slate cupola, which clashed with the red and white geometric pattern of the striped buttresses, the interior was far more restrained with a distinctly modernist accent including an abundance of stark white marble and granite.

Olivia disliked the bronze crucifix on the high altar, claiming that Christ looked like the Wicker Man, however Markham found the tortured twisted lineaments very moving. Most striking of all was the magnificent baldachin in the form of an aluminium crown of thorns, composed of multiple interlocking rods, suspended from a circular lantern made up of thick slabs of coloured glass set in resin and concrete. Multiple dark little chapels — some enclosed by blank walls and others merely alcoves under a low balcony — were dotted round the perimeter, with the emphasis again on stark modernity and minimalist coloured glazing.

An exception to the prevailing simplicity was a chapel dedicated to The Forty Martyrs whose avant-garde design had sharply divided Bromgrove opinion in approved you-either-love-it-or-hate-it fashion. There were no holy men and women with haloed heads. Instead, it featured what was known as the sunburst fresco, a painted reredos with abstract geometric shards of white and grey against a yellow background, beneath which was a rectangular Perspex tabernacle ornamented with brightly coloured wood-block symbols of Christ's passion against swirling concentric patterns in blue, red and green. By contrast with her antipathy for the bronze crucifix, Olivia highly approved. 'It feels very hopeful,' was her verdict. 'There's this sense of stepping into a new reality,' she said. 'Perfect freedom . . . a new creation outside time and space.'

Standing now in the far-left hand aisle of the cavernous cathedral, Markham wished he could tap into some of that hopefulness, but his current mood was very flat despite the beauty of the setting, enhanced by hundreds of flickering votive candles, magnificent floral arrangements and the sweet woody scent of incense.

His attention wandering between hymns, he glanced towards a reproduction of Pietro Cavallini's *Last Judgment* on the wall adjacent to their pew in the north aisle.

It struck him that the angels' faces were notably smooth and unwrinkled, presumably because sin and suffering were to them a distant dream, guessed at but never experienced. Glowing with a radiance not of this world, they knew nothing of the failure pit in which fallen humanity floundered around.

Remembering Charles Larrain, Isobel Farquhar and Carmel Scarron, he sent up a heartfelt prayer that they had now climbed out of this failure pit to be given that new start which would somehow transform what had gone before . . .

Not far from the painting was an icon he did not recall having seen before. A Madonna with warm, almond-shaped brown eyes that were both sorrowful and tender. He felt they looked deep into his soul as though they felt the profoundest compassion and could read him like a book. Unlike the angels, *she* did not hold herself aloof and seemed to say that all was not lost. He felt he could have gazed on the image forever.

But Olivia was nudging him as the congregation launched into *O Come, O Come, Emmanuel*, Noakes's bass lurching through the lyrics in a manner which drew many an amused glance their way. Muriel was fortunately not there to witness his one-man desecration of Christmas classics, preferring to await them back at the homestead.

By the time the Advent candles were lit, some of Markham's despondency had lifted. He had a feeling of being on the right side which would — which *must* — eventually prevail.

All that came to be had life in him and that life was the light of men, a light that shines in the dark, a light that darkness could not overpower . . .

At that moment, Carton Hall's memento mori and brooding effigies seemed as alien as some strange blight. Casting off their influence, even for a short time, felt like a reprieve from prison. Sometimes at church services, he found himself sensitive to unusual changes in atmosphere connected with the presence of evil. On this occasion, however, his inner antennae did not pick up on anything. Not a twitch. Perhaps it really was a case of light vanquishing the dark.

None of the principal Twisses or their staff attended the cathedral service, though he spied Gerard and Stella in cordial conversation with Frank and Anna Harte. The vicar's wife gave him a friendly wave, while strained smiles were all the acknowledgement he received from her companions. Being very much off duty, he made no attempt to gate-crash the little gathering.

As Noakes hastened ahead to announce the guests' impending arrival, Olivia drew her arm through Markham's.

'I think George may already have got stuck into the vino,' she laughed. 'I'm sure I detected a whiff of *eau de Beaujolais* contending with his aftershave.'

Markham chuckled. 'He knows how uptight Muriel gets when it comes to entertaining his boss . . . hardly surprising he needed to fortify himself.'

'God Gil, her lady of the manor routine is excruciating. Not sure *I* can face it without a *vat* of something to perk me up and keep my grin in place . . . especially if she does her usual thing of vamping you while giving me the look she reserves for shady customers.'

But as it turned out, all went reasonably well.

Olivia's heart contracted with pity as she observed how, from the combined effects of hostess anxiety and central heating turned up to the max, Mrs Noakes's normally rigidly controlled perm had dropped, falling into wispy corkscrew spirals that gave her the appearance of having suffered an electric shock. Her dress, obviously new, was an extraordinary brocade creation that contributed to the impression of a sofa on legs, and heavy makeup had become caked around her eyelids and jowls.

The gracious lady routine was as cringeworthy as Olivia had feared, however, while daughter Natalie — whose Oompa-Loompa fake tan and sulky expression marred naturally pretty features — seemed hell bent on giving the impression that she belonged to the waxed jacket set, name dropping and yammering on about county shows in a manner that would have been poignant were it not so ridiculous.

Noakes, needless to say, saw nothing amiss, beaming with pride at his harem and delighted at how the boss managed to draw his girl out, requesting her opinion of the Twisses and their entourage. It was obvious to Olivia, even if the doting father was oblivious, that Natalie had failed to ingratiate herself with the 'nobs', though she said Charles Larrain was always charming and complimentary whenever she visited the Artisan Centre. Probably wanted free membership at the Harmony Spa courtesy of Natalie's entrepreneur fiancé, Olivia thought before reproaching herself for being catty.

Intriguingly, Natalie mentioned that she had come upon the vicar and Larrain a few times 'looking very cosy'. Frank Harte, like Larrain, met with her approval, no doubt because Harte was notably easy on the eye. On hearing her dismiss Anna Harte as 'standoffish' and 'snotty', Olivia reflected that she would have enjoyed being a fly on the wall when the stroppy uber-chav encountered the priest's refined spouse.

Olivia had a feeling that both Muriel and Natalie had been knocking back the Baileys prior to their guests' arrival, which at least meant that 'the missus' overlooked Noakes's more flagrant faux pas, including the shuffling bemusement which saw him mistake Olivia's gift of crystallised ginger for bath salts. Another dodgy moment came when he greeted production of the chocolate log with a jovial 'Mum's Gone to Iceland' before sheepishly adding 'Only kidding' as a crimson tide rose up Muriel's neck and she looked poised for a major sense of humour failure. But Markham's cast-iron old-world charm carried them through.

Well aware that Natalie suspected her of latent uptown girl tendencies and keenly resented anything that smacked of 'talking down', Olivia left the floor to Noakes's two women and, to Markham's amusement, behaved as demurely as a nun (aside from due appreciation of the Pinot Grigio for its anaesthetic properties). As the afternoon progressed, Muriel unbent to the extent of confiding her views on the delicate subject of Noakes's retirement from CID, indicating that she preferred him to go into 'private security' or 'corporate crime fighting' as opposed to anything more vulgarly downmarket.

'*Bloody hell, Gil,*' Olivia said as they walked back to the Sweepstakes, 'talk about delusions of grandeur! It's obvious she wants him suited and booted rather than skulking round in a flasher mac like Bromgrove's answer to Columbo! And she's counting on *you* to see he takes the white-collar route.'

Markham didn't share in her scathing appraisal. 'I'll do whatever I can for Noakesy, you know that Liv.'

Her wrath subsided.

'I know, I know.' Suddenly she skidded slightly, clutching him for support. 'I feel totally stuffed after eating so much. Not to mention pie-eyed from all that Pinot Grigio.'

'Well, I think you won Muriel's heart by your appreciation of her efforts.'

'You were no slouch yourself in that department . . . quite the trencherman,' she observed.

'I aim to please,' was the mild reply.

'You did that alright. They were putty in your hands.' She giggled. 'Talking of putty, where are we going to stick that *hideous* Christmas prezzie?'

He grinned. 'Now, now, Liv, that's no way to describe Turkish handmade pottery.'

'Turkish my backside . . . And you can bet she'll expect us to give it pride of place, so we can't even "recycle" it.' She bit her lip. 'I know the crystallised ginger was a bit naughty, but at least you pitched in with perfume for the two of them. Natalie'll probably *drench* herself in the stuff seeing as it came from you.'

'*Miaow.*'

'Put me in my place over the Christmas decs too,' Olivia muttered before breaking into an arch falsetto. '*Aye laike to stick with tradition, Gilbert . . . We put the tree up on Christmas Eve and it comes down on Twelfth Night . . .* Felt like telling her to stick her John Lewis table piece where the sun don't shine.'

Gently, he put her hand into the pocket of his Burberry.

'You handled it well, sweetheart. And our tree is a work of art . . . even if those Santa swizzle sticks Noakesy gave you are something of an eyesore.'

They trudged on in companionable silence. Then Olivia said, 'Natalie didn't have much time for the reverend's missus, did she?'

'Not exactly a meeting of minds, I imagine.' But Markham's mind travelled back to Natalie's observation about Charles Larrain and Frank Harte appearing to be on friendly terms.

Time to take a closer look at the Reverend Frank Harte.

11. PRIME SUSPECT

Monday 20 December saw the team back at Carton Hall in their improvised incident room.

It was another bitterly cold day, with a weak winter sun gleaming palely on the snow-covered forecourt and on lawns that ran down to shrubberies and giant monkey-shaped topiary. Noakes liked the simian curios scattered throughout the house but was less sure about the garden. 'Squirrels an' bunny rabbits are okay,' he opined. 'Kiddies like that kind of thing. But them shapes look like bogeymen or summat.'

Bogeymen.

The word hung in the room's chill air. A red-eyed Annette Sullivan had wheeled in a trolley with coffee and biscuits, but there was otherwise no sign of the family or staff. After the triple tragedy that had struck Carton, this was hardly surprising.

Pulling their chairs round the elegant rosewood writing desk which now sported an incongruous array of electronic devices, the team looked expectantly at Markham.

What he said came out of left field. 'I want to consider the possibility that the vicar might be our man,' he told them.

Noakes's jaw dropped.

'The *padre?*' he echoed. '*Mr Harte?*'

Doyle looked equally thunderstruck. 'But he's *got* to be kosher surely, guv.'

'Why?' came the calm response. 'Are you assuming that a man of the cloth is incapable of murder?'

'It's not just that,' Doyle said slowly. 'He's probably the most normal out of the lot of them. The family might be barking, but he comes across as a stand-up guy.'

'Yeah, okay for a sky pilot,' Noakes conceded.

Burton, brown bob swinging and intelligent brown eyes alert with interest, leaned forward. 'What makes you think it's him, guv?' she asked.

'Actually, it was something Natalie said when we were sampling Mrs Noakes's wonderful hospitality yesterday.'

Now Noakes was leaning forward too, keen to hear what the boss had to say.

'Natalie mentioned having come across Mr Larrain and Frank Harte together a few times. "Looking very cosy" was how she put it.'

His wingman was divided between pleasure that the apple of his eye had been singled out and disappointment at the meagre intelligence.

'Well, that ain't really enough to get excited about is it, guv . . . Thass what sky pilots do, right . . . go round an' chat to folk . . .' Inspiration struck him. 'Harte could've been trying to convert Aznavour. Y'know, make him give up perving or whatever he got up to with Tricky Dicky.'

Exercising visible restraint, Burton said, 'But sarge, even if the family didn't like the relationship, Richard Twiss and Larrain were consenting adults and most people wouldn't call it "perving".'

'A sky pilot might,' was the stubborn rejoinder. 'An' it didn't jus' have to be about S.E.X. . . . If the pair of 'em were into the occult an' that, satanic practices or wotnot, then the vicar might want to set 'em straight.'

'Mr Hassett said they went through some sort of intense religious phase when they had the idea of refurbishing the parish church,' Burton said thoughtfully, 'but the vicar put the mockers on the scheme when people objected to its being Papist.'

'Well, there you go then.' Noakes was relieved to have found common ground. 'Harte were most prob'ly trying to make it up to Larrain by being extra nice . . . keep him in the fold an' coming to church even if he wouldn't let him plonk candles an' cushions an' stuff all over the shop.'

'Pretty much everybody else was wary of Larrain or at odds with him,' Burton mused, 'with the exception of Claire Mawdsley and in the end she was screwed by him too . . . Seems odd that the vicar of all people would have been chummy with him, especially as it was him and his wife who had to do a mop-up job on Claire after Larrain had chewed her up and spat her out. In the circumstances, I just don't buy the idea of Harte undertaking some kind of pastoral outreach . . .'

'Which means there has to be some other connection between Harte and Larrain,' Doyle concluded. 'One we haven't sussed yet.'

'So, what do we do then?' Noakes sounded mulish, still struggling with the notion of the parish priest as their poison-fixated killer.

'Kate, I want you and Doyle to do some discreet digging,' Markham instructed. 'With the emphasis on *discreet*.'

'Yeah, Sidney'll go ape if he thinks you're sniffing round the vicar,' Noakes warned. 'An' it'd bring the bishop down on us like a ton of bricks.'

Thinking of that pompous, slab-faced clergyman whose company he had been forced to endure at Bromgrove Council's latest 'Value-Based Initiative', Markham silently felt the truth of this observation.

'You don' want to let Harte's missus get wind neither,' Noakes continued sententiously. 'Not to mention Bromgrove Uni . . . They'd freak right out at the idea of students getting mental health treatment from a serial killer's wife.'

'Kid gloves I promise, sarge,' Burton said. But the DS didn't look mollified by her reassurance.

'Noakes and I are going to see Nathan and find out if he's been able to tighten up the psychological profile,' Markham told them. 'We can float the idea of Mr Harte as prime suspect past him and see what difference that makes to the psychological profile.' *If any.*

His wingman looked pleased at the prospect of a session with Professor Finlayson, finding old Shippers good value when it came to discussing true crime, even if the psychologist was even worse than Burton when it came to interminable digressions about 'diagnostic coefficients' and other dry as dust speechifying. Maybe once they'd finished with Frank Harte — which had to be a dead end (excuse the pun!) — he could get Shippers on to Crippen or Florence Maybrick or the Hay Poisoner . . . That last name brought Noakes up short as he recalled that Herbert Armstrong had been a respected solicitor and pillar of the community. Perhaps his Nat was on to something after all . . .

Markham watched Kate Burton as she shifted a pile of papers and files from the writing desk onto a neighbouring Regency drum table, experiencing a rush of affection at the sight of his colleague's beagle-like scurrying. Burton never groused at being assigned the unglamorous spadework that others so often shirked, even though her rank entitled her to demand 'juicier' assignments. He felt a familiar twinge of compunction at this reminder of her willingness to accept a lesser role but told himself that should Noakesy finally retire, this was bound to result in a closer professional partnership with Burton. Uneasily, he wondered what Olivia would make of any such rapprochement given her jealous insecurity where Kate was concerned. Well, he would cross that bridge when he came to it.

'Any luck with the data on minors, Kate?' he asked, recalling the previous discussion about the possibility of their killer having experienced some kind of early-life trauma.

'Nothing useful on the system as far as we can see, guv,' she replied. 'But I've been on to the council and someone from the Education Welfare Service promised to get back to me this morning about critical incidents in schools. Child Protection and other records go back quite a way, so maybe something will emerge from that.'

'Excellent, keep on it, Kate.' Seeing that Doyle didn't look too enthused by the prospect of a tête-à-tête with some council paper-pusher, Markham smiled at him. 'We're getting closer, Sergeant. And sometimes it's the superficially boring legwork that provides the breakthrough.'

The gangling redhead blushed at the implied reproof but sat up straighter. 'I'm with you, sir.'

'And see if you can find Christopher Hassett,' the DI continued. 'He might be willing to talk about the vicar. Only, don't be obvious about it. Give the impression you're after background detail, trying to understand the local set-up, that kind of thing.'

A thought occurred to Doyle. 'What about reporters? They're bound to be sniffing around now there's been three deaths, no matter what we say about Farquhar and Scarron being tragic accidents.'

'Put the Press Office on to it,' Markham instructed. 'They can stonewall the vultures.'

Noakes smirked. 'Now Barry Lynch is free an' single again, he'll want to be hands-on, if you get my drift.' From the frown which crossed Burton's face, it was clear that she did.

Once Markham and Noakes got outside, it was noticeably colder, the sun having disappeared behind a ceiling of thin grey cloud. Again, the DI had that sense of liberation, as though something oppressive had been lifted from his chest.

Gazing up at the mansion, he felt that if he looked closely enough, he would see gnome-like faces and forms leering through the ancient stones on which the frost and ice laid damp fingers. Perhaps that had been the attraction for Charles Larrain and his killer . . . not just the hall's death masks and effigies, which seemed like the symbols of some unknown faith, but a shadowy uncanniness that lurked in its depths and touched everything with preternatural horror. For

Markham, when inside the building, there were moments when he experienced a sensation of throttling fear and naked terror which left him short of breath and dry-mouthed, as though the very bricks and mortar urged him to get away while he still had the chance.

Wryly, he imagined the DCI's likely response to any disclosure of these psychic twinges. Sidney had no time for his gift, if such it was, for filling the frame of things with faces and forms. 'We don't want namby-pamby visionaries in CID, Markham,' he was wont to say snappishly. Sidney had no time for monsters, other than those of the human variety . . .

Noakes, though shuffling his feet to stop them going numb, waited patiently while his guvnor 'went off on one', breath spiralling like light steam into the frosty air. He understood the DI's need for these moments of communion with his surroundings (or trances, as Doyle irreverently termed them) and felt Markham's reputation for refinement shed its lustre on his sidekick.

After a decent interval he said hopefully, 'D'you reckon we could swing by the uni canteen for summat to put us on, guv?'

Jolted out of his meditation, Markham regarded his wingman with resigned good humour. 'You're like those dromedaries that lay down a fat store in case of famine, Sergeant.'

Not the most flattering comparison, but since the reply meant 'Yes', Noakes decided he could live with it.

Once in Markham's car, with the heater switched on, they drove in amicable silence for a time before the DI asked, 'Did Muriel ever have anything to do with Frank Harte, Noakesy? I don't recall her saying much about him yesterday.'

'*Nah*. She heard about him telling folk to call him *Mister Harte* instead of *Father* an' clamping down on statues an' candles an' the rest of it. She didn't like that, see. Says it's a shame, dumping the old ways. It's the thin end of the wedge cos next thing you know they'll be getting rid of tradition an' the royal family an' *everything*.'

'*Ah.*' Markham recalled Mrs Noakes's recent flirtation with Roman Catholicism which, while it lasted, had proved as diverting as it was unexpected. Taken with her intransigence on the subject of unnecessary informality and bad manners, even the Reverend Harte's youthful good looks were unlikely to breach the citadel of Muriel Noakes's preconceived opinions and prejudices. Like most of her ilk, he suspected Noakes's formidable spouse endowed her Maker with those qualities prized by the Women's Guild, which left little room for an un-English bohemianism.

'I reckon our Natalie likes him, though she ain't usually keen on sky pilots . . . couldn't stand the chaplain bloke at Hope who kept telling the kids to come to Jesus an' confess their sins.'

Markham bit his lip at the thought of a teenaged Natalie Noakes taking on some hapless clergyman. Talk about an unequal contest!

But the DS was speaking again, and now he sounded uneasy.

'Are you *sure* about it being the vicar, guv? Like the lad said back there, Harte's practically the only one who's halfway normal.'

'I'm not sure at all, Noakesy. But Natalie's comment set me thinking.'

'You mean like an intuition?' Despite his respect for the guvnor's hunches, the DS was dubious.

'I don't know what it was, but I suddenly had this urge to check him out.'

'Oh aye.'

They had arrived at the university's psychology department.

'Looks like a gulag,' Noakes grunted, surveying the bunker-style concrete building with disfavour. He had recently watched a documentary on Stalin's Russia and considered much of the university's 'brutalist' architecture would fit right in. Heaving himself out of the car, he pronounced, 'Right, let's get some tea an' bacon sarnies, then we'll be ready for whatever Shippers throws at us.'

They had barely finished eating when Markham's mobile rang. At the look on his boss's face once he had ended the call, Noakes prepared himself for a change of plan.

'That was Kate,' the DI said. 'Philip Twiss has turned up dead in suspicious circumstances. She didn't want to go into too much detail over the phone, but apparently it's carbon monoxide poisoning.'

The DS gaped. 'You mean he *gassed* hisself?'

'Unlikely. He was found in an outhouse on the estate. There were two propane tanks that had been left running and the shed doors were shut, so he would have died from CO2 fumes.'

'Accident?' Noakes asked the question without much hope.

'It looks like he'd gone to meet someone, and there were signs that he'd been drinking. But he took a heavy blow to the back of his head, making it likely he was knocked unconscious.'

'Not killed outright then?'

'According to Kate, he may have crawled over to the doors, but he wasn't strong enough to push them open because they were barricaded from the other side.'

'Well, he were a bit of a shrimp compared to the rest . . . a bit puny,' Noakes recalled. 'So it'd be easy pickings. Wouldn't take much bottle to knock him out.'

'Yes, it looked like he had scoliosis or stunted growth,' Markham agreed. 'That would have put him at a disadvantage to start with, especially if he'd been drinking. Once he came round from the blow, the gas would've done the rest. The leak would have brought on a sudden bout of weakness and incoordination — muscular problems, of that sort — so he'd have been too dizzy to get away—'

'An' chummy had barricaded the doors,' Noakes concluded grimly. 'So it's murder then.'

'If Kate's right, we're definitely looking at foul play. Dimples is there now.'

Noakes whistled in dismay. 'Christ, it's like the hall is *cursed* or summat.'

Markham ignored the profanity, a cold clutch of dismay squeezing his stomach and turning his limbs to lead. His heart meanwhile seemed to be thudding against his ribs as though it would burst out of his chest. 'Let's get back to the hall,' he said tersely.

'What about Harte?' the DS asked.

Markham was brusque. 'That'll have to wait.'

'Did Dimples say when the lad died?'

'Sometime yesterday evening . . . around eight.'

Noakes groaned. 'So far virtually none of the potential suspects have an alibi worth anything, an' you can bet it's the same spiel for this one . . . They were having their tea, watching telly, drinking Ovaltine, take your bleeding pick.'

The DS plucked his Day-Glo mustard hoodie from the back of his chair. Irrelevantly, Markham reflected that there was no chance of his wingman blending in with the hall's undergrowth in such vibrant mufti. Along with the flopping red-brown trousers, he was more likely to be taken for an exotic species of grouse. *The lesser spotted Noakes*.

The flare of amusement steadied him and brought his heart rate back within normal limits. He found himself once more able to think clearly.

'Kate said her checks with the council turned up something interesting, but she wasn't sure how significant it was,' he told Noakes as they returned to his car. The DS looked sceptical but seemed to sense that Markham needed encouragement.

'Happen it's summat to do with that early-life accident or trauma thingy, the one that Shippers said sent matey round the twist.'

Markham nodded. His instinct — the infamous 'flair' anathematised by Sidney which he sometimes distrusted but was loath to ignore — told him there was something to be learned from the council data. However, their first priority was to take a look at Philip Twiss.

* * *

'At least this time, I don't have to hedge my bets, Markham,' Dimples greeted him on their arrival at the derelict shed tucked away on the perimeter of Old Carton Woods, which formed part of the estate. 'As you can see from that cherry-red discolouration, there's no doubt about the CO_2 poisoning.'

Squatting down and gently tilting the dead man's head, he added, 'This wound points to him having been bashed with something heavy.' He looked around at the pieces of rusting machinery strewn across the asphalt floor. 'At a guess, I'd say a jack or wheel wrench, possibly an oil pump . . .' The pathologist indicated the two gas cylinders in a mesh cage whose wire door hung drunkenly on broken hinges. 'The valves on those were opened, and with the victim out sparko like that, it might only have taken around forty minutes or so.'

Only.

Dimples got up and moved over to the far wall directly opposite the doors. 'There's blood by these packing cases — looks like they were used as makeshift seating — so I'd say the attack took place here.' He retraced his steps towards the floor. 'We've got a trail of blood leading across the floor and halfway up the doors, which tells me he tried to heave himself upright and force his way out.'

'But a workbench was rammed against the doors on the other side, and he didn't have the strength to force them open,' Burton said quietly.

'Who found him?' Markham asked.

'One of the groundsmen,' she told him. 'Only does checks now and again . . . the last time was a week ago. He noticed the workbench jammed against the doors and thought it was odd. I've sent him back to the Hall with Doyle so he can give a statement. He was pretty shaken up.'

'Why didn't he keep the shed locked?' Noakes demanded. 'I mean, they've got propane in here for chuff's sake.'

'The padlock's broken, sarge,' Burton replied. 'He meant to get it fixed but somehow it slipped his mind. And anyway, the cylinders were in that storage cage, so he figured they were safe—'

'Till someone turned up with a pair of wire cutters,' Noakes interrupted witheringly.

'It's an out-of-the-way place,' Markham said, walking to the doors and contemplating the dell which seemed to cower beneath a hard, steely sky, its holes, stumps and hollows black against the white snow. Even though he couldn't see it, he sensed Carton Hall brooding close at hand, dense, menacing and massively solid in its winter demesne.

The pathologist's voice recalled him to the scene. 'There's an empty bottle of Merlot behind the packing cases. Looks like he was taking swigs from that. His attacker could've brought the booze, encouraged him to wet his whistle, having slipped something into it beforehand . . . a strong sedative . . . Phenobarbital or another barbiturate. It would have made him drowsy, so he didn't really register what was going on.'

Markham looked down at the pitiful corpse of Philip Twiss, his once handsome face congested and contorted, the eyes filmy as though a veil had come down. When he first saw him, despite his lack of inches, Markham had been reminded of Renaissance gallants in a historical picture book. There was no trace of that devil-may-care glamour now.

The DI became aware of figures clustering outside: SOCOs, paramedics, uniforms.

'There's nothing more we can do for him, Markham,' the pathologist said, signalling discreetly to the stretcher party.

Except find the bastard who did this, the DI thought with a surge of rage as assorted personnel went about their business. Moving like shadows all around him.

Words from Isobel Farquhar's obsequies came back to him as he stood in the squalid, ramshackle shed. He could hear the Reverend Frank Harte's voice as clearly as if the priest stood there next to him:

The dead know not anything, neither have they any more a reward; for the memory of them is forgotten. Also

their love, and their hatred, and their envy is now perished.
Neither do they have any more a portion for ever in anything
that is done under the sun.

The Good Book was wrong about that, he reflected grimly, at least so far as he and the team were concerned. Whatever it took, and wherever the trail led, they would see that the murdered dead were *not* cast off nor denied their portion of justice.

He became aware of Kate Burton's gentle *Ahem*.

'Sir,' she said with gentle insistence, 'we may have got something.'

* * *

Back at the hall, they huddled round the fire while Burton told her story.

'The council put me on to a Mrs Carter who was a social worker with the safeguarding team. She's retired now but still totally on the ball. There'd been a case of accidental poisoning at Old Carton Girls' Prep School in 1979 . . . at least that was the decision of the school's directorate. Only, Mrs C wasn't comfortable with it.'

'Why not?' Noakes demanded belligerently.

'She had misgivings about the decision but was overruled by her superiors.' Burton riffled through her notebook then resumed. 'The children in question were best friends and both came from good families. They'd been messing around one lunchtime in an unlocked science lab and one of them poured some acetone into the other's thermos for a lark.'

'*A lark*?' Noakes said incredulously.

'They were seven and eight years old, and it was only the top two classes who used the lab for practicals, so it was feasible to assume they didn't appreciate the dangers. The school was adamant it was a genuine accident and wanted the whole thing squared away with the least possible fuss . . . The child who'd ingested the stuff luckily only swallowed a small amount before being sick, so there weren't any lasting ill-effects. Her parents were very reasonable about it all and didn't want a hoo-ha either.'

'Makes a change,' Noakes grunted. 'Parents today would be gagging for compo.'

Markham's eyes were intent on Burton's face.

'But Mrs Carter wasn't satisfied,' he prompted.

'That's right, guv,' Kate nodded. 'She was uneasy about the so-called prank . . . felt there was more to it than met the eye. There'd apparently been some squabble or falling out between the girls, due to the older girl's possessiveness and her friend chumming up with another kid, though they'd made up before the incident. Mrs C wasn't convinced by the youngster's expressions of remorse . . . felt it was an act and her colleagues were taken in by it because the child was pretty and came from a middle-class background.'

'Was there a psychological assessment?' Markham asked.

'Yes, but it didn't turn up anything significant . . . some histrionic and narcissistic traits, but otherwise no significant markers. Plus, lots of kids have exclusivity issues and ideal friendship scenarios, so in that context her responses fell within the normal range.'

Markham was frowning, obviously deep in thought but to Noakes, it all sounded a bit thin. 'Was there owt else which made Mrs Carter suspicious?'

'She heard an older pupil say something about this girl always hanging round the lab even though her class didn't have lessons in there. One of the teachers shut her up sharp-ish, but it was an odd thing to say.'

'Right.' Noakes was ready for the Big Reveal. 'Which of that bunch of weirdos,' he jerked a stubby thumb towards the door, 'are we talking about? If this lab incident happened in 1979, that'd make 'em . . . lemme see . . . forty-one, for-ty-two.' He screwed up his eyes. 'So that only leaves Metcalfe an' the clever clogs daughter . . .'

'Catherine Metcalfe and Margaret Twiss,' Burton amended punctiliously. 'Stella Twiss, Frances Farquhar, Lady Edith and Irene Clark are all older.'

'An' the Mawdsley one's got an alibi for Larrain,' Noakes added, 'cos she were staying over in Birmingham that night.'

'There's someone you've forgotten,' Burton pointed out quietly. Then, as they stared at her expectantly. 'Anna Harte.'

'*The vicar's missus!*' Noakes was stunned.

'Yes.' Burton held his eyes. 'She was the eight-year-old who poisoned her classmate.' She paused impressively. 'So, it puts her in the frame.'

Noakes clearly didn't like the way this was going. '*Knock it off,*' he protested. 'Mrs Harte with a thing for poison an' murder . . .'

'*Said no one ever.*' Clearly Doyle disagreed with Burton about the latest development being enough to indict Anne Harte. There was an accusing note in his voice as he appealed to Burton. 'You said the prof's friend called the Hartes a rock-solid couple, ma'am . . . and friends of Philip Twiss into the bargain. They're not screwy like the others.' Reddening slightly, he added, 'It's not just because Mrs Harte's a looker. You can tell she's a really nice, down-to-earth woman. It can't be an act. She's a mental health adviser, for God's sake. The university would've rumbled her yonks ago if there were any question marks . . .'

An eerie moaning sound cut him off.

'It's just the wind getting up,' Markham said, reflecting that the building's acoustics doubtless added fuel to stories of ghostly revenants.

'So, we're agreed, then,' Noakes said pugnaciously. 'This St Trinian's bollocks about Mrs Vicar is a big fat time-waste.'

'*No.*' Markham's tone was so peremptory that it sounded like the crack of a rifle shot.

The team waited, watching him.

Finally, he said, 'I see now how it might have come about.'

And slowly, carefully, he proceeded to lay out the case for a new prime suspect.

12. BOLT FROM THE BLUE

Markham knew he had to bring the team with him on this. Burton looked willing to be convinced, but her colleagues were united in their scepticism.

'Doyle, when we were canvassing suspects, you speculated that it might have been Frank Harte who was involved with Larrain,' the DI began.

'Bit of a long shot really, guv,' the young detective protested. 'I realised practically the minute I said it that the idea was ridiculous.'

'But *was* it?' Markham pressed him. 'Everyone assumes the relationship between Larrain and Richard Twiss had to be sexual, but what if it was never consummated? Or even if it was, why should Larrain have restricted himself to *one* partner? If he was a sexual predator, he could well have had his eye on the vicar . . . might even have seduced him already for all we know.'

'But all we've got to go on is Natalie saying that Larrain and the vicar looked to be pretty tight. No disrespect, sarge,' Doyle added with an awkward duck of the head in Noakes's direction, 'but she might've got the wrong end of the stick and the vicar was just being friendly . . . If everyone else was giving Larrain the cold shoulder, maybe he thought it was the Christian thing to do.'

'But what about this incident with Anna Harte when she was a kid at school?' Burton asked.

'*What about it?*' Noakes challenged. Not normally noted for endorsing the conclusions of social services, on this occasion he switched horses. 'The council checked everything out an' signed it off . . . Hell, even the parents of the kid who drank the stuff accepted it were an accident. Jus' cos some old biddy's got a *hunch*, that don' mean Anna Harte's up there with Myra Hindley.'

Burton flushed but stuck to her guns. 'Obviously we'll need to get her in and take a statement, but Mrs Carter was all there. She'd obviously thought about it on and off over the years—'

'Didn't do owt about it, though, did she?' Noakes interrupted. 'Didn't pester the council to dig deeper.'

'She didn't have the *clout*, sarge. And back then, folk were wary of pointing the finger. There were the school and parents to be reckoned with, not just the council. And her colleagues weren't going to back her up. As far as they were concerned, it was Case Closed.'

'So what are we saying then?' Doyle rumpled his ginger thatch in an unconscious imitation of Noakes whose own dishevelled coiffure now looked more aging punk rocker than sober policeman. 'That Anna Harte developed some fixation about poison dating from when she was a kid and it kept getting worse until something happened which set off a killing spree?'

Markham knew better than to start talking about *A Christmas Carol*, especially to any audience which included George Noakes, but he remembered now how Olivia's comments about the theme of traumatised childhood had struck a chord with him . . . as though they offered a clue to the personality of their killer.

'Mrs Carter felt the child who poisoned her classmate — the child we now know to be Anna Harte — had an unnaturally *possessive* attitude towards her friend who, by the sound of it, tried to pull away,' he pointed out.

'That's right, guv,' Burton said. 'Though after what happened, the school made sure to split them up and both sets of parents agreed it was for the best.'

'What if the eight-year-old Anna Harte saw poison as a way of *punishing* her friend for rejecting her?' Markham said quietly. 'What if it went further than that, so a connection between control of a prized possession and poison somehow got embedded in her psyche?'

'Too many ifs,' Noakes grunted. 'An' anyway, that makes her sound like Jeffrey Dahmer or Nilsen . . . the kind of creep who goes round pickling body parts.'

'But a traumatic separation experience in childhood *can* trigger psychological disorders including necrophilia,' Burton said eagerly. 'It's textbook Freud.' She flipped through her neatly tabbed notebook as Noakes and Doyle exchanged ironic glances above her head. 'Yes, here it is . . . In *Totem and Taboo* he talks about the "you" you may have forgotten and—'

'I don' want to hear about Freud.' Noakes pronounced it *Frood*. 'Him an' the other one, Jung, them two to have got a lot to answer for, if you ask me.'

Burton ignored this sweeping dismissal of Western psychoanalytic theory. 'If Anna Harte felt threatened in some way by Charles Larrain, she might've resorted to poison again,' she persisted.

'How would Larrain have threatened her, ma'am?' Doyle asked.

'By rejecting her in favour of her husband.' Burton sounded increasingly sure of her ground.

The youngster's jaw dropped. 'You mean she was in love with *Larrain?*'

'Yes, but it was *Frank* he wanted . . . Don't you see, it was a replay of what happened to her as a child. Her love-object wanted someone else, *and she just couldn't bear it.*'

'It's possible this wasn't the first time Anna Harte resorted to poison to gain her own ends,' Markham said gravely. 'I'm willing to bet there are other episodes in her past

. . . incidents that didn't go as far as murder . . . unexplained sickness or accidents involving her intimate circle.'

Doyle had listened intently.

'There's this film me and Paula watched the other day,' he told them. 'Called *Phantom Thread* . . . A woman keeps poisoning her bloke with wild mushrooms because she figures it's the only way to stop him leaving her. While he's all vulnerable and weak, it means he's dependent on her, in her power.' He bit his lip awkwardly. 'Paula didn't reckon much to it.' Privately, Burton reflected that having a helpless male in her power sounded right up Paula's street.

'Take my advice, lad, choose summat nice an' safe next time,' Noakes advised in the manner of an elder statesman. 'You don' want her thinking the job's messing with your head.'

'Yeah, but it was dead convincing, sarge. You could see how it might happen.'

'*Exactly*,' Burton said triumphantly. 'If Anna Harte wanted Larrain but couldn't have him, then she was going to make damn sure nobody else did.'

'He was *hers* at the end,' Doyle said thoughtfully. '*All hers*.'

Markham could see his arguments were having some effect and pressed home his advantage. 'If Anna shared Larrain's interest in memento mori and funerary objects — which would be in keeping with a pseudo-necrophiliac personality — then that was another reason for her to stage his death in the Tapestry Room at the hall,' Markham observed. 'With the added attraction that she could observe his lingering agony and savour the experience undisturbed.'

'*Jesus*,' Noakes said with feeling.

'That was a prayer I trust, Sergeant.' Markham's tone was flinty.

'I jus' can't get my head round it, guv,' his wingman said contumaciously. 'I mean, the woman looks like Alice in freaking Wonderland, but you're saying she got off on watching Aznavour spew his guts out an' foam at the mouth like he had rabies?'

The DI unbent. 'That's *exactly* what I'm saying, Noakes,' he replied in a gentler tone.

'Nat said she saw Aznavour an' the vicar cosying up to each other, but she never said owt about *Anna* sniffing round him.'

'Doesn't mean it didn't happen,' Doyle pointed out. 'She'd have been careful not to advertise it . . . probably used to that what with being the vicar's wife and having to keep a front up.'

'Every community is a neighbourhood of voluntary spies,' Markham murmured.

Noakes recognised one of the guvnor's quotations. 'Yeah, as in you have to look out for the nosey parkers,' he translated.

Again, the DI echoed Olivia's description of their killer, privately marvelling at how accurately it fitted Anna Harte.

'It was the perfect camouflage,' he said. 'She *groomed* the locals to ignore what was happening right under their noses.'

Burton nodded vigorously. 'She had a position which kind of made her immune: the vicar's wife.'

'Like Caesar's wife, above suspicion,' Markham said as though to himself.

Noakes wanted to head off any boffin-type digressions. Once the boss and Burton got started, there was no knowing where it might lead.

'What about the others then?' he said forcefully. 'Izzy an' Carmel an' Phil . . . What went on with them three?' At least he hadn't said 'Mrs Thing', Markham reflected wryly, and had managed to remember which son it was. Two out of three represented an improvement of sorts.

'They must have seen or guessed something,' Doyle said. 'Something which pointed to Anna.'

Noakes scratched his chin. 'Izzy were old school,' he said. '*She'd* have gone to the police if she thought Anna had poisoned Larrain . . . *wouldn't she?*' It sounded almost like a plea.

'Maybe she saw or suspected something but delayed doing anything about it,' Doyle speculated. 'I mean, it's a big thing accusing the vicar's wife. She'd have wanted to be sure.'

'Maybe for some reason she thought Anna knew who it was,' Burton chipped in. 'Or she could've seen something but not connected it with Anna being the murderer. Either way, she could've said something which made Anna nervous that Isobel was on to her.'

'Isobel hesitated,' Markham concluded, nodding. 'And her hesitation was fatal.'

'What about Carmel?' Noakes asked before answering his own question. 'Blackmail, I s'pose? Wanted to lay something by for that scrote of a son.'

'Yes, I think that's right,' Markham agreed sadly. He had taken to Carmel Scarron, despite what he suspected was a well-worn impersonation of a golden-hearted mop lady. 'Greed or strong maternal instincts got the better of her natural good sense.'

'Plus, Anna could've spun her a sob story about what happened with Larrain,' Doyle pointed out. 'She might've said she only planned to make Larrain sick by way of payback, but things went wrong . . .'

'Payback for what?' Noakes queried.

'Oh, she'd have made something up I reckon,' Doyle replied. 'Maybe she said he tried it on with her . . . or claimed he'd had a spat with her and the vicar . . . anything that sounded halfway convincing.'

Burton saw the logic. 'That barney Larrain had with Patrick, and Larrain throwing his weight around — not to mention him setting the Twisses at each other's throats — would've made Carmel sympathetic to Anna.'

'Plus, Aznavour most probably looked at her like she were dirt,' Noakes put in. 'No love lost there.' He cogitated some more. '*Hey*,' he said, '*that's* how it might've played out with Izzy. Anna could've spun her a yarn about Aznavour copping a feel or being a letch an' that's why she hated him.'

'Somehow I don't see Isobel Farquhar being as credulous or as easily imposed on as Carmel Scarron,' Markham observed, 'but it could have happened like you say.'

'Presumably Philip Twiss was on to Anna as well,' Doyle took up the tale.

'Nathan's friend Mike said the Hartes were friends with Philip,' Burton reminded them. 'Even if he suspected Anna, he'd have been on her side because of the family hating Larrain for his hold on Richard . . .'

'But he *must've* realised she were mad as a box of frogs and freaking *dangerous*,' Noakes burst out. 'I mean, she'd killed *three* people. What made him think he wouldn't be next?'

It was a reasonable question.

Doyle ruminated. 'He might've wanted to persuade her to turn herself in . . . or even help her do a runner.'

'He'd been drinking in that shed,' Markham pointed out. 'So his defences were down.'

'If she came over all damsel in distress, he'd have fallen for it,' Noakes suggested, unconsciously influenced by the knight-errantry that characterised his own attitude towards Olivia. 'But as for the idea of her clobbering him with a wheel wrench or whatever Dimples said she used . . .'

'He never saw it coming,' Burton said. 'Like the boss said, he was lulled into a false sense of security after she lured him out there for a heart to heart.'

'Are we really saying the woman's got this kink about poison all because she fell out with her bestie back when they were schoolkids?' Doyle still struggled with the notion of refined Anna Harte harbouring such latent aggression. 'To be honest, my money was on Christopher Hassett because of the way he bought into all that House of Valois stuff . . .' He paused. 'You could tell he was almost, well, turned on by it.'

'I wondered about it being one of the Twiss siblings,' Burton joined in. 'There is something dysfunctional about the family, I could see it warping them big time. And Lady Edith came across as repellent . . . ruthless enough for a killer.'

'There were any number of possibles,' Markham agreed. 'The way the aunt and uncle seemed estranged from the main branch of the family threw up questions . . . And there was that rapacious events manager looking to get her claws into Michael Twiss. I doubt whether we'll ever get to the bottom of what went on at Carton Hall.' Some stones were best left unturned.

Noakes's mind was running on the Valois dynasty. 'Wonder if Anna Harte modelled herself on one of them aristos in that weird exhibition . . . Catherine de Medici an' that crowd. She seemed pretty interested in that legend about those lovers with the poncey names.'

'Tristan and Iseult?' Markham said slowly. 'Yes, that's true . . . And Olivia told me Anna waxed lyrical about some figurine Sir Simon had bought at auction, a statuette of Olympias — Alexander the Great's mother who was rumoured to be a prolific poisoner . . .'

'Oh yes, I overheard them talking about that,' Burton chipped in eagerly. 'Olympias was married to Philip of Macedonia, but on their wedding night he had a dream of her poisoning snakes which freaked him out.'

Noakes wasn't renowned for his love of classical antiquity, but he looked interested at this. Happen he could look it up and impress Nat with more historical nuggets . . .

Markham was animated. 'When the time comes for a psychiatric evaluation, along with the fractured developmental history, I'm sure we'll find Anna Harte had a deep-rooted fascination with poison from her earliest years.'

'Yeah, but why *poison*?' Noakes, like Doyle had difficulty mapping the features of a sexually sadistic killer onto the vicar's wife with her swan-necked blond beauty and perfect self-possession.

'Nathan says poisoners are often childlike and manipulative at the same time,' Burton replied. 'Permanently immature . . . hell bent on making the world the way they want it but well able to calculate how to achieve their aims.'

'I guess poison gives them a good chance of getting away with it,' Doyle observed with practical good sense. 'No need for any physical confrontation.'

'And it suits the sociopathic killer,' Burton went on. 'Helps to turn their victim into an object with no feelings.'

'*Scary*,' Noakes said with feeling. Then, 'Mind you, she got physical with old Phil, didn't she . . . bashed him over the bonce before turning on the gas.'

'Philip was a *friend* and there was blood,' Markham said. 'It got messy . . . untidy. The experience may have thrown her off-kilter . . .'

'As in you think she's going to give herself away cos it's kind of given her a shock?' Noakes demanded.

'Well, that's our best chance, isn't it?' Doyle reasoned. 'Somehow we've got to hope she panics, takes a risk, and then we catch her in the act.'

Noakes wasn't sure he liked where this was going. 'What kind of risk?'

Burton spelled it out. 'She goes after someone else who has to be eliminated.'

The DS stared at her. 'Like who?'

'Claire Mawdsley,' she said softly.

'*Tricky Dicky's ex*?' he exclaimed incredulously. 'You mean set her up for a slug of Harpic or Domestos or whatever the chuff takes Anna's fancy this time round?'

Doyle came to Burton's support. 'Some kind of stake-out's the only way we can get her. Unless Dimples or forensics perform a miracle, we can't make a murder charge stand up.' He made a rueful face. 'And the clock's ticking. With Philip Twiss dead, there's no way of avoiding a press conference—'

'Unless we can convince Sidney that an arrest is imminent,' Markham finished heavily. He got up and began pacing, winding up at the window which framed the bleak outdoors like a steel engraving: hard-edged, desolate, bleached of colour.

Then he wheeled around, his tall dark figure suddenly energised.

'Let's do it then,' he said. 'We get Sidney onside and then brief Ms Mawdsley.'

'Good luck with convincing her Anna is loony tunes,' Noakes said with an expressive shrug.

'No one can ever be sure what goes on in friendships,' Markham countered. 'I detected a certain reserve on the subject of the Hartes when Kate and I had that meeting with Ms Mawdsley at the Grapes. I specifically recall her saying she "cut ties with pretty much everyone at Carton, which was a shame because she was good friends with Margaret and Pip." It sounded to me like she had side-lined her erstwhile confidantes at the vicarage.'

'That don' mean to say she thought Anna were a poisoner,' Noakes objected.

'Perhaps not,' Markham answered. 'But her *subconscious* might have prompted her to put distance between herself and the Hartes.' The austerely handsome countenance betrayed impatience. 'The important thing is that she comes on board.'

'What about a cover story?' Noakes again.

'Nathan will help with that,' the DI replied. 'Best to keep it simple . . . She could say she'd noticed something between Anna and Larrain and it made her wonder or there'd been some gossip about the two of them, which got her thinking . . .'

Burton's solemn little face was intent. 'Or she could pretend Philip Twiss confided that Larrain boasted about Anna coming on to him then freaking out when she discovered he was interested in blokes.'

Doyle joined the fray. 'How about she'd noticed the Hartes' marriage was in trouble and Anna seemed on edge, not herself, and it was obvious Frank was worried about her?'

'I think you're getting the hang of this.' Markham's encouraging smile transfigured his features. 'A combination of "plot-lines" should do it. Plus, Ms Mawdsley may be able to tell us about any incidents from their past — anything we can use as a lever to open the floodgates and provoke a response from Anna. If there were displays of possessiveness or any over-intense attachments, these might plausibly cause a girlfriend who knew her well to suspect she killed Larrain.'

Noakes pursed his lips, seemingly bent on playing Devil's Advocate.

'Don' forget she's a mental health adviser at the university,' he said. 'They must've checked her out.'

'Checks don't pick up on everything, sarge,' Burton said crisply. 'Easy enough to game the system if you know how.'

'So are we going after her medical records?' Noakes wanted to know.

'Not sure how useful they'll be at this point,' Markham told him. 'And we don't want to run the risk of alerting her. Better to catch her on the back foot via Ms Mawdsley.' Forestalling any further Methuselah-like objections, he continued, 'Obviously we'll mount full surveillance and leave nothing to chance.'

'The DCI'll need some persuading,' said the voice of doom. 'I mean, *the vicar's wife* . . . She an' Sidney's missus most prob'ly do flower arranging together.'

'That's why we've got to convince him that Anna Harte is our killer, Noakesy.' Markham held his wingman's gaze. 'The four of us singing from the same hymn sheet.'

'Oh aye.'

It was enough.

* * *

Events moved swiftly on their return to the station.

They were admitted to the DCI's outer office by his new PA, a bespectacled bustling bantam of a woman with grey crinkly ram's wool hair and an enormous bosom who reminded Markham of his old Cub Scout leader Mrs Crane.

Noakes, too, was nostalgic.

'She's like my old Sunday School teacher,' he murmured reminiscently. 'Gave me Green Shield Stamps when I did Daniel in the Lions' Den.'

Rather an apt analogy, the DI thought, as the team was ushered into the inner sanctum.

While they waited for Sidney to conclude a testy phone conversation about overtime (always a vexed subject), Markham's eyes wandered over the Hall of Fame, as the photomontage which took up the whole of one wall was irreverently known.

There were no recent additions of minor royalty or local celebrities in the pantheon, but he soon found what he was looking for. Yes, there it was . . . a picture of Sidney and the Chief Constable with Sir Simon and Lady Edith at some shindig or other, probably organised by the Heritage Committee.

As always, Sidney's strident honk was profoundly irritating, but Markham reminded himself to cut the man some slack, thanking his lucky stars that *he* didn't have to be a desk warrior.

The DCI looked better than he had up at Carton Hall. Warmer for a start, his well-appointed office boasting radiators that actually *worked*, unlike those in CID. The goatee he had formerly cultivated was gone (presumably on the basis that it detracted from the Bruce Willis 'hard man' buzz cut), and his eczema appeared to be in retreat. All helpful portents.

The office sported a vast mahogany desk of majestic dimensions, topped with photographs of Brunhilde-like Mrs Sidney and startlingly well-scrubbed teenaged boys whose short back and sides haircuts and uncompromising muscularity suggested they were shoo-ins for Sandhurst. An absence of files and paperwork implied that this was the uncluttered domain of a man with a mind like a steel trap — a man in control (or a man who crapped on everyone else, as Noakes was wont to put it).

At least Sidney had stopped displaying testimonials over the sideboard, finally secure enough in his pre-eminence not to require this evidence that he was a master of the universe. Or more likely, Brunhilde had told him it was vulgar.

Markham knew he was on something of a losing wicket when it came to persuading his wingman and Olivia that a better understanding had sprung up between himself and the DCI. Even so, he sensed hopeful portents for the future.

Sidney's room, unlike the DI's own poky cubicle, had a fine view out towards St Chad's snowy terraces, pristine and spotless in their winter drapery. Markham suddenly wished that his mind, attuned as it was to squalid human misery and malice, could be wiped clean of the detritus that came with his job, leaving him open to the magic of Christmas.

Christmas.

Just days away now.

And a killer still to catch.

Sidney was winding up his conversation with a look of '*To the victor, the spoils*', though his mood of complacent self-satisfaction dimmed somewhat as his eyes passed over Noakes's mustard and maroon ensemble. Happily, Burton and Doyle were there to divert his attention, and he could always comfort himself with the reflection that DS George Noakes would soon be just a bad dream.

Smoothly, Markham launched into an unflashy but convincing recital of the facts, making the case for Anna Harte as their new prime suspect in the Carton murders.

Sidney listened attentively, nodding appreciatively as Burton followed up with some well-judged observations culled from Freud's *Psychopathology of Everyday Life*. Noakes had not demurred at the guvnor's suggestion that his fellow DI should cover the profiling angle. 'Yeah, you an' her can give it the old one-two, boss . . . make Sidney think he's thought of all the clever Dick stuff hisself' — this being his wingman's idea of a compliment.

'What of the risk to Ms Mawdsley?' Sidney enquired at the conclusion of their presentation.

It was to the DCI's credit that Claire Mawdsley's safety was the paramount concern, trumping the disquiet he undoubtedly felt at the notion of the vicar's wife being a serial killer. Markham again appreciated the recent shift in Sidney's approach.

'Round-the-clock surveillance once you give us the go-ahead, sir,' Markham said promptly. 'Assuming Claire agrees to help us, Professor Finlayson will work on a script and agree a location for the interview with Mrs Harte. Probably not a good idea for her to wear a wire, but we'll establish clear sightlines and have all access and exit points covered. There's still an element of risk, sir,' he admitted frankly, 'but we don't think Mrs Harte will launch a physical attack. She's more likely to bring poison along and look for an opportunity to administer it once she's lulled Claire into a false sense of security by some form of self-serving confession.'

'But you said she violently assaulted Philip Twiss — knocked him unconscious,' Sidney objected. 'What's to stop her doing the same to Ms Mawdsley?'

'Direct physical violence is *atypical* for a poisoner, sir,' Burton responded. 'For some reason, Anna's plan for that particular encounter went terribly wrong and she lost control of events . . . Either Philip Twiss said something that pushed a button — penetrated her defences — or he suddenly realised the danger, so she had to act quickly.'

'Alternatively, he didn't go under quickly enough, and she simply panicked,' Doyle added.

'Dr Davidson did say there was a considerable amount of Phenobarbital in Philip Twiss's system. Enough for him to go out like a light, only for some reason he didn't,' Markham elaborated. 'It's probable Mr Twiss had an unusually high tolerance due to being on heavy doses of opioids over the years for a spinal condition. I won't bore you with the science, sir. The bottom line is that things didn't go according to plan.'

Sidney considered this for a moment. 'Didn't the housekeeper at the hall also end up in a pool of blood?' he asked beadily.

'Yes, sir,' Burton told him. 'But she was overcome by insecticide fumes and knocked herself out on the kitchen table, so that was *inadvertent*.'

Markham's fellow DI wore what Noakes thought of as her Head Prefect face on as she expounded the team's theory.

'Actually, sir,' she continued, 'we think all the ugliness and mess with Carmel Scarron may have ratcheted up Anna's anxiety levels, which is why she lost her touch when it came to Philip Twiss. Watching Charles Larrain suffer was fine because that was about sexual jealousy and revenge, all tied up with the attraction to poison and watching its effects. But the murders of Isobel Farquhar, Carmel Scarron and Philip Twiss were a whole different ball game — born out of *necessity* and *the need to avoid discovery*. She still used poison because, well, you could say it was like her comfort blanket — a compulsion — but those three people weren't enemies in the same way as Larrain, so there was an impulse to distance herself from the physical reality of their deaths.'

With a squeamish expression, Sidney countered, 'Nonetheless, they suffered agonising deaths, Inspector.'

Markham took over. 'That's correct, sir. But according to Professor Finlayson's profile, while the killer is likely to lack empathy — in line with a stunted emotional development — the need to maintain their self-image will have fostered an aversion to bloodshed.'

'We're talking about an overriding urge to keep the ego intact, sir,' Burton followed up eagerly. 'Like you said at the criminology conference last year, self-deception is integral to narcissistic personality disorder.'

Markham heard this with some amusement. Given Slimy Sid's predilection for having others "ghost write" his speeches, it was more than likely the DCI had plundered Nathan Finlayson wholesale.

Still, it appeared to have done the trick. Sidney jutted his jaw forward in the manner of a potentate receiving tribute.

'What about the Reverend Harte?' he asked after an interval of peacocking. 'Are you going to speak to him?'

'Arguably he has a right to know, sir,' Markham conceded. 'But he might be resistant—'

'Prob'ly he'd want to have it out with her,' Noakes pointed out helpfully. 'It ain't every day you find out your old woman gets off on arsenic.'

Sidney looked as if he could well have dispensed with this parenthesis before smiling benignly at Burton. 'Remarkable how Mrs Harte managed to sustain her role as a respected mental health counsellor given the empathetic impairment,' he commented.

'You mentioned *mirroring* in that paper you wrote on psychopathic coping traits, sir. "The Hollowness of the Serial Killer". The way Bundy and, er—' with a self-conscious look at Noakes — 'Shipman mimicked those around them.'

Noakes and Doyle glanced at each other before looking quickly away.

'Indeed, Inspector,' Sidney mused. With a poor attempt at humility, he added, 'I had no idea my words made such an impact.'

Noakes looked as though he might throw up, but Markham found something touching about the glow of delight that momentarily illuminated Sidney's features, Kate Burton being so transparently in earnest that it was impossible to suspect her of insincere flattery.

'Are we good to go, sir?' he enquired, capitalising on the goodwill engendered by the psychoanalytical debate.

'Yes, Inspector. I'm prepared to authorise surveillance of the suspect on the basis of what you've told me, but time is of the essence.' His clammy avuncularity towards Kate Burton was replaced by slit-eyed steeliness. 'Presumably I can advise the chief constable that an arrest is imminent?'

Noakes watched admiringly as his elegant pinstriped boss calmly replied, 'You may, sir,' smirking as he registered the correction of Sidney's syntax.

If the guvnor ever decided to take up poker, he'd be a dab hand at it.

Disconcerted by the way Markham's 'useful idiot' was grinning at him, the DCI hastily brought the meeting to a close.

* * *

Late that evening, back at the Sweepstakes, an exhausted Markham put Olivia in the picture as they compared notes on the sofa.

Full of admiration for the way Kate Burton had handled herself, he realised too late that his panegyrics were not going down well.

'Are you sure you're not being railroaded into this, Gil?' Olivia said with a distinct chill in her voice, shrugging out of his embrace.

'*Railroaded*? What d'you mean, Liv?'

A crimson streak appeared across her transparent skin, but she plunged ahead.

'Well, from what you say, it seems to me that Kate's pulling the strings here.'

Markham gazed at her steadily. 'That's unfair, Liv. It was *Kate* who got us that breakthrough with the council.'

The warm partisanship acted on her nerves like the scraping of fingernails across a chalkboard. 'I thought it was *you* who came up with the idea of childhood trauma, not her.'

'It was a joint effort, Liv.' Now his tone was disdainful, almost disappointed. 'And she handled Sidney brilliantly.'

'Quite the little operator.'

The words were out of her mouth before she could help it and Olivia felt a pang of self-reproach at the sight of Markham's tired white face and heavy eyes, noticing for the first time little glints of silver in the black hair above his ears. But some perverse impulse prevented her from retracting what she had said.

'What's this all about?' he asked quietly. 'I never took you for the jealous type.'

'Typical male.' She rolled her eyes. 'Reducing it to a catfight.'

'Liv, for God's sake,' he burst out, 'how else am I supposed to take it? You never seem to think straight when it comes to Kate.'

There was something in his dogged weariness that implied he had long been aware how she felt about Kate Burton. Her attempts to hide it obviously hadn't worked. The awareness that he had known her secret all along sent all the blood suddenly rushing to her heart, leaving her deathly pale.

'You care about her more than you do me,' she said curtly.

'She's my *colleague*, Liv. It's a question of *respect*.'

'It's more than that,' came the emphatic reply.

He looked at her in stupefaction, hardly able to credit this discordance after their closeness the previous evening. Outside it was sleeting again, gusts of wind bringing driving rain and hail against the living room window, enhancing the sense of indoor comfort by the outdoor contrast. He longed to be able to savour it without quarrelling over Kate Burton.

'Now's not the right time for this,' he protested. 'Not when we're so near to closing this investigation and making an arrest.'

'There's never a right time,' she said with a scorching glance. 'Not while I'm playing second fiddle to your job.'

Markham's face too was very pale, and the well-moulded forehead and lips were tightly compressed.

'You're being unreasonable, Liv,' he said with some bitterness. 'I've asked you to marry me—'

'As a consolation prize to keep me sweet.' She choked a little as she said these words.

'*No.*' Fire came out of the dark sombre eyes. 'Because I *love* you.'

She made an impatient movement, knocking a coffee cup off the low glass table in front of the sofa.

'Leave it,' he said, but she ignored him, retrieving it before disappearing into the kitchen as though grateful for the diversion. On her return, she scrubbed the discoloured carpet savagely as though for dear life before vanishing once more.

Markham waited patiently, though with a sinking sensation of having reached a crisis. Deep down, he knew that he had not allowed himself to face up to Olivia's jealous resentment by acknowledging it directly.

And now he was paying properly for his cowardice.

Olivia reappeared again clutching a large class of red wine and stood by the window.

Her next words took the wind out of his sails.

'I think we need a holiday from each other,' she said dully. 'That'll help us find out where we're at.'

'I know where *I'm* at,' he said incredulously.

'I don't think you do,' was the cold retort. 'But anyway, I've made up my mind. School breaks up tomorrow and I'm going to stay at Mum's. She'll be glad to have me now the rest had to cry off.'

There was something implacable in her expression which made her suddenly look much older.

And the next minute she was gone, holding up a peremptory hand to forestall further argument. It wasn't the first rupture between them, but there was an irrevocability about the gesture.

The storm outside abated, but Markham felt as if he had been lifted up by a whirlwind and set down in a still and awful place.

13. AN END AND A BEGINNING

Markham remained where he was until he heard the front door of the apartment close behind Olivia. Then he wandered into the kitchen and reached for the red wine. Aware that he needed to eat, he retrieved a ready meal from the freezer — the first that came to hand, such was his lack of interest in food — and slammed it in the microwave. Minutes later his supper was ready, and he adjourned once more to the sofa.

The meal tasted like sawdust, but somehow he forked it up, registering belatedly that it was one of the M&S vegan range to which Olivia had endeavoured to convert him (she knew Noakes was a lost cause).

Returning to the kitchen, he opened a second bottle, despite knowing he couldn't risk a hangover the next day.

Suddenly he remembered what Kate Burton had told him about how she felt when her father died. 'It was just like it says in that poem, sir . . . "Funeral Blues", I think it's called. Or maybe "Stop all the Clocks". I remember that first line because it's just what I wanted to do. Only somehow I couldn't, you know . . . Then I thought how Dad wouldn't want me to freeze-frame life like that. He'd have told me to pull my finger out and go on putting the scumbags away.'

Markham knew that poem off by heart. It was one of his and Olivia's favourites.

And now he murmured the words to himself. Words that conjured up a world of pain that Markham himself was all too familiar with.

Olivia was his world and in an instant she had gone.

But like Kate Burton, he couldn't afford to make time stand still.

Not if he was going to do his job properly.

However, despite his best efforts, he could not stop brooding over what had gone wrong with his partner. It came to him again that Olivia recognised something in Kate Burton that he had missed. That there was something between them that he had not fully appreciated or acknowledged. Maybe Olivia knew better than he did what it was that he needed.

He tried to make sense of it.

Kate Burton was *peaceful*, he concluded. It was as though she was the conduit leading him to a more humane and restful aspect of himself . . . as though through her he somehow rediscovered the mother — the gentle feminine influence — he had lost.

God, that all sounded too creepily dysfunctional and Oedipal for words, as well as uncomfortably reminiscent of the peculiar relationships at Carton Hall . . .

He shook himself. Took a hefty swig of red.

Whatever the nature of his feelings for Kate Burton, it definitely wasn't about sex, he told himself.

Or was it?

If he were being honest, he could admit that Kate had a grave, old-fashioned charm of face and character which appealed to him strongly, albeit she lacked Olivia's romantic allure, brilliant colouring and flashing repartee. Whenever he looked at his colleague's simple expressive face or she lifted her honest eyes to his, he experienced unalloyed pleasure.

She did him good.

Perhaps it was the fact she possessed a freshness and innocence that Olivia had lost somewhere on her travels, leading to occasional outbursts of mistrust and suspicion, even against him. It seemed to him too that her diatribes against those she considered unbearably PC somehow partook of this bitterness against the world in general.

He knew that Olivia resented the perfect confidence that existed between himself and Kate . . . that it somehow made her feel insecure, shut out. Maybe she even suspected him of discussing her with Kate, though in fact neither of them ever broached matters of the heart.

Perhaps that was because they both sensed it was dangerous territory . . . a door they couldn't open.

Round and round went his thoughts, as though he was wandering in some infernal maze.

Was he being an archetypal chauvinist? he wondered. Attracted to Kate as the 'little woman' who demonstrated a flattering subservience towards him both professionally and personally?

No, that made Kate sound like one of those Victorian heroines fainting by turns on the chaise longue with smelling salts to hand.

His colleague was feisty in her own way. Granted, a different way to Olivia. But God knew, only a mixture of guile, tact and good humour could ever have tamed Noakes to the point where he was prepared to overlook her being an 'intelleckshual' who always seemed to have her nose in a book and was a walking incarnation of woke to boot.

His smile turned to a grimace as he weighed up the probability of Olivia's departure becoming known at the station. The bare prospect of his private life becoming the stuff of canteen gossip felt like red hot needle-points all over.

Gulping down more wine, his gaze fell on the Christmas tree over by the bay window. Olivia had done a wonderful job, her innate artistry turning the artificial pine into something out of a fairy tale. With a sharp pang, he recognised little felt woodland creatures among the baubles and realised he had seen something similar at the Artisan Centre.

Old Carton. His job.

He needed to get a grip. However callous his words to Olivia, he couldn't afford to lose focus at this stage of the investigation. Not when they were so near to snaring a very dangerous killer.

His thoughts turned to the meeting with Claire Mawdsley which had followed their session with Sidney . . .

Despite the woman's apparent incredulity in the face of the team's suspicions about Anna Harte and revelation of the episode in her childhood, he could not help feeling that at some level it wasn't news to her and subconsciously she may have realised her friend was a sick woman.

'I knew Anna and Frank were going through a rough patch,' she told them defensively, 'but thought it was just a case of the seven-year itch, plus they were both so terribly busy . . . ships that passed in the night.' Confronted with the notion of her friend's infatuation for Charles Larrain, she reminded them that it was Anna who put her back together after she was dumped by Richard Twiss in favour of Larrain.

'Anna hated Charles as much as I did,' she insisted. 'I never picked up on there being anything remotely sexual.' When the subject of Anna's possessive streak came up, she turned evasive. 'Doesn't everyone go through phases like that?' was the tart rejoinder, but her grey-green eyes seemed suddenly opaque as though turned inwards at something only she could see. Then the moment was gone, and her gaze was clear again, but Markham was convinced there was something floating beneath her conscious awareness that could not rise to the surface. Perhaps it never would.

Noakes came into his own against this obduracy, surprisingly gentle as he always was with those who found their world tilting the wrong way up and the old certainties gone forever.

'If we're right about Anna, then she needs your help, luv,' the DS told her. 'Prob'ly deep down she wants to be caught an' get it all off her chest.'

'You mean spend the rest of her days in a psychiatric unit?' was the agitated reply.

'The poor lass is mixed up in her head,' Noakes said even more gently. 'Must've been hell carrying all that around an' trying to keep the show on the road. Mebbe if she'd got help sooner, it wouldn't have got on top of her.'

'I wondered why she never had children,' Claire said, then bit her lip as though trying to recall the words. But that single utterance held a wealth of meaning.

'A mental hospital don' mean her life is over,' Noakes persisted.

'If she's killed four people, it does! They'll never let her out.' There was a note of suppressed hysteria in the woman's voice.

'Look, it's all about making her better, not jus' throwing the book at her.'

Markham was pretty sure Noakes had his fingers crossed behind his back when he said this.

'Why does it have to be me doing the police's dirty work?' Her voice was shrill and querulous like a child's.

'Because your head's screwed on the right way an' you know it's the right thing to do,' Noakes retorted promptly, as if it was blindingly obvious.

And suddenly with that, she capitulated . . .

Now, slumped on the sofa, Markham contemplated their choice of venue for this crucial encounter, recalling the discussion with Nathan Finlayson.

The psychology professor had suggested the beech grove by the Pavilion in the hall's grounds. 'Mrs Harte's bound to be in a highly febrile state of mind . . . Proximity to the mausoleum should help unleash the demons.'

'You mean cos she's got this necrophiliac thing going, an' the wood being smack next to a load of mouldy old Twisses is bound to set her off?' was Noakes's blunt response. 'As in she'll whip out weed killer?' he added pointedly, just in case the professor didn't follow his drift.

'Something like that,' Finlayson agreed tranquilly.

'The mausoleum's a weird place for a meeting. Won't she smell a rat?' Doyle wanted to know.

Noakes involuntarily screwed up his face at this, as though assailed by the whiff of long-dead Twisses.

Finlayson shook his head. 'It's in the open,' he told them. 'And to use the vernacular, I think it will press her buttons. It wouldn't surprise me if Mr Larrain and his, er, intimate circle used the mausoleum as a trysting place.'

'You know, Tricky Dicky's the spit of Rasputin with that long black hair an' scowl,' Noakes said unexpectedly. 'I can jus' see him an' Aznavour getting their jollies from having orgies an' stuff next to a cemetery.'

Registering Finlayson's surprise, Markham said, 'Long story, Nathan. Let's just say Rasputin's been a recurring motif ever since an investigation at the Newman.'

'You must tell me about that some time, Inspector,' the other replied, his eyes kindling with interest.

'He's probably one of Harte's pinups,' Noakes grunted, his mind travelling down the delightful byways of his dog-eared true crime library. 'Russian holy man from the time of the Tsars. Everyone hated him an' wanted him dead, so they fed him cakes laced with cyanide all washed down with a bottle of poisoned Madeira, but that didn't kill him so they shot him, only he *still* wouldn't stay down so they ended up chucking him in the river . . .'

Doyle was impressed. 'Bloody hell, sounds like *Fatal Attraction* or something . . . y'know, that one with the bunny boiler Michael Douglas can't finish off.'

'Yeah, totally way out,' Noakes agreed. 'The bloke who arranged it were a psycho cross-dresser . . . almost as freaky as old Grigor.'

Doyle was engrossed. 'Didn't Boney M. do a song? Something about Rasputin being a massive ladies' man and screwing anything in a skirt—'

'Including the Russian queen,' Markham concluded drily. 'Look, if you two have quite finished with nine-teenth-century Russia's answer to Harvey Weinstein, I'd like to get back to our stakeout.'

'Sorry, sir,' Doyle mumbled, but Noakes didn't look remotely contrite.

'There's a bird hide on the side of the wood nearest to the mausoleum,' Burton resumed.

Noakes stroked his chin. 'Oh yeah, the scratty little cabin with them peephole thingies,' he mused.

'There'd be enough room for the four of us . . . provided we budge up,' Doyle added, trying not to look at Noakes's paunch.

'What if it's pissing down an' Harte decides she wants to keep dry?' the DS demanded. 'Or she might want to take a look an' make sure no one's snooping.'

'I've checked it out, sarge,' Burton told him. 'You can lock the door from the inside and pull up the shutters. The whole estate's technically a crime scene after what happened to Philip Twiss, so it'll just look like the police have sealed everything off.' She consulted her diagrams. 'In front of the hide there's wooden decking under an awning . . . a sort of covered porch or veranda for shelter with a bench . . . somewhere for people to sit when they've had enough of the wildlife.'

Noakes needed convincing. 'Does it mean we'd be near enough to grab the lass and get her out of there if Harte kicks off?'

Burton stuck to her guns. 'Nathan says Anna sees violence or bloodshed as verboten — an absolute no-no.'

'Hard to believe when you think what she did to Philip Twiss's head . . . looked like grapefruit pulp once she'd finished with him,' the DS observed laconically. 'Aznavour an' Izzy didn't look too pretty neither.'

Burton shook her head decisively. 'That wasn't meant to happen. It's not part of her preferred M.O., sarge. Nathan says the clinical differentials rule it out.' Twitching her glasses more firmly onto her nose, the DI flicked through her notebook again. 'Based on what happened with her at school, he thinks there may have been some sort of abuse going on at home.'

That brought them up short, though as he heard the words Markham remembered Olivia talking about Scrooge in *A Christmas Carol*: the 'glimmer of abuse' and painful memories that had to be exorcised.

'Like what?' Doyle asked, mystified.

'She was an only child . . . had a lot of time off sick. They thought her mother was just one of those fusspot parents, but looking back now . . . It's possible her mum *made* Anna sick as a form of gaining status—'

'You mean Munchausen syndrome by proxy,' Noakes interrupted, dipping once more into his true crime rolodex. 'Like Beverley Allitt who murdered all them babies.'

'Well, definitely some form of factitious disorder, though mum was never caught in the act or anything like that,' Burton agreed. 'Anna could've internalised the abuse . . . come to see drugs and toxins as a means of control. Ultimately a source of gratification.'

Markham contemplated his colleague, thinking that there was something almost comically incongruous about the Girl Guide earnestness with which she propounded her theory of the regressive personality.

Throwing circumspection to the winds, Doyle shook his head. '*Christ*, it's beyond me.'

'If we take what Shippers says on trust, then we can rule out a Slice N Dice scenario,' Noakes concluded.

'That's about it, sarge,' Burton said simply. 'The script's watertight now, so Anna's not going to suspect a police trap, and anyway, Nathan says her judgement will be impaired after what happened with Philip Twiss . . . it will be almost like she's got PTSD.'

Noakes was ready for a play-through. 'Okay, here we go,' he said, hands spread on the chunky thighs like a veteran mansplainer. 'Claire phones Harte an' suggests bringing booze an' rugs an' summat to eat . . . plastic cups, the whole caboodle . . . kind of a *picnic* cos that'd be a fun way to catch up. Then when they get there, she comes over all matey an' confidential, says she jus' wants Harte to explain stuff that's been bothering her, like she wants her old mate to say not to worry an' it don' add up to diddlysquat.'

'And she behaves a bit *dippy*,' Doyle joined in. 'Says she fancied meeting up by the mausoleum on account of it being ever so *romantic* so Anna thinks she's getting off on the cloak and dagger stuff. Gives the impression she doesn't believe Anna's the killer in a million years, just wants a few things cleared up.'

'Exactly.' Burton was evidently pleased at how they reeled it off.

Markham took up the reins. 'Claire has to come across as unstable and potentially indiscreet,' he said. 'So she asks what *really* happened between Anna and Larrain. Was it true what Philip Twiss said? That she'd made the moves on Larrain, only he wasn't interested?' The DI raised a forefinger. 'It's *vital* that Claire strikes the right tone . . . vague mistrust tinged with prurient curiosity that hasn't exactly flowered into full-blown suspicion but represents enough of a threat that Anna decides to kill her.'

'D'you reckon her acting skills are up to it, guv?' Doyle asked.

'I'd say so,' Markham replied. Wryly he added, 'She came across earlier as desperate to believe that we've got it wrong and her old friend couldn't possibly be the killer. Her head's all over the place, so Anna will pick up on the undercurrents of instability and confusion. As a counsellor, she's used to seeing people in various states of distress and from that point of view, Claire comes across as the genuine article.'

Noakes was impatient for the climax. 'Alright then,' he said. 'At some point during the picnic, Anna's heard enough and decides Claire's for the chop . . . or the bleach or whatever chuffing drug she's brought with her.'

'Claire acts all oblivious at first,' Doyle continued. 'Pretends she doesn't notice what Anna's doing cos she's busy wittering on about feeling all *emotional* being back at the hall. It brings back memories of Richard Twiss and their fling . . . how could he treat her like that blah blah.'

'So Harte feels confident enough to slip something into the booze,' Noakes said with grim satisfaction. 'But then suddenly Claire pulls a big dramatic number, starts shrieking.' In a niminy-piminy voice he trilled, 'Hey, what d'you think you're doing . . . What were you up to then? I saw you put something into my drink.' Voice rising an octave and clearly enjoying himself, the DS continued shrilly, 'Were you trying to poison me? You were, weren't you.' With an affectation of extreme terror, piggy eyes straining out of their sockets, he reached an ear-splitting crescendo. 'OMG, it was you all along . . . you're the Carton killer.'

He wound up his performance with an air of one expecting a round of applause and curtain calls, leading Doyle to oblige with an ironic slow handclap.

Noakes, looking slightly disappointed, resumed in his normal tones, 'Claire makes out like she's frozen with terror, can't move kind of thing . . . she don' try to run away or owt like that . . . Then she asks *why*, like she's playing for time, says she *wants to understand* an' mebbe she can help.'

Burton nodded, fluffing out her chestnut bob as though clearing her head.

'If Nathan's right, she won't be able to resist the chance to release the tension,' she said.

'So she'll spew her guts,' Noakes said more prosaically.

'And when she's done venting, she'll try to force-feed the drugs to Claire,' Doyle wound up. 'And that's when we charge to the rescue. Bingo!'

'*Ackshually*,' Noakes considered Burton with narrowed eyes.

She braced herself.

'Looks like Shippers has covered all the angles . . . Yeah, the boy done good.'

Thinking back over it now, Markham recalled how Kate's homely little face had glowed with delight at the compliment to her fiancé (all the more precious considering its source), a shy smile breaking out like sunlight on a landscape.

He realised his hands were stiff and sore, clenched together as if by that tight painful grasp he could deaden the anguish of Olivia's departure. His feelings for his sharp-clawed feline partner were complex but they ran deep, and a bitter pang over their quarrel made him heart-sick.

Olivia was diametrically different from Kate, but they *clicked*.

And not just in the bedroom.

His partner had a power of fascination which was nothing to do with her striking looks. Witty, iconoclastic, clever, flirtatious. Even when the wit was pungent and touched with bitterness, it drew him in. Kept him alive, vital. Their shared literary interests and love of the arts (in the early days, Sidney dubbed her 'Markham's blue-stocking lady friend') meant that he never tired of her company . . . even when doubts and suspicion caused it to curdle.

He knew that at times he had withheld himself from her in a way that must have hurt, compartmentalised his life, focusing on the box marked CID and relegating her to Miscellaneous.

He knew there was some justice in her complaint that there was 'never a right time' for honest communication between them. He should have grasped the nettle sooner and fixed the Kate Burton problem . . . found a way to reassure her that his colleague and Nathan Finlayson were right for each other and happy together . . .

But still an insidious siren voice kept goading him, whispering 'What Ifs' . . .

Everything was wrong and the world out of joint, but he had to concentrate on plans for the following day. *Had to*. Resolutely stoppering the bottle of red, he headed for his study, determined to stun himself into numbness as soon as he could by reviewing the manila folder marked *Operation Carton Hall*.

Later that night, despite sticking at it well into the small hours, Markham slept badly.

In his dreams, he was back at the hall, trailing his fingers along the dark oak panelling and wainscoting of endless winding corridors, passing old embroidered chairs, ponderous busts and antique cupboards until he rounded a corner and came upon a cabinet inlaid with enamelled miniatures set into the carved woodwork. Peering closer, he recoiled with a shock of recognition as first Olivia, then Kate Burton and finally Anna Harte looked up at him with dead upturned faces. Then, whirling upwards, they turned into a trio of avenging Furies who pursued him back the way he had come, their unearthly keening ringing in his ears.

He woke up in a cold sweat that required three cups of black coffee to subdue.

By contrast with his turbulent mind, it was a beautiful tranquil winter's day. The landscaped gardens outside his windows glittered with hoarfrost and a robin perched somewhere nearby singing its heart out. Even the leafless trees looked less forlorn than on the previous day, their fine articulation of branches, boughs and slender twigs like a delicate tracery against the bright blue sky.

He had arranged to collect Noakes at nine.

Noakes.

His wingman would be upset by the merest hint of 'trouble at t'mill'. In some bizarre way, Noakes was like the child he and Olivia had never had. The three of them formed almost a surrogate family unit which it would be heresy to shatter. Plus, his incorrigibly uncouth sergeant's fealty to Olivia was strong, their relationship complicitous and affectionate to a degree that was hard for onlookers to fathom. Certainly Muriel did not care for it at all, but Noakes had proved unexpectedly stubborn in his allegiance and his wife had learned to accept this unaccountable preference.

Ironic that he and Noakes (of all people) should each be in love with two women at the same time. He would have to ensure that his number two had no inkling of the rupture with Olivia until they had put the Carton case to bed.

Today's stakeout was his last throw of the dice. Unless they could wrap it up, 'Blithering' Bretherton or another officer higher up the food chain would take over. Philip

Twiss's death made it imperative that the poisoner should walk into their net.

Markham looked out towards the neighbouring cemetery and its shrouded sleepers.

He thought of Charles Larrain and Isobel Farquhar, denuded of all dignity as they retched and spasmed in their hideous final agony . . . then of Carmel Scarron and Philip Twiss, spared similar horrors but no less dead and cold for all that, banished to that shadowy bourne from which no traveller returned.

Once, when he and Olivia were watching the film *Dead Poets Society*, his partner had been struck by a scene where Robin Williams's school teacher encouraged his pupils to listen to the pictures of long-dead students and hear their ghostly whisper: *Carpe diem*, seize the day.

'It's the same for you and your murder victims, Gil,' was Olivia's matter-of-fact observation. 'You hear them in your ear all the time, don't you? Only with them, it's a plea for vengeance.'

'Not vengeance,' he muttered to himself before draining the last of his coffee and heading to get washed and dressed. '*Justice.*'

* * *

Noakes *did* notice that the guvnor was looking grey and grim, but he accepted the explanation of a restless night readily enough.

The DCI had agreed that their operation to snare Anna Harte should be as low-key as possible save for the perimeter of Carton Hall's estate being discreetly secured, ostensibly as part of ongoing forensics but in reality to ensure that no ramblers or curious day-trippers inadvertently stumbled on the stakeout. Claire Mawdsley had made her phone call and was primed for the encounter, a CID-issue smartphone with audio recorder in her pocket to catch the killer's confession.

Arriving at the bird hide with Burton and Doyle, Markham was vividly aware of the hall's gables and mullioned windows in the distance and the Pavilion close by with its shelves of 'mouldy Twisses'.

As they set up inside, Burton's thoughts were running on the strange family at the heart of it all.

'All that historical stuff — the exhibition and stories about poisoners — had me convinced there was some kind of connection between the killer and the Valoises,' she commented ruefully. 'But in the end, it was nothing to do with them at all.'

'Who can say how it influenced Anna or preyed on her mind,' Markham said. 'You talked about her *internalising* things, so it's quite possible the hall's legends and general uncanniness brought out impulses that she thought were safely buried.'

Noakes's mind was on other things. 'Smells musty in here.' He wrinkled his nose fastidiously. 'Bloody weird place for a picnic if you ask me.'

'In here maybe, sarge,' Doyle replied, 'but that decking and the veranda's quite picturesque. Y'know, kind of like a log cabin or one of those chalets when you go skiing.'

'Oh aye.' But Muriel wasn't particularly keen on Abroad, and as for strapping yourself to a pair of sticks and hurtling down the mountainside . . . talk about Kamikaze. Mind you, Nat was quite keen to try yuppie stuff like that.

'They'll be here shortly,' Markham's voice cut across these reflections. 'Everything ready?'

'Yes, guv,' Burton confirmed. 'Claire's word-perfect and I don't reckon she'll panic.'

'Better not,' muttered Noakes dourly.

Now all they had to do was wait and listen.

* * *

Claire Mawdsley was indeed word-perfect and very convincing. 'Like Bridget Jones on amphetamines,' as Noakes said afterwards. Breathless, gushing, nosy and insinuating. A credit to Nathan Finlayson's patient coaching.

Anna Harte sounded the same as usual. Gentle and refined, the melodious contralto in sharp contrast to the other's high-pitched prattle. So unaltered were her tones, that Markham experienced a moment of sharp self-doubt. Had he been mistaken about this woman? Had he jumped to the wrong conclusions? Looking down at Kate Burton's tightly clenched small hands, he knew she was asking herself the same questions. His colleague looked up at him with a tense yet trustful gaze, and in the gloom of the hut he felt rather than saw Noakes's eyes bore into them.

But then came Claire's shrill accusation that Anna had put something in her drink and the following dry words put an end to all doubts.

'So, you got there in the end, Claire. How clever of you. I suppose that means I'll have to kill you as well.'

Until that moment, Markham hadn't realised he was holding his breath.

The killer might as well have been talking about the weather. There was something more chilling about her quizzical politeness than any amount of invective.

Claire held her nerve and pleaded for an explanation as primed. 'Help me to understand it all,' she said.

And out it came, delivered with no variation of tone or manner.

In the end, it was just as Markham had suspected.

Anna loved Charles Larrain but he had 'betrayed' her, though not a word passed her lips about him turning his attentions to her husband. Doctoring the vape kit and hip flask was child's play given his fetish for the Tapestry Room. It was easy to slip out to the hall because Frank had taken a sleeping pill and was out for the count.

Isobel Farquhar must've found out something. She looked at Anna 'queerly' after Charles died, as though she knew something discreditable about her. More than that, though, she dropped a pointed hint about having a duty to be 'completely honest with the police'.

Carmel Stratton saw Anna up at the hall the night Charles died, after she'd followed him there. God knows why the housekeeper was snooping around, but afterwards she tried to blackmail her, all the while professing fulsome sympathy on account of the dead man being a bully and all-round nasty piece of work. The combination of insect spray and gas was meant to kill her, but she collapsed and knocked herself out, as though it was somehow fated to end that way.

Philip Twiss was *never* meant to happen, only he'd guessed about her feelings for Charles and noticed something was wrong with her marriage. Plus, Charles had joked to Richard about even the vicar's wife having the hots for him.

It was when speaking about Philip that the first cracks appeared in Anna's composure, her speech more halting as though something under the surface was trying to force its way through. She began to talk more quickly too and stammered slightly over some words . . .

Then a mass of ice slid off the roof of the hide with a hiss.

There was an eerie silence afterwards. The four detectives willed themselves into stillness, but it was too late, something in Claire's expression must have given the game away.

'So *you've* betrayed me too,' the killer said, quietly.

'*No, Anna, no!*'

Springing through the door, Markham saw Anna Harte, like a film in slow motion, raise something to her mouth and crumple from the bench to the ground.

Doyle and Burton bundled Claire out of the way as their colleagues crouched over the slight form which was now thrashing and convulsing so violently that it took all their strength to pinion her. Markham began abdominal thrusts but knew in his heart it was useless.

Somehow the repetitions felt like sobs coming from deep inside him.

'She's gone, boss,' Noakes said at last placing a hand on the DI's arm. 'You can leave it now, she's gone.'

Blond hair streaming out on either side like angel's wings, Anna Harte's face showed bright and clear again as the horrible purple colour of suffocation faded, the hint of a smile on her lips.

The Carton Hall killer had escaped her earthly reckoning.

* * *

'I reckon the Rev guessed it was her,' Noakes declared as the team enjoyed a drink in the Grapes two days later, their cosy booth shutting out a waning winter afternoon and outer chill.

Burton gave a resigned sigh. 'If he did, he's not saying.'

'I doubt we'll ever know,' Markham observed quietly. 'And with the community closing ranks to protect him, the police won't get a look in.'

Noakes winked. 'Rikki-Tikki-Tavi's being ever so *caring*, so looks like Frankie's given him the glad eye . . . It's gotta be *lurve*,' he added as Doyle spluttered into his Grolsch.

Burton didn't rise to the bait. 'The man's personal life is none of our business,' she said firmly, privately hoping that Richard Twiss and the vicar would be able to salvage something from the wreckage.

'I'll never forget Anna's voice at the end,' Noakes continued. Markham noticed that 'Harte' had given way to the use of her first name, as though that unforgettable moment on their knees in the snow had imbued his wingman with compassion for the poisoner. 'She sounded like she were reading the news . . . all calm and polite.'

'What was it that Isobel Farquhar found out about her?' Burton enquired, her mind busy with loose threads.

'We'll need Frances to confirm it,' Markham said, 'but I suspect her mother might have discovered something about what took place at Old Carton Girls' Prep School and traced it back to Anna.'

'Even though she'd changed her name and everything?' Doyle asked.

'Isobel had contacts at the council through her husband who served on committees of one kind or another when he was alive,' Markham replied. 'If by some fluke it happened that tittle-tattle or a piece of gossip came her way, she could have made the connection with Anna.'

'Didn't believe she was a killer, though,' Doyle ruminated.

It was a mistake that had cost Isobel Farquhar dear.

'Imagine her having that kill-pill ready,' Noakes said after a long pause.

'Phostoxin,' Markham amended. 'Most likely she got it online.'

Burton shivered, though it was toasty warm in their cubicle.

Time for a change of subject.

'Have you made a decision about next year, sarge?' she asked Noakes.

'Thass my Crimbo present to Sidney.'

Three pairs of eyes were riveted to his face.

'I'm putting in for retirement,' he told them, attempting a grin. 'So they can dig out one of them manky carriage clocks, cos I'm finally ready to *doooooo* it.'

The DS sounded insouciant but looked anxiously at Markham who forced a smile.

'Nice one, Noakesy,' he said, with more enthusiasm than he felt. 'You've earned it, though God knows who's going to fill your shoes.'

Knowing Sidney, he thought, some brown noser-cum-spy.

Noakes puffed out his chest. 'I've been offered security manager at Rosemount.'

Doyle was impressed. 'Isn't that the posh retirement home over by Bromgrove Rise?'

'Yeah.' The other tried to look casual but failed by a mile. 'My missus is best friends with their office manager an' she tipped her the wink I might be in the market for summat *corporate.*' He beamed round the table. 'I've got a decent pension but don' want to hang my boots up yet.'

Hats off to Muriel and what Olivia termed her 'gush of infinite nothings', thought Markham wryly. This time it had certainly brought results!

After a time, Burton and Doyle made their excuses, leaving Markham and Noakes together.

'How's your Liv then?'

'Mercy dash home, Noakesy.' He was amazed at how relaxed he sounded. 'Her mum's been taken poorly. Once I've dotted the i's and crossed the t's on Carton, I'll be joining her.'

How easily the falsehoods rose to his lips. But this was his wingman's moment of glory and he resolved to let nothing spoil it.

'Let's get the drinks in,' he smiled. 'I want to toast Rosemount's new supremo.'

A new chapter was dawning for the team with more adventures on the horizon.

Bring it on!

THE END

ALSO BY CATHERINE MOLONEY

THE DI GILBERT MARKHAM SERIES
Book 1: CRIME IN THE CHOIR
Book 2: CRIME IN THE SCHOOL
Book 3: CRIME IN THE CONVENT
Book 4: CRIME IN THE HOSPITAL
Book 5: CRIME IN THE BALLET
Book 6: CRIME IN THE GALLERY
Book 7: CRIME IN THE HEAT
Book 8: CRIME AT HOME
Book 9: CRIME IN THE BALLROOM
Book 10: CRIME IN THE BOOK CLUB
Book 11: CRIME IN THE COLLEGE
Book 12: CRIME IN THE KITCHEN
Book 13: CRIME IN THE SPA
Book 14: CRIME IN THE CRYPT
Book 15: CRIME IN OXFORD
Book 16: CRIME IN CARTON HALL

Thank you for reading this book.

If you enjoyed it please leave feedback on Amazon or Goodreads, and if there is anything we missed or you have a question about, then please get in touch. We appreciate you choosing our book.

Founded in 2014 in Shoreditch, London, we at Joffe Books pride ourselves on our history of innovative publishing. We were thrilled to be shortlisted for Independent Publisher of the Year at the British Book Awards.

www.joffebooks.com

We're very grateful to eagle-eyed readers who take the time to contact us. Please send any errors you find to corrections@joffebooks.com. We'll get them fixed ASAP.